短篇小说集（英汉对照）

云与影

Clouds and Shadows

[加] 格伦·W. 阿诺德　著
刘新慧　译

世界知识出版社

图书在版编目(CIP)数据

云与影 /（加）格伦 · W. 阿诺德著；刘新慧译. —北京：世界知识出版社，2017.1

ISBN 978-7-5012-5395-1

Ⅰ.①云… Ⅱ.①格… ②刘… Ⅲ.①短篇小说—小说集—加拿大—现代 Ⅳ.①I711.45

中国版本图书馆CIP数据核字（2016）第322612号

图字：01-2016-9734号

Flight was first published in the winter 2010 edition of *North American Review.*

责任编辑	张迎辉
责任出版	赵 玥
责任校对	张 琨
书 名	云与影 Yun Yu Ying
作 者	[加] 格伦 · W. 阿诺德
译 者	刘新慧
封面摄影	[加] Craig Arnold
出版发行	世界知识出版社
地址邮编	北京市东城区干面胡同51号（100010）
网 址	www.ishizhi.cn
投稿信箱	734660862@qq.com
电 话	010-65233525（编辑部） 010-65265923（发行） 010-85119023（邮购）
经 销	新华书店
印 刷	北京艺堂印刷有限公司
开本印张	880×1230毫米 1/32 6¾印张
字 数	275千字
版次印次	2017年1月第一版 2017年1月第一次印刷
标准书号	ISBN 978-7-5012-5395-1
定 价	26.00元

目录

Weathermaker

I am the Weathermaker.

This isn't some quaint nickname, though. I really do make the weather.

I just don't understand how I do it. Nobody does.

I have never let any of the Companions call me this before, and they never tried. They were all professionals, and they understood that I was unique, that I was special, that I needed to be handled very carefully.

I knew right away, though, that this new one—Elena—was different. When she first strode into my room two months ago, she flung the curtains open, took a look outside at the steely pillows of clouds that were

天气制造者

我是天气制造者。

这可不是什么打趣逗乐时用的绰号。我真能制造天气。

我只是不明白自己是如何造的。没人知晓。

以前我从不允许任何一个陪伴者这样称呼我，也从未有人试过。她们都是专业人士。她们明白我与众不同、我很特别、我需要被谨慎对待。

一见到她——这位叫作伊莲娜的新陪伴，我就明白，她与别人不一样。两个月前，她第一次踏入我的房间时，猛地打开窗帘，看着窗外即将往外吐雨的硬云

just starting to spit rain, and said "Come on Weathermaker, get up. We've got work to do."

团，说道："天气制造者，起床了。我们有活要干。"

Still groggy, I rolled out bed and groped for my robe. The first feature I noticed about her was her wrists. They were slender and beautiful, threaded with tight tendons that implied strength. Of course I found them attractive—she was chosen specifically for me. I stood there, staring at her, taking in the rest of her features: the coarse, black hair that curled up into masses of frantic ringlets, the thin lips that smiled easily, the expressive eyes the colour of polished walnut. She was perfect, at least superficially. But of course, they knew this.

我还没完全睡醒。我从床上爬起来，找着自己的睡袍。我首先注意到的是她的手腕：纤细、美丽、肌腱分明，暗示着力量。理所当然，我认为它们很有吸引力——她是专门为我选的。我站在那儿，盯着她看，其余美色尽收眼底：粗糙的黑发向上卷成一簇簇疯狂的小卷；嘴唇细薄，笑起来很容易；眼睛会说话，是那种打磨过的栗色。她很完美，至少表面如此。当然，他们知道这一点。

For her part, she seemed to understand her role very well. She looked at me, up and down. I suddenly remembered I was naked and quickly covered myself with the robe. "Don't worry about that," she said, "I'll be seeing much more of that later. For now, though, we have work to do." As she walked out of the room, she turned and smiled, adding "and make sure you have a good breakfast. You'll need all the

就她而言，她似乎很明白自己的角色。她上下打量着我。我突然意识到自己还光着身子，就赶快用睡袍裹上自己。"用不着担心那个，"她说，"以后我还有机会看到更多。但现在我们得工作了。"当她走出房间时，她转过身来，笑着说："早餐一定要吃好。今天你需要一切能够获得的能量。"

energy you can get today."

I couldn't help but grin. The speckles of rain stopped and a rent in the grey curtain of clouds appeared, pierced by a hazy shaft of buttery light that reached toward the canopy of the damp cedars that surround the villa. I was already beginning to feel good about this one.

But that was two months ago. Now she is more worried. Now she is more serious. She thinks I am losing control. I wonder what else she thinks.

****

I was six years old when I first became aware of what I could do. Mom, Dad, my sister Beth and I were at the summer fair. It was the usual road show of stomach hurling rides, glutinous, greasy food, slimy, serpentine hucksters and other sparkling entertainments. It was magical; it dazzled with intense colour, sound, stimulation. It was also hot. The prairie summer sky glowed like a blue popsicle, the sun tingled and burned our skin, made black spots appear in front of my eyes as my sister dared me to stare at it.

我只能呲牙一笑。雨点停了下来。灰色的云中出现了帐篷的形状，被一道不甚分明的奶油色光轴刺破，向下照射在别墅周围潮湿的香柏树冠上。我已经开始对她产生好感。

但那已经是两个月之前的事了。现在，她担心得更多、变得更严肃。她认为我正在失控。我不知道她还有什么别的想法。

****

六岁时，我首次意识到自己能做什么。当时，妈妈、爸爸、姐姐贝丝和我正在一个夏季集市上，也就是人们通常看到的路边表演，比如让人五脏六腑颠倒的过山车、黏乎乎的油腻食品、狡猾的商贩和五花八门的游戏等。它简直奇妙无比：夺目的色彩、刺耳的声音、强烈的刺激；当然，天也很热。夏季草原的天空像蓝色的冰棒一样闪闪发光。太阳灼伤了我们的皮肤；当姐姐怂恿我盯着太阳看时，我眼前出现了黑色的斑点。

Dad had been very tolerant as he took me on ride after ride—bumper cars, the Ferris wheel, the small rollercoaster—but I wanted more. I pointed, pulled on his sleeve. "That one! That one!"

父亲一直很宽容，带着我一次次地坐碰碰车、摩天轮、小型过山车等，但我还要更多。我扯着他的衣袖，用手指着高喊："那个！那个！"

"No, you can't go on that one yet. You're still too small. Maybe next year."

"不，你还不能坐那个。你还太小。或许明年吧。"

His reasoned tone didn't satisfy me. I had heard the screams, the laughs from the people riding the Zipper. I didn't care about the rules. I stomped my foot, clenched my fists. "I want to go!"

他语气诚恳，但并不能说服我。我听到了喊叫声、欢笑声，那是坐摩天轮的人发出的。我才不在乎那些规则呢。我跺着脚、握着拳头，高喊着："我要坐！"

Dad's tone was more insistent. "No. See the sign there? You're too small."

父亲语气更坚定。"不。看到那边的提示了吗？你还太小。"

I was breathing harder, and I could feel the mucous thickening in my throat. I was going to cry. I didn't want to be a baby, but that lump in my throat was like a hot stone, and I wanted to expel it, scream my anger at the world. Then, I felt something change, like the sudden dimming of a room when a curtain is drawn. My skin felt like it was detaching from my bones, floating away from me, autumn

我喘着粗气，觉得喉咙的粘膜在增厚，我要哭了。我不想表现得像个婴儿，但喉咙里哽着的那块东西就像一块热石头，我要把它挤出来，喊出我对世界的愤怒。接着，我感到了异样的变化，就像是窗帘被拉上，房间突然暗了下来一样。我的皮肤好像从骨头上脱离、漂移出去，就像树叶在秋风中被卷起。我的身体似乎也和

leaves caught in an updraft, as if my body were being separated from something deeper inside. My anger turned to fear, and I did start to cry.

Dad had that look I had seen before. He wanted to comfort me, but he knew he couldn't give in to my tantrum. Mom stayed back, understanding the dynamic. Then, something changed in Dad's face. His eyes, which had been tightly focused on me, suddenly glanced up at the sky, his mouth opening slightly. His face looked as if he were seeing something that had no right to exist. His expression scared me, but still I followed his eyes. The brilliant blue sky had been replaced by a roiling, angry, dark cloud—purple and green and black—like scummy pond water boiling on a campfire. It quickly expanded across most of the sky, blocking the sun, chilling the air. Then, without warning, a brilliant flash burned my eyes and a thunderous crack split the air, shaking the ground, vibrating my bones. I opened my eyes just in time to see the Zipper tipping over on its fulcrum, its two sides folding up like a pair of scissors.

体内更深层的某样东西分离。我的愤怒变成了害怕。我真的开始大哭。

父亲脸上出现了我以前见过的表情。他想安慰我，但很清楚不能向我的坏脾气妥协。母亲不插手，知道其中的微妙。就在这时，父亲脸上的表情开始变化。他原本盯着我的眼睛突然投向天空，嘴巴微微张开。他脸上的表情就像看到了本不该存在的东西。他吓着我了。我顺着他的目光向上看。湛蓝的天空被急速翻滚、来势凶猛的浓云取代——紫色的、绿色的、黑色的——就像满是腐质的池水在篝火上沸腾。浓云快速扩散，遮住了太阳，使空气骤然冷却。接着，没有预示，一道闪电灼疼了我的眼睛，一声炸雷在空中响起，撕破空气、震撼大地，我全身的骨头都快被震得散架子了。我睁开眼睛，正好看到摩天轮在它的支架上倾翻，两边合起来，成了一把剪刀状。

The remainder of my memory of this moment is not like a slow-motion video, but rather, a series of still images; a photo album where the pictures are distorted by the filmy, protective cover. There is one image of the Zipper halfway to the ground, its structure bent at an impossible angle, one end blackened, the individual cars full of faces, bare-toothed screams and widened eyes. There is another image of the structure as it first impacts the oily tarmac, the internal supports bending, the metal of the cars deforming. Then the image of one of the cars bouncing off the ground, its sides crushed by the impact, an arm protruding from the wire cage, bent backwards at the elbow. Then the image of the same car as it rolls over my mother. Both her hands are up, pure instinct and reaction. Her eyes are closed, her mouth turned down in a grimace of brief but instantaneous awareness of what was about to happen. There are no images after this one; I flip through all the pages of my album, trying to find something, but there is nothing left, until the last page.

我对这个时刻存留的记忆并不像一部慢速录像；相反，它更像一系列静态的图片，一本相册，照片由于被罩上了一层保护膜而变了形。其中有一张是正在向地面坠落的摩天轮，以一种不可能的角度折断了。一端已经变得焦黑。那些坐在一个个车斗里的人面目狰狞、呲牙咧嘴地喊叫着，眼睛瞪得大大的。另一张则是同样的摩天轮刚触地的样子，地面油腻腻的；它内部的支撑物弯了，车斗的金属架变了形。接下来的一张是其中一个车斗落地弹起的情形，四周被撞击得不成样子，一只手臂从车斗里伸出来，胳膊肘处向外反转着。再接下来的一张是同一个车斗碾压在我母亲身上的情景。出于本能的反应，她双手向上伸着。她双目紧闭，嘴角向下拉扯，片刻间已经意识到将要发生什么。这是最后一张照片。我翻遍了相册，直到最后一页，极力想要找出些什么，但什么都没留下。接着，我又找到了另一张照片。

There I find one more picture.

My father's face.

He is standing high above me. The venomous cloud frames him. His face is twisted, trying to cope with too many emotions at once. I can barely recognize him, and I am scared of him. The other pictures are silent, but this last image speaks. My father's eyes burn through me, and as they drill into my core, his voice repeats, over and over:

You.

****

A large, grey gull cruises in a lazy circle over the water. Elena strokes my hair, smoothing the wind-tangle. "Your stats have been good," she says. The gull suddenly drops, then in a flutter, lands on the small, foamy curls. "But there've been some problems."

"Problems?"

We are walking on the beach. Our feet sink, sand collapses inward on our steps. Green, silty water tries to erase our progress, dirty foam snakes across the smooth sand. The sky is grey but the clouds are

那是父亲的脸。

父亲站在那儿，高出我许多。邪恶的云团包裹着他，像是照片的框架。他的脸因瞬时间要承受如此多的情感而变形。我几乎认不出他了，他让我害怕。其他照片都是无声的，唯独这张是有声的。父亲目光灼灼；当它们刺穿我，灼进我的内核时，父亲的声音一遍又一遍地重复着：

你。

****

一只大个的灰色海鸥在水面上懒惰地打着旋。伊莲娜轻抚着我的头发，把被风弄乱的头发抚平。“一切数据显示良好。”她说。海鸥突然向下飞，拍打着翅膀，落在堆满泡沫的漩涡上。“但还是有些问题。”

“问题？”

我们正在海滩上散步。脚沉入沙子，水慢慢把沙粒冲回到我们留下的脚印里。绿色的、不怎么干净的海水试图冲刷掉我们留下的痕迹，肮脏的泡沫像蛇一样窜过平滑的海

starting to break up, jagged azure scars begin to appear. The air is sweet with cedar and damp moss; Elena holds my hand.

滩。天空是灰色的，但云团正在消散，锯齿状的蓝色开始斑斑点点地出现。空气里有香柏木和湿苔藓的甜味。伊莲娜握着我的手。

"Yes. That gentle rain in northern Vietnam turned into a hailstorm. The snow in southern Chile was too wet. The sun afterward came too quick and caused an avalanche."

"是的。越南北部温柔的雨变成了冰雹；智利南部的雪又太湿，太阳随后来得太快，引起雪崩。"

The ocean starts swelling a little stronger; the gull bobs and sways on the surface. "Was anyone hurt?"

海水开始上涨，势头更猛。海鸥在水面上翻飞、打旋。"有人受伤吗?"

"No, it was just a small slide in a remote area. No serious issue really, but I'm just a little concerned about you. Are you feeling okay?"

"没有，只是在一个偏远的地区有小面积积雪滑落，没什么大不了的；我只是有点担心你。你感觉好吗?"

It always comes to this. Everyone depends on my happiness. Or sadness. These give sun and rain. Nobody ever wants my anger or despair; these can result in thunderstorms, hurricanes, tornados. The companion's job is to keep my balanced, focused. Elena has been the best so far. But I still make mistakes. "I feel fine," I lie.

最后总是会回到这个问题。每个人都仰赖着我的幸福或悲伤，它们意味着晴天或雨天；没有人想要我的愤怒或绝望，它们会导致雷暴、飓风和龙卷风。陪伴者的工作就是让我保持平衡和专注。伊莲娜是迄今为止最好的，但我仍然会犯错。"我感觉很好。"我撒谎道。

We've finished our morning

早上的事情已经做

session. I try to get much of the day's work out of the way early. Most places in the northern hemisphere wanted sun, not surprising really as this is the prime time to ripen summer crops. Sun is usually pretty easy; I just need to be happy. Elena takes care of this as best she can. The American Midwest, Ukraine and some parts of northern Africa were looking for rain, to alleviate recent dry spells. This is trickier; the smaller pockets always are. We will have to work on this after lunch.

完，我试图让一天的工作早点结束。北半球的大多数地方想要太阳，这不奇怪，因为这是夏季农作物成熟的最好时节。要太阳通常很简单，我只需要快乐。伊莲娜尽其所能保证这一点。美国中西部、乌克兰和非洲北部的一些地区正在求雨，以缓解最近的干旱。这有些棘手，区域越小越是这样。午饭后我们就得处理此事。

The day always starts in the Globe Room—a converted barn in the trees on the back of the property. Elena is a technical wizard; she pulls up the holographic globe that displays real-time atmospheric conditions, summarizes the previous night's weather, reviews my performance compared to expectations, and then provides the standing orders for the day. I don't know where these orders come from. None of the companions will tell me. They are well trained.

每一天都是从地球室开始。这是一间被改造的谷仓，坐落在房子背后的树丛里。伊莲娜是技术向导，她会把显示实时大气状况的全息地球仪拉到跟前，总结前一天晚上的天气状况，把我的表现和预期的进行比较，作出评估，然后把当天要处理的订单递给我。我不知道这些订单来自哪里。我的陪伴者中没人告诉过我，她们都训练有素。

Elena releases my hand and puts her arm around my waist, her

伊莲娜放开我的手，用胳膊搂住了我的腰，把头依

head on my shoulder. The breeze coming off the ocean stirs the waves of her ebony hair. I pull her closer. I know her job is to build me up, make me feel good, but I can feel tension in her body. She knows she has to be careful how she presents any criticism, knows that the correct equilibrium must be maintained. I learned from previous companions not to push them, not to interfere with their plans. She pulls me closer, hugs me, strokes my back. My fingers move in her hair as I watch the gull take off from the choppy water and fly into the emerging sun. I wonder how much she really understands about the mistakes, about me.

在我的肩上。海风习习，吹动着她波浪般的乌发。我将她拉得更近。我知道，她的工作是让我渐入佳境、心情好，然而，我却能感受到她体内的紧张。她知道，当她提出批评时，她必须小心翼翼、权衡利弊。从以前的陪伴那儿，我学会了不给她们施加压力，不干扰她们的计划。她把我拉得更近，拥抱我，抚摸我的背。我的手梳理着她的头发，看海鸥从波涛汹涌的水面飞起，冲向正从云中探出头的太阳。我想知道她对我犯的错、对我本人到底了解多少。

****

Elena has dimmed the lights. We are in the Focus Room of the barn. On the wall, a series of images are projected. Most of the images show rural areas, fields of golden, whiskered wheat silhouetted against an impossible, blue sky, oceans of emerald sugar beet leaves, neatly order rows of gnarled, tied grape vines, sunflowers blocking the sun,

****

伊莲娜已经把光线调暗。我们在谷仓的聚焦房里。一系列图像被投射在墙上。大多数图像显示的是农村地区：一片片金黄色的、留着胡须的小麦背衬着看似不真实的蓝天；绿色的甜菜叶像海洋般铺开；一行行葡萄树，其弯曲的藤条被整齐地拢在一起；向日葵挡住了

their petals like translucent flames. On the bottom of the screen, names scroll with the images: Zhytomir, Kharkiv, Poltava, Sumy, Mykolayiv. This step is important: Elena needs to make sure I know where to focus my attention. I relax as she flips through these bucolic images, reciting a list of statistical and geographic information about Ukrainian agricultural production. Her research, as always, is thorough. She wants to immerse my consciousness completely in the essence of the place.

As the last of the rural images settle into my mind, she begins describing recent meteorological conditions. The images change to sky shots: white, cumulus cotton balls that slowly flatten and morph into a greyer nimbostratus layer. The region, Elena explains, has had a good growing season, but recent dryness has started to wilt the crops. A day or two of sustained, light rain would be ideal. The image of the developing rain cloud loops repeatedly, a computer-generated distortion of the heavens. My limbs relax and I start to wonder what

太阳,其花瓣像半透明的火焰。在屏幕的底部，滚动着不同地区的名字和图像：日托米尔，哈尔科夫，波尔塔瓦，苏梅，尼古拉耶夫。这一步很重要：伊莲娜要确保我知道在哪里集中我的注意力。当她翻动着这些乡村图像时，我身心放松，同时背诵着一长串有关乌克兰农业生产的数据和地理信息。和往常一样，她的研究做得缜密、全面。她想让我的意识完全沉浸在这个地方的本质之中。

当最后一幅乡村映像在我的脑海中定格时，她开始描述最近的气象状况。墙上的映像也变成了各种天空的形态：白色的、棉花球般的云团慢慢变平，变成了灰色的雨层云。伊莲娜解释说，该地区一直都有一个良好的生长季节，但最近的干旱使庄稼开始枯萎。一两天持续的小雨将是十分理想的。逐渐形成的雨层云翻腾、循环着，这是电脑生成的、扭曲的天空。我四肢放松，开始想象今天她要怎样帮我导入。

trigger she is going to use today.

Then, slowly, the music begins to fade in from the surrounding speakers. I instantly recognize the sparse piano chords. I draw in a deep breath. It's been several years since a companion used this. Part of the companion's job is to keep me surprised. I can't become numb to the triggers.

This one should work.

I close my eyes and let the familiar story of the song—the hired assassin as a sympathetic character—infiltrate me. Does a bad action taken make a person bad? I have thought about this often.

I can feel my breathing increase as the pulse of the music picks up. The assassin is beginning his preparations for his target. My palms are damp.

The assassin holds his breath, readies, then fires.

Then the tempo slows. This is where it should start happening—the assassin's flashback to his childhood after he kills his target. This part of the song, the haunting lyrics of childhood abandonment and loneliness, always used to make

慢慢地，音乐从周围的扬声器中淡淡流出。我马上就辨识出了这稀疏的钢琴和弦。我深吸了一口气。几年前的一位陪伴用过这个。陪伴工作的一部分是让我保持惊讶，不能对触发物无动于衷。

这个应该管用。

我闭上眼睛，让这首歌里熟悉的故事——一位有怜悯心的雇佣杀手——渗透我。做过一件坏事就能让人变成坏人吗？我常常思考这个问题。

随着音乐脉冲的提升，我能感觉到自己的呼吸在加快。刺客正准备刺杀目标。我的手掌湿漉漉的。

刺客屏住呼吸、准备、开火。

接着，音乐节奏放缓。这里应该是效应发生的地方——刺客杀了目标后开始回忆童年。这部分歌词令人感慨、难忘，讲述的是童年被遗弃、孤独的故事，总是会让我泪流

salty streams of tears run down my cheeks.

满面。

I swallow, put my hand to the dry, papery skin on my face.

我咽下口水，把手放在我干爽、纸一般的脸皮上。

Elena is looking down at a computer monitor. She is not frowning, but her face is creased with tension. The last chord fades, its echo burrowing into the corners, and Elena turns up the lights. She has cut the projection of the images. She doesn't say anything.

伊莲娜低头看着一台电脑显示屏。她不是在皱眉头，但脸上由于紧张而拉出了褶子。最后的和弦隐去，回声消失在各个角落。伊莲娜打开了灯。她已经关掉了投影仪。她什么也没说。

"It didn't work, did it?"

"没起作用，对不对？"

She tries to hide her disappointment. She knows she has to be careful here. The goal was to make me feel sad, but not like a failure. I never used to fail. I touch my face again. There is no burning behind the eyes, no thickening of mucous. I haven't responded to the song at all.

她试图掩饰失望。她知道她必须小心。目标是使我感到悲伤，而不是失败。我过去从未失手过。我又摸了一下自己的脸。眼底没有灼疼的感觉，喉咙里没有增厚的黏液。我对这首歌根本没有反应。

Elena sits on the arm of the chair, puts her hand on my shoulder. "I don't understand. That song always used to work. I just don't feel anything." My words are flat, like a grey cloud smothering the sky.

伊莲娜坐在椅子的扶手上，把手放在我的肩上。"我不明白。"我说道，"那首歌一直都管用的。我只是没感觉。"我的话瘪瘪的，就像令天空窒息的灰云。

She strokes my neck. "It's okay. Maybe you're trying too hard."

伊莲娜轻抚着我的脖子说："没关系。也许你太努力了。"

"You mean I should try not to feel anything?"

I can tell from the slight pressure of her nails on my flesh that I have annoyed her. "No, of course not." She stands up, smoothes the creases in her skirt. "Maybe we should take a break, a few days away from it."

And do what? I know we can't go anywhere—too risky to let me out in the real world. I don't want to fight with her, though, so all I ask is "What about the weather?"

"The weather existed long before you were around…"

She doesn't finish the sentence, but I know what she's holding back:

…and will be around long after you are gone.

****

Elena peers up between the cedars, trying to find the sky in the narrow window between the whispering branches. The walk in the rainforest was her idea; she knows it relaxes me. She consults her handheld monitor. I don't need to look up; I know the sky is the colour of flat steel. She presses a few

"你的意思是我应该尽量不去感觉吗？"

这话惹恼了她，我能感觉到，她放在我脖子上的手指在稍稍用力："不，当然不是。"她站起来，把裙子上的褶子弄平。"或许我们应该休息一下，离开几天。"

做什么呢？我知道我们不能去任何地方——让我回到外面真实的世界里风险太大。但我不想和她争吵，我只好问道："那天气咋办？"

"在你出现之前天气就存在了……"

她没说完这句话，但我知道她咽回去的那部分是什么：

……在你消失后它仍然会存在。

****

香柏树在低语，顺着其树枝间狭小的缝隙，伊莲娜向上看，试图看到天空。在雨林中散步是她的主意，她知道这会让我放松。她查看着手上的监控器。我不需要向上看，我知道天空是扁钢一样的颜色。她在监控器上按了几个按钮，然后皱眉。

buttons on the device then frowns. This is first explicit expression of disappointment I've seen from her.

"It's getting worse, isn't it?"

She looks up, suddenly aware that I am watching her. She snaps the monitor shut. Her expression loosens a little, her face once again professionally neutral. "Virtually every weather station is reporting the same thing. Thick, stratus clouds. A grey blanket, but no rain. No sun either. The uniformity and scale of it is unprecedented."

I sit down on a crumbling tree stump, finding just enough support. "I really want to help. I want…to be useful."

She puts her hand on my shoulder and for a moment, I try to imagine that there is genuine affection in the action. Her touch makes me think of last night, her naked leg flung over mine, her hand stroking, threading the hair on my chest. Sex with Elena is always exhausting, always energetic, always perfect. Yet, I am usually disappointed after sex—fulfilled, of course, with my cells still vibrating, my synapses still raw from their

这是我第一次见到她明显表示的失望。

"情况越来越糟，是吗？"

她抬起头，突然意识到我在看她。她啪地合上监控器。她的表情放松了一点，脸上再次呈现出职业化的、中立的表情。"几乎每个气象站都在报道同样的内容：厚层云，像灰色的毯子，没有雨，也没有太阳。其一致性和范围之广都是前所未有的。"

我坐在一个年久风化的老树桩上，只想支撑一下自己。"我真的很想帮忙。希望自己……有用。"

她把手放在我的肩膀上。那一瞬间，我试着想象，她的举动里是有真感情的。她的触摸让我想起昨晚：她的裸腿缠在我的裸腿上，手不停地抚弄着、捋顺着我的胸毛。和伊莲娜做爱总能让我筋疲力尽，每次都是激情四射、完美无憾，但每次做爱后，我通常会感到失望。当然，我的身体得到了彻底满足——每一个细胞还在颤抖，大脑神经突仍处

explosive firing—but I always feel a heavy gravity pulling me down. I always think there should be more. The moment is exquisite, but it is just a moment. It's like a rent in a thick, grey layer of clouds, briefly opening to let in a shaft of blinding sunlight, and then closing again, leaving a featureless blanket stretching from horizon to horizon. And after the moment, when her slick, warm flesh is pressed against me, her lips feathering my neck, I think that she is just doing her job, looking after my needs. I sometimes wonder if she actually feels anything for me. It is possible, I suppose. It's also possible that she is well-trained actor. We never discuss love. We both understand that this would make it difficult to do our jobs.

"I know you want to help," she says as she strokes my hair. "Something's going on with you right now, and we need to try to figure it out."

I rest my head against her chest. How can I explain? I've tried to feel something, anything. I've looked at the pictures of my family, my mother's smile, so different than that

在爆燃后的生疼、茫然状态——但我总会感到一种沉重的地球引力把我往下拉。我总认为应该再多点什么。那一瞬间很微妙、很短暂，就像厚厚的、灰色云层中的一个帐篷，快速打开门，让一线炫目的阳光泻进，然后再把门关上，留下一个毫无特色的毯子，从地平线的一端延伸到另一端。那一刻过后，当她光滑温暖的肌肤压在我的肌肤上、她的嘴唇轻啄我的脖子时，我认为她只是在做她的工作，照顾我的需要。有时我真的想知道她是否对我有感觉。我想是可能的。当然，她也有可能是训练有素的演员。我们从不谈爱情。我们都明白这点，否则我们的工作将很难进行。

“我知道你想提供帮助，”她一边说着，一边抚摸着我的头发，“你现在有些状况正在发生，我们需要试着找出答案。”

我把头停靠在她的胸部。我该如何解释?我一直试着感觉什么，任何东西。我看家人的照片，那里有妈妈的微笑，完全不同于最后

final grimace seared into my memory. I've read that final letter from my father after he sent me away, those words—I love you but I can't accept you. I've looked at all the letters I sent him, returned unopened. I've tried all the other triggers, the music, the food, the sex. Everything that worked before doesn't work now. I've even tried pain, a searing, throbbing agony that spread up my arm, past my elbow, as I yanked unsuccessfully on a pair of vise grips clamped to the nail on my right index finger. The pain was real enough, as were the briny tears that stained my cheeks, but there was no emotional response. No fear, anger, joy, anything. I just can't feel anymore.

的、那深深印在我记忆里的表情。我读父亲把我送走后寄给我的最后一封信、那些话语——我爱你，但我无法接受你。我看着寄给他的所有信件，都原封退回。我试过了所有其他能使我有触动的东西——音乐、食物、性。以前起作用的所有东西现在都不起作用了。我甚至试着感受痛，我用一把大力钳夹住我的右手食指，让灼痛穿过肘部，顺着手臂蔓延——还是没用。痛是真实的，咸咸的泪水沾满我的脸颊，但就是没有情感反应。没有恐惧、愤怒、快乐，什么都没有。我不能感觉了。

Elena continues to absently twine my hair as she stares, with eyes the colour of a faded leaf, at the seamless layer of dull putty that covers the sky. "This is serious," her voice is almost a whisper, "and something needs to be done."

伊莲娜凝视着无缝、沉闷的灰色天空，继续心不在焉地拨弄着我的头发，眼睛的颜色像褪了色的树叶。“这很严重，”她的声音如呢喃呓语，“得做点什么。”

But what? Does she know?

但做什么呢？她知道吗？

****

Years of hyper-awareness of

常年对情感保持高度的

my emotions have numbed me, like sleeping on your arm. First there is discomfort, then pins-and-needles, then nothing, not even motion. The alarm clock could be ringing, but you can't shut it off because your arm just lies there like a dead thing. You can even consciously give the command to your arm to move, but nothing happens because the nerve has been compressed to the point that no signal can get through. If you wait long enough, the nerve will eventually wake up and the pins-and-needles will start again, then feeling will come back. I hadn't thought about my problem this way before, but it seems appropriate. Except I've been waiting for a while now but I still don't feel even a hint of a tingle.

警觉已经使我麻木，就像胳膊被人睡久了的感觉。首先是不舒服，然后是发麻，然后就什么都感觉不到了，甚至连动都不能动；即使是闹钟响了，你也不能把它关掉，因为你的手臂躺在那里，就像是死了一样。你甚至可以有意识地命令你的手臂移开，但什么也没有发生，因为神经被压迫到了极点，信号无法通过。如果你等的时间足够长，神经最终会醒来。先是麻酥酥的感觉，接着感觉就会回来。以前我从未像这样考虑过我的问题，但这样考虑似乎很恰当。只是眼下我已经等得有些时间了，仍然感不到一丝的悸动。

****

I am on the beach. Elena had suggested I walk down there by myself. She knows me well, knows that I sometimes need moments to stare at the sea, to gaze at the empty horizon, looking for a boundary that doesn't exist. The sky is still grey, of course, but the breeze has picked up,

****

我在海滩上。伊莲娜建议我独自去那儿。她很了解我，知道我有时需要盯着大海看，盯着空空的地平线，寻找一个不存在的边界。当然，天空还是灰色的，但微风已经吹起，把满是泡沫的波浪推到岸边光滑的沙滩

lapping foamy waves up onto the smooth sand. When the water retreats after crashing down, it sounds like someone shaking a saltshaker inside my head, agitating the crystals.

上。当水在岸边击碎、开始回流时，那声音在我听来就像有人在我的脑子里摇着盐罐、里面的晶体被搅拌一样。

I spend over two hours on the beach. The sun is probably starting to set, but the uniform pall of the sky makes it difficult to tell. I head to the Globe Room, expecting to find Elena. She always works late into the evening.

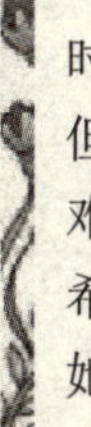

我在海滩上待了两个小时。太阳或许正开始西落，但一色、单调的天空让人很难判断。我向地球室走去，希望在那儿能找到伊莲娜。她总是工作到深夜。

I push the door open. The Globe Room is dark. I turn the lights on but the room is empty. I don't call out. I work my way across the room and throw the switch for the holographic globe. It stutters and flickers for a moment, then comes to life, a slowly rotating orb almost completely engulfed in a dull blanket of cloud. I want to touch it, somehow scrape that blanket away, but I know there is nothing really there. It is just an image of something that is real.

我推开门，地球室里漆黑一片。我打开灯，房间是空的。我没有喊叫。我摸黑走过房间，打开了全息地球仪的开关。它噼啪闪烁了片刻，接着运行起来。一个慢慢旋转的球体几乎完全被毯子一样的云包裹着。我想触摸它，以某种方式把那层毯子刮掉，但我知道那里其实什么都没有。它只是一个真实物体的映像。

I then check the Focus Room, the kitchen, the recreation room, the utility barn. She is not in any of these rooms. I feel something

我接着又查看了聚焦室、厨房、娱乐室、多功能谷仓，任何地方都找不到她。我感到体内某样东西开

tightening inside me. I go to my bedroom and put my hand on the bed. The sheets are cold.

I then go to her bedroom. I rarely go here, as she always comes to me when I need her. I knock on the door, and then feel silly, as we are the only two residents of the villa. She would know who it is. There is no answer. I push the door open. Something doesn't feel right in the room. The walls are bare. Although I have only been in this room a few times, I know she had hung some fairly neutral landscape pictures. I hesitate, then enter the room. There are no signs of her existence at all: not a hairbrush on the night table, not a carelessly discarded sock, not a single wrinkle on the bed quilt. I start pulling open drawers. They are all empty.

I sit for a moment in the vacant room. It doesn't just look like she left; it looks as if she had never been here at all. I feel myself starting to shake. I bolt out of her bedroom, then run back through the Globe Room, through the hologram, bisecting the earth, outside toward the beach. The sun is barely

始收缩。我走进自己的房间，把手放在床上，床单是凉的。

我接着走向她的卧室。我很少来这儿，因为当我需要她的时候，她总是去我那儿。我敲门，接着意识到自己很蠢，因为整个别墅就我俩住；不用敲门，她也知道是谁。没人应答。我推开了门。房间里的某样东西让我觉得不对劲——墙是空的。尽管这个房间我只来过几次，我知道她曾在墙上挂了几幅相当中立的风景画。我犹豫了片刻，走了进去：没有任何她曾经存在过的痕迹，床头柜上没有梳子，没有乱扔的袜子，床单上连一个褶子都没有。我开始把抽屉一一打开，它们都是空的。

我在空房间里坐了一会儿。看起来她不像是刚离开，好像是从未来过。我觉得自己开始颤抖。我匆忙离开她的卧室往回跑，穿过地球室和把全球分解成局部的全息图处理室，向着海滩奔去。太阳几乎看不分明，在厚厚的云层后发着苍白的

discernible, a pale glow behind the thick clouds. I find a log on the beach, stripped smooth by years of relentless waves before chance deposited it here, and I lay down. I breathe quickly, the sand pressed wet against my cheek. I don't understand this; I am feeling…what? Not nothing, not a void, but something. My chest feels fractured, cramped, compressed. She's just the Companion, just doing her job, trying to help me do mine, trying to help me be useful, trying to help me redeem myself. I wipe a clot of sand from the corner of my eye and see for the first time the change in the sky. The uniform, steely plate of cloud is beginning to bubble, to roll and twist and turn in on itself, curling into dark, horn-shaped coils. The sky is darkening, the flush of the setting sun disappearing quicker than it should be. I burrow deeper into the sand, hoping for…escape? A sudden flash brightens the sky, illuminates the gnarled, black clouds and their twisted contours. The bang of the thunder is loud, shaking the soupy sand that embraces me. Then a fat drop of rain strikes my ear, making it

光。我在海滩上发现了一根原木，经过多年海浪的冲刷，已经变得光滑；或许只是一个偶然的机会它被带到了这里。我躺了下来。我呼吸急促，任沙子湿湿地压在我的脸颊上。我不理解这些，我正感觉到……什么？不是什么都没有，不是一片空白，而是有些什么。我的胸部感到破裂、抽搐、收缩——她只是一个陪伴而已，只是在做她的工作，帮我做我的工作，帮我变得有用，帮我自我救赎。我从眼角擦去一小坨沙子，第一次看到了天空的变化。千篇一律的、铁板一块的云开始起泡、滚动、扭曲、向内翻滚，卷曲成乌黑的、喇叭状的线圈。天空变暗，夕阳消失得比平常更快。我更深地被沙子覆盖，希望……逃避吗？突然一个闪电照亮了天空，照亮了疙疙瘩瘩的乌云和它们扭曲的轮廓。响亮的炸雷声，震撼着像汤汁一样包裹着我的沙子。接着，一颗大雨滴落在我的耳窝里，冰冷的雨水顺着耳洞往里流淌，我的耳朵开始鸣响。然

ring as the cool liquid dribbles down deep. Then another drop, And another. The sporadic drops quickly turn into a downpour, a torrent. I am being pounded, drenched. I think I hear a shout in the distance, but the sound is engulfed by another thunderous concussion. The sky has disappeared now; there are only blinding flashes and streams of water running into my eyes. I work my way under the log as best I can, keeping my head out of the mire that is quickly liquefying around me. Another bark of thunder and I hear a tree snap and crash to the ground. I know this is me; I know I am doing this. But it seems out of control, like when I was six, but worse, because it is more powerful. It's like an ice-dam in the spring has suddenly cracked and shifted, and all the weight of the meltwater behind it suddenly races and floods the waterway. I don't know what to do, so I just bury myself deeper.

It lasts for hours, maybe days; I don't know. The sky is black like a crow's wing. If there is any sun, it doesn't show. The wet sand has slopped over my inert body, pinning

后是另一颗、再另一颗；这些坠落的雨滴很快汇成了一条小溪、激流。我被击打着、湿透了。我想，我听到远处有一声喊叫，但那声音被吞没在另一个雷鸣的震动中。天空已经消失了，现在只有让人睁不开眼的闪电和小溪般流入眼内的雨水。我在圆木下尽我所能地挣扎着，把头伸出正在我周围快速变稀的沙泥潭。又是一个炸雷，我听到一棵树折断、倒下。我知道这是我，我正在发挥作用，但一切似乎失去了控制，就像我六岁时所发生的那样，但这次更糟，因为一切都来得更凶猛，就像春天里的一个冰坝突然爆裂、移动，它后面积起来的、融化了的冰水突然释放、奔跑，冲毁了水道。我不知道该怎么办，我只是把自己埋得更深。

它持续了几个小时，也许几天。我不知道。天空是黑色的，像一只乌鸦的翅膀。如果有太阳，它也没有露脸。湿沙子在我僵硬的身

me under the log. Only my head has stayed above ground. Finally, the rain begins to slacken, slowing first to a drizzle, then a shower, then nothing. I shake some of the water off my head. I am weak and my arms and legs feel cemented in place. The tension in my chest has unwound itself; this is where I belong, and I know I must sink deeper.

体上滑动，让圆木下的我感到刺痛。只有我的头部还保持在地面以上。最后，雨开始慢下来。先是变成了蒙蒙细雨，然后是阵雨，然后就停了。我把水从头上甩落。我很虚弱，胳膊和腿里像灌了水泥一般。胸膛里充斥的张力已经解除。我属于这里，我知道我必须沉得更深。

Then, a hand, on my head, stroking my hair, pulling it out of my eyes, wiping my brow. She whispers. I am sorry. Please, let me help you.

然后，一只手放到我的头上，抚摸我的头发，把眼睛里的头发拨了出去，擦着我的额头。她在小声说话。我很抱歉。请让我帮你。

I blink twice, and then can see again. Her eyes are soft and concerned and there is truth in them, a truth I have never seen before.

我眨了两次眼睛，然后我又能看到东西了。她的眼光柔和，充满了关爱，里面有真理，以前我从未见过的真理。

Behind her head, the clouds begin to clear and a hint of blue, just a sliver really, starts spreading, slowly ripping apart the raven-shroud across the sky.

她头后的云开始变得晴朗，一丝蓝色——其实只是细细的那么一点点，开始蔓延，逐渐把笼罩着天空的黑色裹尸布扯破。

The Last Concert

最后的音乐会

I can still recall it: the day music ended.

Julian remembers that date as he circles the dressing room for the seventh time in five minutes. As he paces, he drums his fingers against his thighs, trying to keep them limber, trying to smooth out the arthritic twinges that pulse in his knuckles.

Stay loose. They need to hear you, hear the music.

He sits down in front of the mirror, pastes a stray, grey hair down with his left hand. Staring at the old man looking back at him, he sees sagging, Basset hound eyes. *Those eyes used to be so bright, so alive…*

***我**仍能回忆起那天：音乐结束了。*

当朱利安五分钟内在更衣室里走第七圈时，他记得那个日子。他迈着步子，手指像敲鼓一样地击打着自己的大腿，试图让它们保持灵活，缓解关节炎引起的指关节痛。

放松。他们需要听到你、听到音乐。

他在镜子前坐下，用左手抿着下压一缕灰色的头发。盯着镜子里的自己——那正回视着自己的老人，他看到的是下垂的、巴吉度猎犬一样的眼睛。*那双眼睛曾是那么明亮、那么鲜活……*

Shaking his head, he displaces the grey strand again. *I mustn't think like that. This is my only chance. Make it good. Make them understand what music really is*.

他摇了摇头，那缕灰色的头发又被弄乱了。*我不能这样想。这是我唯一的机会。一定要做好。让他们明白音乐到底是什么。*

He smoothes the ends of his black bow tie, smiling as he thinks of how hard it had been to find one that wasn't pre-tied. The knot is perfect, he knows, even after all these years without practice. *Everything's automatic now, everything's easy. Everything except me.*

他抚平黑色领结的边角。想着竟然费这么大的劲儿才找到一个事先没有打了结的领结，他笑了。结打得很完美，他深知这一点，即使这么多年没练过了。*现在，一切都是自动化，一切都变得容易了。一切——除了我。*

Standing up, he brushes his satiny lapels and then tents his fingers, slowly stretching the ligaments, stimulating the fine muscles in his hands. He checks the clock on the wall one last time and then opens the door to the dim hallway. *Just wait for the call now, any moment*. He lets a nervous smile crease the corners of his mouth. *It's show time*.

他站了起来，梳理着光滑的翻领，然后手指像帐篷一样地拱起，慢慢拉伸关节处的韧带，刺激手上健美的肌肉。他最后再次确认了一下挂在墙上的钟表，打开通向昏暗走廊的门。*现在只等一声召唤了——任何时刻。*他把一丝紧张的微笑抿向嘴角。*是表演的时刻了。*

****

September 12, 2057. That was the date.

Julian remembers it. He had been there, and as young and serious

****

2057 年 9 月 12 日。就是这个日子。

朱利安记得这个日子。他就在那里。作为一名年轻

music student, he understood the significance of the day. The location was Carnegie Hall. Enrico Kieso had played a tribute to Brahms. The hall was not even one quarter full. Old Kieso didn't understand at the time and he bristled at the media's insensitive questions, but Julian somehow knew that this was the last performance of live music to ever be heard by human ears. The rain pounding on the pavement that evening had driven the inevitability of the moment into the deepest cells of Julian's brain, the steady rhythm of the drops slapping the cement like a mocking tattoo.

Kieso's performance had been excellent, though not brilliant, but the sparse crowd was barely able to sustain its polite applause for more than a few seconds. They all wanted to get back home, back to their see-me units, back to hear, to feel, to taste and touch the music in ways the old man on the stage couldn't possibly reach with his playing. As a student of music, Julian had felt it necessary to try the see-me, to see if he could understand the addictive quality of the Cerebral-Musical-

的、严肃的音乐系学生，他知道这个日子的重要性。地点是卡内基音乐厅。恩里科·吉索演奏了一首向勃拉姆斯致敬的曲子。大厅里坐了不到四分之一的人。老吉索对媒体麻木不仁的提问表示愤怒。他当时并不知道，但朱利安却以某种方式得知，那将是人耳能听到的最后一场现场演奏会。那天晚上，雨击打着人行道，把那不可避免的时刻敲进朱利安大脑最深处的细胞里。雨滴拍击水泥路面的稳定节奏像是嘲笑的鼓点。

吉索的演奏虽然谈不上是精彩绝伦，但从头到尾都很出色。然而，稀疏的人群只是给了不超过几秒钟的、礼貌性的掌声。他们都想着回家，回到“看我”的组合单元里，去听、去感受、去咀嚼、去触摸音乐，其方式是舞台上的老人以他的演奏方法永远无法做到的。作为一名音乐系学生，朱利安觉得有必要尝试“看我”，以验证自己是否能

Enhancement device. Three days before Kieso's concert, he had reluctantly agreed to use the device in the controlled environment of one of the college's music studios. His professor had been raving about the unit, claiming that it would completely revolutionize the experience of enjoying music and the role of the musician. Julian had been sceptical, believing with youthful and reckless strength of conviction that the purity and truth of music could not be replicated by a machine.

够理解音乐强化设备令人上瘾的特质。在吉索表演的前三天，他勉强同意在学院的一间音乐工作室里使用这种装置，而且是在受控环境下。他的教授一直力荐这个设备，声称它将彻底改变享受音乐的过程和音乐家的角色。朱利安对此一直持怀疑态度。以年轻人特有的直率，他坚信音乐的纯粹和本质是任何机器都无法复制的。

The device itself was quite simple and unassuming, looking much like a set of triangular headphones, but Julian immediately sensed its power. As he listened to Beethoven's Moonlight Sonata, he felt warmth spreading through his body, a slow and glowing whiskey-burn that grew in his belly, then started poking at his brain—a gentle prodding at first, then more insistent, more urgent, until it started to feel as if the inner core of his soul were being pulled out of his body and held up for inspection under glaring sunlight. But the experience was not unpleasant. Rather, the music spoke

这个设备本身很简单、毫不起眼，看起来就像一套三角形的耳机。然而，朱利安立即就感觉到了它的力量。当他听贝多芬的《月光奏鸣曲》时，他感到一股暖流传遍了全身，先是腹部感受到了威士忌能带来的灼热，它运行缓慢但给人以华丽感；然后它开始抨击他的大脑——先是像温柔的针刺，但这种感觉变得越来越持续、紧迫，直至他觉得灵魂的内核被拉出了体外，暴露在耀眼的阳光下接受检验。然而，这种经历不是不愉快；

to him, but not in the simple way of words. The music actually became part of him, as if it were infusing itself into his cellular structure, coiling around his DNA, asserting itself into his personality. The music knew him, understood him. And as the tones stroked his mind, they began to strengthen, amplify his emotions. He had been nervous before the experiment, and this feeling of anxiety grew stronger and stronger as the music progressed. He could feel the slickness of his palms as he gripped the arms of the vinyl chair, the thumping of his heart trying to shatter his ribs. The tension became almost unbearable, a skull-cracking pressure that almost blinded him. Then something odd, something beautiful happened. The bile churning in his stomach turned sweet, the squeezing pain in his skull released, his limbs relaxed, his palms turned cool. This was the power of the see-me. It used the music to draw all his negative emotions out and invert them back onto himself. Weakness became strength. Fear became confidence. Melancholy became joy. As the

相反，这是音乐与他的对话，只是运用的方式不是简单的文字而已。音乐已经成为他的一部分，就像是已经融进了他的细胞结构，在他的 DNA 周围环绕，成为他个性特征的一部分。音乐认识他、了解他。一旦那些调子触击到他的大脑，它们便开始增强、扩大他的情感。实验前他一直紧张；随着音乐的进行，这种紧张感变得越来越强。他双手紧紧抓着乙烯基材料做成的椅子把手，手掌里满是滑腻的汗水；怦怦跳的心似乎能破肋而出。这种紧张力变得几乎无法忍受，一种能让头盖骨崩裂的压迫几乎让他的眼睛看不见任何东西。然而，接下来发生的事情奇怪而美丽。他胃里翻腾的胆汁开始变甜，挤压他头骨的疼痛开始释解，他的四肢放松，手掌变凉。这就是“看我”的力量。它用音乐把他所有的负面情绪吸出体外，把它们转化并输回到他的体内，弱变成了强、恐惧变成了自信、忧郁变成了快乐。随着奏鸣曲蜿蜒流出乐谱，朱利安感到幸

sonata wound its way through the final bars, Julian felt a blissful happiness filling, expanding, lifting him. He was unaware of the sticky chair he sat in, the stale air that stung his nostrils. All he knew was the music massaging his soul.

福与快乐在体内充斥、膨胀，把他向上提升。他已经感觉不到屁股底下坐着的、黏糊糊的椅子和刺激他鼻孔的浑浊空气。他知道音乐是他灵魂的按摩师。

When the music had ended and the headphones were lifted off his head, it was as if a part of his body had been amputated. Julian had never tried drugs, but he imagined that the shaking spasms of withdrawal must feel something like the emptiness that flooded into his veins and brain when the see-me stopped. His immediate longing for more, the aching need to strap the headphones back on convinced him that he would never touch a see-me again. In that moment, he understood the power of the machine, understood how it was going to change the world.

当音乐结束、耳机被从他头上摘掉时，就好像他身体的一部分被截掉了。朱利安从未尝试过吸毒，但他想象快感消退时那令人颤抖的痉挛一定像“看我”停止以后涌进他血管和大脑里的空虚。他马上渴望得到更多。那种要重新戴上耳机的需求是如此灼人，以致他深信永远不会再碰“看我”了。那一刻，他明白了机器的力量，明白了它将如何改变世界。

It was addictive. And it was beautiful.

这是上瘾，这是美丽。

****

A knock rattles the door.

He is escorted backstage by the old, hunched custodian—a man who

****

有敲门声。

他被一个驼背的老管理员带到后台——一个看起来

seems even older than Julian. They don't exchange any words, but Julian imagines that the man, if he isn't too senile, can probably remember live music. Although he moves with a slow shuffle, there is a certainty and purpose in his progress that makes Julian think the man has walked these backstage corridors many times. Julian wonders if the man has ever used a see-me.

比朱利安还老的人。他们没有交换任何语言，但朱利安猜想，如果那个人不是太老朽的话，他或许还记得现场音乐是怎样的。尽管他动作缓慢，但一举一动充满了肯定和目的性，这让朱利安相信这男人在后台的走廊里已经走过很多次了。朱利安想知道这个男人是否用过“看我”。

With a gentle push on the shoulder, the custodian guides Julian into the dark shadow of the curtain, and then retreats. Julian clasps his fingers together and stretches them, bending them back, opposing their natural direction. *Okay, okay. Just relax*. He pushes his way through the curtain and is momentarily halted by the light. He purposely doesn't look at the audience. He hasn't asked about the ticket sales. It doesn't matter. If only one person shows up, it is still a victory. He assumes most of the people there are curiosity seekers, experience hounds, and maybe a few who just want to mock him.

管理员在朱利安的肩膀上温柔地推了一下，把他带到幕布的阴影里，然后退下了。朱利安两手扣在一起，拉伸手指，尽量把它们往后扳，和它们自然弯曲的方向相反。*好吧，好吧。只需要放松*。他推开幕布走了出去，刹那间被灯光止步。他故意不去看观众。他还没有问过票卖得怎样。没关系。哪怕只有一个人出现，那仍是一种胜利。他猜想坐在那儿的大多数人是为了猎奇、获取经验，或许也有少数人只是为了想嘲弄他。

But by the sound of the applause, Julian knows that there is

然而掌声告诉他，这里有不止一个人。掌声来自各

more than one person here. The sound of clapping hands comes from all directions, filling the room. As his eyes recover from the shock of the spotlight, he carefully makes his way to the piano. His fixes a gaze on the glistening black Steinway, one of his own. Nobody knows how to tune it anymore, so he did it himself earlier in the day. The long arc of a scratch down the side also shows him that there aren't any movers who know how to handle a piano now, either. Still, none of that matters to him. He is here, on the stage again, recreating a distant memory, and an audience is waiting; waiting for him, and not a see-me.

个方向，充斥着整个房间。当他的眼睛从聚光灯的照射下恢复常态，他小心翼翼地走向钢琴。他注视着闪闪发光的黑色施坦威钢琴，那是他拥有的其中一台钢琴。已经没有人知道如何给它调调了，所以，今天早些时候他自己已经调好了调。钢琴侧面有一道长长的划痕，弧形的，这告诉他，现在已经没有多少搬家公司知道如何搬运一台钢琴了。不过，这一切对他都不重要。他就在这儿，再次登上了舞台，再创一个遥远的记忆，而且观众在等待，等待他，而不是"看我"。

The applause, more curious than enthusiastic, trails off as he pulls out the bench. He flips the tails of his tuxedo out with a flourish. Settling himself onto the hard wood of the seat, he carefully opens the folio of sheet music he had laid out earlier. He won't have a page-turner tonight, but it doesn't matter, as he knows this piece intimately. The sheet music is mostly for show, to let the audience see something from the past, something that they have

当他拉出板凳时，好奇多于热情的掌声渐渐停了下来。他用力掀起燕尾服的后叉。在实木板凳上坐定之后，他小心翼翼地打开了早先放在那儿的对开本乐谱。今晚他不会有一个翻页人，但没关系，因为他如此熟知这首音乐。乐谱大多是在作秀，为的是让观众能够看到过去的某样东西、他们已经忘却或从来就不知道的东西。他选择了肖邦的《圆舞

forgotten, or maybe never even known. He has chosen Chopin's *Valse, Opus 69, Number 2*—one of his favourite waltzes.

曲，作品 69 号，第 2 乐章》——一首他喜欢的华尔兹舞曲。

The room is silent now. He clears his throat, shifts slightly on the bench and curves his fingers over the keys. A brief pause, then the notes begin. The first section is slow, sweet and Julian closes his eyes as his fingers dance gracefully on the gleaming ivory. He sways slightly as he feels the swirling melody wind up his spine and settle in his chest. The notes flow, a gentle breeze tickling his skin.

大厅沉寂了下来。他清了清喉咙，在凳子上稍微移了移，手指拱起放在了键盘上。停顿了片刻，音乐响起。第一部分缓慢、甜美，朱利安闭上了眼睛，任手指在熠熠闪光的、象牙色键盘上优雅地跳跃。当他感到摇摆的旋律顺着他的脊椎袅袅上升、在胸部落定时，他也轻轻摇摆起来。音符在流淌，犹如微风拂着他的肌肤。

Julian is barely aware of the audience as he changes to the major key. The tempo builds, and he opens his eyes to focus a stare on the black and white patterns in front of him. As the speed of the piece increases, he starts to make a few mistakes. He covers these well, but they still bother him. He had wanted to be perfect, but it has been so long…

当他移到大调时，他几乎意识不到了观众的存在。节拍在加快，他睁大眼睛专注地盯着面前黑、白键构成的整个键盘。随着音乐速度的提升，他出了几个小错。虽然他掩盖得还不错，但还是为此受到了困扰。他想要完美，但时间太长了……

He is vaguely aware of movement, of shapes in the audience drifting away into the deep shadows. He clenches his teeth together as he switches back to the minor key. He

他模模糊糊感觉到有动静，观众席里有人影移动到更暗的阴影处。当他切换回小调时，他咬紧了牙关。他知道他必须在这里全神贯

knows he has to concentrate here, but he also has to pour his soul into it now. This is where the music shakes his bones, where he peels off his shell for all to see. Julian is working hard now, his hands a blur of gnarled, hairy flesh, but he is making more mistakes. He feels the music moving up his throat, entwining his spinal column, saturating his brain. It is all coming out now, all the passion and the pain, all the hopes and regrets of a career that never happened, a desire never fulfilled; it all flows out of those ancient fingers, all the music that was only ever played for his ears alone, and fills every corner, every empty space in the room.

注，投入灵魂。这里就是音乐能震撼他骨头的地方，是他能揭去外壳向世人展示自己的地方。朱利安现在更卖力地弹着，多骨节、多汗毛的手因飞舞着而变得模糊，但是他犯的错更多了。他感到音乐正在向他的喉咙移动、盘绕他的脊柱、浸透他的大脑。现在，一切都释放出来了——激情、痛苦、生涯中永远没有实现的希望和遗憾、一种永远无法满足的欲望——这一切都从他那古老的手指中流淌出来；那些只为自己的耳朵演奏过的全部音乐现在充斥在大厅的每一个角落、每一寸空间。

As he approaches the end, drops coalesce in the corners of his eyes, prisms that distort but cannot hide the growing emptiness of the room, the gaping jaws of empty seats. He focuses on his hands, which move like two dancers, flowing and dipping and gliding, the final notes ringing. His head is bowed over the keyboard, tears dripping steadily onto the ivory. After a couple of gulped breaths,

接近尾声时，泪珠在他的眼角聚集。泪珠的棱镜作用会扭曲原物，但不能隐藏事实：大厅越来越空，空座位像张开的大嘴。他专注于自己的双手，它们像两个舞者，移动、俯冲、滑翔，直至最后一个音符被敲响。他低头、鞠躬，眼泪不断地滴落到下面象牙色的琴键上。一两次深呼吸之后，朱利安抬起了头。

Julian looks up.

The room is silent. The room is empty.

大厅里一片沉寂。大厅是空的。

He gazes into darkness, the stage lights piercing his tears, blinding him. The last notes have faded, been embraced by the stale curtains that hang limply at the side of the stage. There is no sound. Then, hesitantly at first, a single pair of hands starts clapping. Julian wipes his eyes, squeezes his temples, and stares into the abandoned room.

他凝视着黑暗，舞台灯光刺穿他的眼泪，令他的眼睛发花。最后的音符逐渐隐去，被挂在舞台边的、软塌塌的旧幕布所拥抱。没有任何声音。接着，迟疑地，一双手开始鼓掌。朱利安擦擦眼睛，挤压自己的太阳穴，凝视被抛弃的大厅。

Back in the far left corner of the theatre the old custodian stands applauding, his hands accelerating, slapping out an increasingly appreciative rhythm. The salvo of echoes bounces, chases the quiet out of the room.

在剧院后面左边的角落里站着老管理员，他在鼓掌。他的手越拍越快，以一种节奏表达着越来越多的欣赏。回声四起、到处跳跃，把安静驱逐出大厅。

Julian eases himself up from the bench, feeling his exhaustion for the first time. He straightens his lapels, smoothes his thin hair back, wipes his hands on the satin strip in his pants.

朱利安放松自己，从板凳上站了起来，第一次感到了疲惫。他正了正翻领，抚平脑后已经稀疏的头发，在裤子的缎带上擦了擦手。

And then, he takes a bow.

然后，他鞠了一躬。

300 km/h

God, Paul used to say, becomes visible at 300 km/h.

He would know if anyone did.

I remember his words as I wait, one foot up, one foot down, left hand quivering over the clutch, right hand cranking the throttle, teasing a growl out of the engine.

I watch the red lights, my heart hammering my ribs. It's been three years since I've done this, since I've raced. I must be barmy for trying this, after what happened. I squish this thought into a little ball, trying to keep of picture of Abs' big smile in the front of my brain.

The lights go out. I release the clutch and the bike leaps. I swing my

每小时 300 公里

保罗常说，上帝会在每小时 300 公里时显现。

他想知道是否有人做到过。

想起他说过的这句话时，我正在等待——一只脚上、一只脚下，左手紧握离合器抖动着，右手转动着油门，惹得马达发出低吼声。

我盯着红灯，心怦怦跳着，击打着肋骨。自从我干起这行，当了赛车手，已经三年了。事情发生之后，我仍尝试做这个，一定是疯了。我把这个想法压缩成了一个小球，努力把阿布丝的大笑刻在脑门上。

红灯灭了，我松了离合。胯下的摩托窜了出去。我甩起

right foot onto the peg, my knee suddenly on fire. God, it hurts.

The first two corners go well. A tight hairpin followed by a sweeping left-hander. The bike feels okay, although my hip and knee are throbbing. I let a couple of young blokes on Triumphs go by. No need to get stupid. This is just for fun.

Turn three, a tight left hander. I'm dropping into my lean when an Aprilia flies by on my left. He's gone in too deep. The wanker wrestles it down, but his back wheel skips a bit and clips my front. Christ, not again. I wobble then straighten it up. My hands are shaking, my guts dropping onto my seat as I run off the racing line into the gravel. The rest of the field goes by as my wheels bite into the grey pebbles. That's it. I'm done. I coast through small stones, looking for a place to park. As I slow, I hear something screaming behind me. This doesn't sound like a street bike. I stop and turn, my foot sinking into the trap. I blink, my spine shuddering as I see those familiar, baby-blue leathers, the helmet with the flaming

右脚搭在脚踏板上，膝盖突然像着了火一般。上帝！好疼。

前两个拐角过得不错——一个是发卡状的小角度，接着是一个大弧度的左拐。胯下的摩托感觉还可以，只是我的髋关节和膝关节都感到刺疼。我让一两个骑胜利牌摩托的小伙子超过。没必要跟他们斗气。我只是骑着玩玩。

第三个弯道是一个很陡的左转弯。正当我的摩托开始向地面倾斜时，一辆亚普里亚牌摩托从我的左侧飞驰而过。他切入得太深，摔倒在地，但他的后轮弹起，卡在了我的前轮上。天哪！再别发生这样的事了。我摇晃着，试图把车子扶正。当我的赛车脱离跑道驶向砾石时，我的手在颤抖，苦胆都吓破了。我的车轮咬进了灰色的鹅卵石堆；这时，后面的选手全都一闪而过。就这样。我完了。我滑行驶过一些小石子，想找个地方停下来。当我慢下来时，我听到身后有轰鸣声。这听起来不像是一辆街头摩托。我停下来，转身，脚陷进砾石里。天啊！我眨着眼，我的脊椎直发抖。我看到了那熟悉的淡蓝色皮衣和有着燃烧

Southern Cross, my ears buzzing with that Suzuki engine that sounds like a bee-hive exploding with nitrous-oxide. My hands are soaked in my gloves; my feet squelch in my boots. I can't believe it. It's Paul.

Paul, who died a year ago today.

****

I've never seen a bloke who could flick a bike through the corners like Paul could. He was the most natural racer that ever straddled a motorcycle, an artist on two wheels. But he was pretty smart, too, at least for a gear-head. Most racers are single-minded: they just want to go fast. And win, of course. Paul was like that too, but he also read books. He was really into meditation, all that eastern philosophy stuff. He said it made him a better racer. It sounds crazy, but it certainly worked for him.

The thing about seeing God became a bit of a joke between us, at least when we could still joke. We'd go out for a romp at Donington and, of course, he'd kick my arse. When

的南十字星图案的头盔，耳边是嗡嗡作响、铃木摩托的发动机发出的声音，听起来像是一个蜂窝在一氧化二氮气体中爆炸。我的手、脚出汗，手套内和靴子里都湿透了。我无法相信，那是保罗。

保罗，一年前的今天去世了。

****

我从没见过任何一个家伙能像保罗那样轻松驾车转过弯道。他是天生的摩托车赛车手，一位骑在两个轮子上的艺术家；而且他也够聪明——至少对于一个只会赛车的人而言。大多数赛车手都只有一个心思：快，当然，还有赢。保罗也不例外，但他也看书。他会真正地陷入冥思——那些东方哲学之类的东西。他说，那样会让他成为更好的赛车手。听起来很疯狂，但对他的确很管用。

关于见到上帝之说已经成了我们之间的一个玩笑，至少在我们还能开玩笑的时候。在多宁顿时，我们会常常溜出去比试比试。当然，他总是打败

we'd get back to the pits, I'd ask him if he'd seen God this time. Sure, sure he'd say. Why do you think I passed you on turn seven? You don't think I could have done it without divine intervention, do you?

我。当我们回到车圈里时，我会问他这次是否见到了上帝。当然，当然，他说。要不然，我怎么会在第七个弯道时超过你呢？你不觉得有神力在助我吗？

Paul wasn't all that religious though, not in the traditional sense. He and I grew up together, raised as dull Protestants on that beautiful, boring emerald jewel at the bottom of the world, New Zealand. Yeah, we're both Kiwis, and we both always grinned when the toffee-nosed Pommies up here would ask us if we were from Oz. We came here together, twelve years ago, to chase a dream. We used to bomb around the hills of Coromandel on our 250's, dreaming of the TT, of the world of Doohan. We wanted to be racers, and although I always felt pretty humble, Paul was convinced that he was going to be in MotoGP some day. I believed him. If you had seen him massaging those curves through the green-velvet hills on the peninsula, you'd believe too. He was like a concert violinist, a poet, a painter of masterpieces. He knew how to make a bike do things that

然而，从传统意义上来说，保罗并不那么信教。他和我一起长大，生活在地球下部、新西兰这块美丽、乏味、绿宝石般的小岛上，过着新教徒的生活。是的，我们都是猕猴桃（新西兰人）。当我们被傲慢的英国人询问是否来自澳大利亚时，都会呲牙咧嘴一笑。12 年前，我们一起来到这里，追逐一个梦想。我们常常骑着 250 立方厘米马达的摩托在克罗曼戴尔山脉驰骋、咆哮，梦想着旅游者杯摩托车赛，梦想着杜汉的世界。我们想成为赛车手。虽然我总觉得自己卑微，但保罗确信有朝一日他会参加世界摩托车大奖赛。我信他。如果你见过他对半岛上那绿茸茸山脉间的曲折小道像按摩一样一遍遍驶过时，你也会相信。他就像乐队里的小提琴手、一位诗人、一个杰出画家。他知道如何让一辆摩托车

shouldn't have been physically possible.

So we came to England, where racing is important and where we could kind-of-speak the language. We were certain this was where we were going to get that break that would let us be racers. We were young, naïve of course, but we also knew that it was going to take some hard work. We both managed to secure one-year contracts on a small team in one of the 125 series. It wasn't much, but it was a start. Paul was utterly brilliant that year, winning the title. I was less than stellar, but I managed fifth overall in the standings. Not great, but I was having fun, and I was genuinely happy for Paul's success. I drank champagne with him as he hoisted the trophy after the final race of the year, grinning as I gave him the winner's shower. This was what it was all about.

Then, two things happened that winter in the off season. I met Abs. And the accident.

****

The Suzuki comes to a stop on

做出看似不可能的事情。

因此，我们来到英格兰。在这里，赛车很被看重。在这里，我们多少可以用这种语言说话。我们确信，在这里我们会有所突破，成为赛车手。我们都很年轻，免不了单纯，但我们也知道，这需要付出努力。我们都设法获得了为期一年的合同，在125系列的一个小队中。这虽不起眼，但却是一个开始。那一年，保罗很出色，赢得了冠军。我没那么耀眼，但也设法在积分榜上排名第五——虽不是很好，但我很开心。我真心为保罗的成功感到高兴。在当年总成绩出来后，他举起冠军奖杯的那一刻，我和他共饮香槟；我向他喷洒着属于胜利者的香槟，开怀大笑。这就是我们想要的。

然而，在那年冬季非赛季时发生了两件事：我遇到了阿布丝，发生了车祸。

****

铃木摩托在跑道上停了下

the track. I lift my visor, wiping the thick fog off its surface. It's definitely him: the stylised number 65, the sponsor stickers, the helmet emblazoned with his Kiwi pride. Despite my leathers, my body is starting to go cold, the liquid in my suit and gloves starting to feel like ice.

He turns his head and looks at me.

I can't see his face, of course. Paul always wore a reflective visor. There's something about the tilt of the head, though, that makes me absolutely certain.

He waves his arm, like he is beckoning me. My feet sink further into the gravel.

He revs the engine, nods his head toward the track.

This doesn't make any sense to me, but I drop my bike into first gear and spin my way through the gravel onto the track beside him.

I am only a couple of metres from him now. He points down the track, clunks his bike into gear, revs it again, and is gone. About fifty metres down the track he looks back again.

来。我举起面罩，把上面那厚厚的雾水擦掉。没错，就是他：65号，字体很时尚，那是赞助商的代号；头盔上印有他作为新西兰人的骄傲。尽管我穿着皮衣，但身体开始发冷，衣服里、手套内的汗开始让我感到像冰一样。

他转过头看我。

当然，我看不到他的脸；保罗总是戴反光面罩，但那头部微倾的样子让我确定，那就是他。

他挥挥胳膊，像是在召唤我。我的脚更深地陷入砾石。

他加大了油门，朝着跑道点了点头。

这在我看来毫无道理，但我还是把车调到第一档。车轮在砾石中打了几个转，跑上了他身旁的赛道。

我离他只有几米远了。他指了指赛道，咔、咔转动车把，上档、加速，消失了。大约在赛道上跑出五十米，他再次回过头来看我。

I can't believe what I'm doing, but I release the clutch and take off after him. My hip throbs, but the chill settling into my bones goes even deeper.

我无法相信自己在做什么，但我松开离合器，跟了上去。我的髋在刺疼，渗入骨髓里的冷变得更深。

****

Paul and I were enjoying our lives as off-season racers. We didn't have much money, of course, but we managed to scrape together enough to pay for the flat we shared and a few bevies with the ladies. We were taking it easy, trying not to think too much of the future. When you're that young, you don't need to plan; you just know something will happen. Well, something did happen. Paul got the call from Honda for a try-out on their 250 GP bike. Although this was still a junior series, it was a big step up. Unbelievably, he managed to convince them to give me a shot as well. I was dead chuffed about this of course, and so was Paul.

****

保罗和我享受着淡季赛车手的生活。当然，我们没有多少钱，但还是能想办法凑够钱合租公寓和偶尔玩玩女人。我们尽量顺其自然，试着不去太多考虑未来。当你那么年轻时，你不需要做计划，你只管去做，让事情发生就行了。嗯，事情确实发生了。保罗接到电话，让他去试车——本田250GP。尽管这仍是一个初级系列，但还是向前迈出了一大步。令人难以置信的是，他竟然设法说服了本田，给我一个试车的机会。我当然高兴得要命，保罗也如此。

So there we were, a cool November morning, grey but not rainy, on the track at Donington trying to show our best stuff. I was nervous, believe me—thought I might event wet my leathers. Paul

因此，在 11 月一个清冷的早晨，我们站在了多宁顿的跑道上，准备展示我们最好的伎俩。天是灰色的，没有下雨。我很紧张。相信我，我的皮夹克可能都是湿的。然而，

though, seemed calm. He wasn't into the meditation stuff yet, but there was something about him that morning, a look in his eyes, like he could see the future. He just seemed so focused, as if nothing around him mattered. We ran a few practice laps and then the clock started. There were five of us out there, all trying to impress, but we weren't really racing; we were just trying to set the best lap time. Our starts were staggered so we'd have room on the track. I started ahead of Paul.

After running about four laps, I could see on the board that my times were pretty consistent with the others, except for Paul. He was running three seconds a lap faster than the rest of us. Three seconds! I couldn't see how I could make up that kind of time, but I tried. Braking later, deeper leans, I tried everything. Paul was a mate, but I didn't want him embarrassing me.

On the last lap, Paul really seemed to want to impress the team bosses. He had made up the stagger and caught me. I couldn't just let him by, though. I wanted to make him earn the pass. I held him off for

保罗看起来很平静。他没有做冥思之类的事情，但那天早晨他是和以往不太一样——他的眼神，就像能看到未来。他看起来很专注，好像周围的一切都不重要。我们先试着跑了几圈算是热身，接着就进入倒计时。有五名车手，都想有出色表现。然而，那并不是真的赛车，我们只想有最好的单圈成绩。我们的起点是错开的，因此在跑道上都有各自的空间。我的出发点排在保罗的前面。

四圈后，我能在计分板上看到，我的用时和其他人基本一致，但保罗例外。他每圈的速度比我们其余的人都快三秒。三秒！我看不出自己有任何赶超这个成绩的可能，但我仍然努力着。我把刹车尽量延后、车身更倾斜，尝试着一切可能。保罗虽是挚友，但我不想在他面前输得太差。

最后一圈了，保罗似乎真的想让车队老板印象深刻，他缩短了车距，赶上了我。我不想让他那么轻易地超过我。我要让他费点劲。我一直挡着他跑了两个弯道；但在下一个弯

two corners, but on the next he took one hell of a dive to the inside. Bloody insane, really. My guts jumped through my teeth. I didn't think there was any way he could hold it. But he did. Or at least, he almost did. His back wheel broke loose for just a moment and skidded out. He shimmied, and started to stand it up, but as he did this his back wheel touched my front. I was still knee down, pushing, and this slight impact created a wobble. Well I knew I was going to have to stand it up to keep control. As I started to shift my weight, my front wheel twisted and I high-sided. Now, I'd gone for many big slides before and gotten banged up, bruised and skinned, but I'd never high-sided.This is very bad. I went over the bars and landed awkwardly on the track. Something in my knee popped in a direction that was never intended, and my brain exploded into a galaxy of red and white stars—it looked like the Kiwi flag. This wasn't the worst of it, though. There was another bloke just behind us in the corner, and he didn't have time to react (I am told—I couldn't

道时，他突然魔鬼般地俯冲到了内侧。他简直是疯了。我的五脏六腑都提到嘴边了。我想，无论如何他都得栽了。但他却做到了——或者说，他几乎做到了。他的后车轮有那么一刻没抓紧地面，向外打滑；他抖动着试图把车立正。他这样做的同时，后车轮已经碰到了我的前车轮。我的膝盖仍然朝下，手在推着车把。这轻微的触碰让我的车颤抖起来。我知道我得先把车立正再找平衡。然而，当我开始把重心提起时，我的前车轮拧着了，我被掀翻出去。到那时为止，我经历过多次大的滑摔——其结果不外是重伤、轻伤或划破了皮，但我从未被掀翻出去过。这很糟糕。我越过车把笨拙地落在跑道上。我感到膝盖里有某样东西向着错误的方向杵出去，脑袋像炸开了花，变成了布满红色、白色繁星的银河——就像新西兰国旗。这还不是最糟糕的。在那个转弯处，我们的身后还有另一个家伙，他根本就来不及反应（事后有人这样告诉我——当时的我根本就

see much of anything at this point) so he ran right over me, catapulting himself into the gravel trap. He was okay, he had a soft landing, but when he hit me, he jammed my leg out of its socket. I tell you, there is no sound worse than a scream inside of a motorcycle helmet. I think I finally passed out from lack of oxygen rather than the head injury. Thank God for small mercies.

弄不清发生了什么）。因此，他就直接从我身上碾了过去，向着砾石坑冲了过去。他还好，着路较轻，没什么大碍；但他撞着我时，我的腿骨被拉出了骨臼。让我告诉你吧，没有任何声音比戴着头盔嘶叫更可怕的了。我想我是因为缺氧而不是脑袋受伤晕了过去。感谢上帝的怜悯之心。

I woke up in the hospital. Morphine is good, but it wasn't good enough. I was eventually able to understand the doctor's psychedelic, medical talk. Seems my knee was blown to pieces, my pelvic joint shattered and the ball-end of my femur chipped where it had pulled out of my pelvis. Plus all my muscles, ligaments and tendons were bruised and stretched out of shape. In summary, I had made a fucking, first-rate mess of my self.

我醒来时躺在医院里。吗啡起了作用，但还不够好。医生的病理谈话总是让人云里雾里，但我最终还是听明白了：似乎是，我的膝盖被撞成了碎片，我的骨盆关节被撕裂，我的股骨球头被从臼窝里拉了出去、撞碎了。除此之外，我所有的肌肉、韧带和肌腱都受了伤或被撕扯得变了形——一句话，我变成了一堆超级废物。

Paul came to see me, but not until two weeks later. He got the spot on the team of course, and immediately after the trial, was whisked away to Japan for fittings. He said he was really sorry about the accident, sorry that he hadn't been

保罗来看我，那是在两周之后了。当然，他得到了队里的那个名额。试车结束后，他随即被带往日本做适应和调整。他说，对于这场事故他感到很抱歉，对于我醒来时他不在身边感到抱歉。总之，是抱

there when I woke up, just sorry. But there was something strange in his eyes, something harder, sharper than I had ever seen before. When we talked of the crash, I told him that he had been too aggressive on that corner. He just shrugged and said "That's racing."

歉。然而，他眼睛里多了一种怪怪的东西、一种我从未见过的东西——既狠又辣。当我们谈起那次撞车时，我说，他太急于求成，转弯处也不减速。他只是耸耸肩，说："赛车就是这样。"

My muscles tightened, despite the morphine. "You had the spot locked up. You didn't need to prove anything."

尽管打了吗啡，我的肌肉却在绷紧。"你已经稳获那个名额了。你无须再证明什么。"

He didn't blink as he leaned forward in the chair. "When you're on the track, you're always racing, mate."

他在椅子里向前探了探身，眼睛一眨也不眨地说："当你在赛道上时，你就在赛车。伙计。"

I had no reply to this as I sunk into the mattress, staring at the ceiling, trying to remember those distant days in Coromandel.

对此我没有作答。我缩在床垫里，眼睛盯着天花板，试图记起那遥远的、我们曾在克罗曼戴尔度过的日子。

****

****

We go through two corners. He stays in front of me, but he doesn't pull away. On that bike, he could easily be gone, but he seems to have a different purpose today. He looks back periodically, making sure I'm still there. I am slow, as I have to wobble the gravel off the tires. The throbbing in my hip and knee

我们已经驶过了两个弯道。他一直保持在我前面，但并没有飞驰而去。一旦跨上那辆车，要离开，对他来说，是分分钟的事儿，但他今天似乎另有意图。他不时回头看看，确保我还跟着。我很慢，因为要晃掉轮胎上的砾石。每次我在摩托车上移动，髋关节和膝

intensifies each time I shift my weight. God, I don't think I'm even going to finish one lap.

He seems to sense my distress. He slows on the straight, letting me catch up. I shake my head at him. I can't see his face, but there is something about the tilt of his head, the flex of his fingers on the throttle that makes me sad, disappointed. Then he does something really strange. He points, first up at the sky, then down the track. I shrug. He makes this gesture again. I make a slashing motion across my throat, pointing at my fiery knee. We just coast for a few moments, side by side. The air is barely a whisper under my helmet when he suddenly swings his bike close to mine.

Then it happens.

****

I eventually got out of the hospital, eventually learned to walk again. It was tough, both mentally and physically. I mean, I knew I wasn't destined for greatness like Paul, but I still had to face the fact that I would probably never get on a bike again. All my dreams, all my

关节处的疼痛就会加剧。老天！我想我可能连一圈都完成不了。

他似乎察觉到了我的沮丧。他在直道上慢了下来，让我赶上。我对他摇了摇头。我看不到他的脸，但当他的头倾斜时，我能感觉到什么；那放在油门上的手指的伸缩让我伤心和失望。然而，他随后做了件很奇怪的事情。他先向上指了指天，然后向下指了指赛道。我耸了耸肩。他又做了同样的手势。我做了一个抹脖子（自杀）的动作， 指了指灼疼的膝盖。我们并排向前滑行了一会儿。我戴着头盔，空气几乎变成了耳语。突然，他摆动摩托车，向我靠近。

后面的事就发生了。

****

我最终离开了医院，学会了再次走路。无论在心理上还是身体上，这都不容易。我的意思是，我知道我天生就不像保罗那样是做大事的人，但我还得面对另一个事实，那就是，我可能永远都不能再骑摩托车了。我所有的梦想和计划

plans had dribbled down the drain, and I was only twenty-two. I really had no idea what to do next.

My doctor suggested that I try Tai Chi to help with my rehabilitation. Now, I was never much into this alternative medicine shit, but I had nothing else to do so I reckoned I'd give it a try.

My instructor immediately made an impression on me. Abigail—Abs she preferred to be called—had an electric smile, long coppery hair, bright green eyes and that beautifully transparent skin that English girls seem to wear so well. She took a special interest in me, as I needed a lot of attention to get my body strengthened, and I was always eager for our sessions, for the feel of her strong hands steadying me as I tried to master Grasp Bird's Tail. She liked me, but she was one of those people who seemed to like everyone. I was smitten, and the slow, painful process of making my body work again somehow seemed more bearable with Abs gently steering me along. We did go out a few times, and there were a few sweet kisses, but eventually she told

都被冲进了下水道，而我才 22 岁。我真不知道下一步该做什么。

医生建议我试一试太极来帮助康复。对这个医学上的旁门左道，我从未正眼瞧过，但我又没别的事可做，所以就想不妨试一试。

老师立即就给我留下了深刻的印象。阿比盖尔——她更喜欢人们叫她阿布丝——有着电人的微笑、古铜色的长发和明亮的绿眼睛；她的皮肤透亮、美丽，似乎只有英国女孩才有此特质。她对我特别感兴趣，因为我需要特别关注，以让自己的身体强壮起来。我总是渴望上课，感受她有力的手稳住我做鹰抓鸡时晃动的身体。她喜欢我，但她似乎是喜欢每一个人的那种人。我被她迷得神魂颠倒。在阿布丝温柔的引导下，那痛苦而漫长的康复过程在某种程度上变得似乎不那么难以承受了。我们出去过几次，有过一些甜蜜的吻。但最终她告诉我，她是真的像普通朋友那样喜欢我，因为她觉得我们之间没有化学反应。我不得

me that she really liked me as just a friend, that she didn't feel any chemistry between us. I had to accept this, but the memory of her lips still made my body ache even after it healed.

不接受这个现实，但每每想起她的嘴唇，我的身体便隐隐作痛，即使在我康复以后也如此。

Paul saw me intermittently. Although his team had local headquarters, he was busy with practicing, promotions and other stuff I guess. Then, once the season started in the spring, he was frequently away on the continent for the races. Since signing with Honda, Paul had become much more serious-minded, and our friendship seemed to have cooled a little. I didn't think that I bore a grudge against him, but somehow it seemed harder to talk to him. He was so focused now he didn't even seem like the same person. He had started getting into meditation—said it helped make him smoother on the bike—and when he found out that I was doing Tai Chi, he was immediately interested. I couldn't believe it. For a bloke who could go so fast to want to do something so slow seemed ridiculous.

保罗断断续续地来看我。尽管他的团队在当地有总部，但他总是忙于训练、促销或别的活动——我猜想是这样的。然而，一旦春天来了，赛季开始，他便频繁去欧洲大陆进行比赛。自从和本田签了约，保罗变得更加认真，而我们的友谊似乎已经变得冷却了一些。我并不认为我对他有不满情绪，但不知何故，和他交流变得越来越难。他如此专注，似乎变成了另外一个人。他已经开始形成冥思的习惯——他说这会让他骑车更顺。当他发现我在做太极，他立刻很感兴趣。我无法相信，一个能把摩托骑得如此快的家伙竟然想去做如此慢的事情，这简直令人匪夷所思。

I introduced him to Abs and knew right away that something was

我把他介绍给阿布丝，立刻便知道他们之间将会发

going to happen between them. Even though he only erratically attended the classes, there was something in the way Abs greeted him that was more than just cordial. They did eventually start seeing each other, at least when Paul was around, which wasn't that often. Sometimes I wondered what she saw in him. He seemed so focused on his racing now, and I couldn't understand how he could give Abs the warmth and attention she deserved. Still, they got on well, so how could I not be happy for them?

生什么。尽管他很不规律地来上课，但阿布丝问候他的方式不仅仅是亲切。他们终于开始见面了——至少是在保罗来的时候，而这种时候并不经常发生。有时我想知道她到底看上了他什么。他现在是如此专注于他的赛车，我无法理解他怎么能够给予阿布丝应得的温暖与关注。然而，他们相处得很好。我还有什么理由不为他们感到高兴呢？

It was near the end of the summer following my accident that I really started to feel I was at a loose end. I mean, I was able to walk again, barely, but I had nothing to do. Paul was now becoming a little famous, as he had just signed a contract for the following season with Rizla Suzuki in the premier class, and he used his contacts to get me a job at Donington. It wasn't much, just general facility maintenance, nothing too strenuous, but at least I got to be around bikes all day. I was grateful to have something to do.

在我出事后的那个夏末，我真的开始感到无所事事了。我的意思是，我又能走路了，当然还不是很好，但我却无事可做。保罗现在变得小有名气。他刚和瑞兹拉-铃木签署了下一个赛季的合同，属于超级赛之类的。利用他的关系，他为我在多宁顿找了份工作。活不多，就是一般的设备维护，不需要太多的体力。然而，我至少又能整天和摩托车打交道了，我对保罗心存感激。

Now that Paul was playing with the big boys, he was away even more, busy with testing, promotional obligations, racing — he was becoming a true professional. The thing is, Abs started going with him to some of his races. I understood this—she was in love with Paul, why wouldn't she follow him? Of course, it meant I got to see a lot less of her. Even though we were just friends, Abs and I had spent quite a bit of time together, and I found that when she was away I really missed her. She had helped me with my recovery more than she knew, keeping my spirits up, giving me something to look forward to each day as she gently pushed me a little further. She really was my best mate after the crash.

现在，和保罗打交道的都是大腕儿。他离家更频繁，忙着测试，忙着尽义务推销，忙着赛车。他正变成一个真正的职业赛车手。问题是，阿布丝开始跟他一起去参加某些赛事。对此，我能理解——她爱上了保罗，为什么就不能跟着他呢？当然，这意味着我见她的机会少了。虽然我们只是普通朋友，阿布丝和我待在一起的时间还真不少。当她外出时，我发现我真的很想念她。她对我的康复所起的作用要远远大于她能想象的。一天天，她温柔地把我向前推，让我精神饱满、有所期待。车祸后，她成了我最好的伴侣。

This was about the time I started sinking. I mean, I'm not generally self absorbed, but as I swept out the garages at Donington that winter, the damp, oily air tickling the back of my throat, the heavy English sky settling like a grey blanket on the washed out green hills, I started wondering why I was there. I mean, life had been so

这时我开始情绪低落。我的意思是，我通常并不自闭，但那年冬天，当我在多宁顿打扫车库时，那潮湿的、油腻腻的空气让我的喉咙深处痒个不停。大不列颠联合王国那厚重的天空像灰色的毯子盖住了已经褪色的青山。我开始质疑，为什么我要待在那里。我的意思是，生活一直如此美好，充

good, so promising a couple of years before and then my best friend almost kills me, steals my girl (well she wasn't really my girl, but it still hurt) then gets me a job sweeping floors. What happened to my life? Paul's life, on the other hand, seemed to be charmed in the extreme. He was making good money chasing his dream. He was starting to get some respect. He finished third in the championship that year, and then won it all a year later. Abs was totally in love with him; in fact, they got engaged after his first season of MotoGP. I guess I had a little too much time to think about things, and I found the bitterness starting to settle into my bones. I started to wonder if Paul had purposely taken me out. I wasn't destined for greatness like he was, but maybe he still saw me as some kind of threat. Whatever the reason, he had changed my life. I might have had a career in racing; maybe Abs would have felt differently about me if I hadn't been a cripple. I don't know. These thoughts started swirling around in my head, bubbling and simmering away like

满了憧憬，直至一两年前——一切都变了：我最好的朋友几乎杀了我，偷了我的女人（当然，她不能说是我真正的女人，但我还是受到了伤害），然后给我找了份扫地的工作。我的生活到底怎么了？相反，保罗的生活似乎美到了极致。他既赚大钱，又能追逐自己的梦想。他开始受人尊重。那一年，他在锦标赛中得了第三名；一年后，他赢得了总冠军。阿布丝完全被他征服了。实际上，在世界摩托车锦标赛第一个赛季后，他们就订婚了。我猜想我有太多的时间去想事情，结果，痛苦开始慢慢沁入我的骨髓。我开始猜测，保罗是不是故意带我出去——我生就不如他，但他或许仍视我为某种威胁。不管原因是什么，他改变了我的生活。我或许本可以靠赛车谋生；如果我没有瘸，或许阿布丝对我的感觉就有所不同。我不知道。这些想法开始在我的脑海中打旋、冒泡、消失，就像泥罐在罗托鲁瓦河中慢慢被吞没那样。我开始花更多的时间打

the mud pots in Rotorua, and I started spending more time dusting the cobwebs in the garage, avoiding Paul and Abs as much as I could. I wanted to forget about them, and for a while I did.

扫车库里的蜘蛛网，尽可能回避保罗和阿布丝。我想忘了他们。有那么一段时间，我还真的忘了他们。

****

We come to a stop on the track. He is only inches away from me, my body is shaking in my suit. He reaches down and grabs my knee. There is a brief, intense pain that shoots lightning bolts through my leg, and then a spreading, cooling numbness. The fire in my knee and hip are gone. His touch is almost not like a touch. I can't actually feel his hand on me, but instead there is merely a slight pressure that completely surrounds my leg, as if I am walking in shallow water. I flex my knee. No pain at all. He lets go and pops his bike back into gear. With a nod, he takes off and I follow, suddenly not feeling awkward on the bike anymore. I don't understand what is happening, but I begin working the bike through the corners, and it feels good.

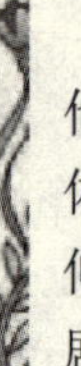

****

我们在跑道上停了下来。他离我只有几英寸远。我的身体在衣服下颤抖。他突然向下伸手抓住了我的膝盖。短暂的剧痛就像是有一枚闪电的铆钉射进我的腿里。然后，一种令我感到冷飕飕的麻木开始蔓延。膝盖和臀部的火消失了。他的触摸几乎算不上是触摸。我实际上并没有感觉到他的手碰到了我的身体；我只是觉得腿被一种轻轻的压力包裹，是那种走在浅水区里的感觉。我弯了弯膝盖，并不疼痛。他松开刹车，再次把车挂上档。他点了一下头，胯下的车窜了出去；我紧紧跟着，突然间不再觉得骑在车上有什么不舒服。我不明白正在发生什么，但我开始驾车穿过弯道，而且感觉很好。

****

Life can be really stupid, really unfair at times. I hadn't seen Paul and Abs for over a year. Paul had just won the championship and I had heard that he and Abs had set a date for their wedding. Good for them, I thought. I needed to get away from the whole racing scene for a bit, so I decided to get some sea air for a few days.

I can still remember where I was when I got the news: leaning on a railing on the seawall in Blackpool. It was January, drizzly, not busy, waves tumbling and turning, thumping and whisking. I had been standing there for quite a while, watching the grey sky settle into the sea, letting my feet grow into the concrete, when my mobile rang. Paul had been in Japan doing some testing. The helicopter that was taking him back to the airport from the track had crashed. No survivors.

I went to the funeral, of course. Like everyone, I was in shock. Still, there was a small part of me that wondered if there was some kind of balancing, some kind of justice at work here. I mean, I didn't wish

****

生活有时真的是愚蠢而不公平。我有一年多的时间没见保罗和阿布丝了。保罗刚刚赢得了锦标赛的冠军。我听说他和阿布丝结婚的日子也选定了。好样的，我想。我需要远离任何和赛车有关的事情——哪怕是短暂的。因此，我决定去海边呼吸几天海洋的空气。

我仍然能记得当获知此消息时我身在何处：靠在布莱克浦海堤的一个栏杆上。当时是 1 月份，下着毛毛细雨，人不是很多，海浪翻滚、转动、击打、搅拌着。我已经站在那儿有一阵子了，看着灰色的天空慢慢落入大海，任自己的脚慢慢在混凝土地面上生根。这时手机响了。那段时间保罗一直待在日本做某种测试。把他从赛道送回机场的直升机坠落。没有幸存者。

当然，我参加了葬礼。像每个人一样，我感到震惊。然而，仍有一小部分的我在想，冥冥中是否有一种平衡、一种正义。我的意思是，我并不希望保罗死，这是当然的啰。然

Paul dead, of course, but the funeral really stung me, brought out all the venom I had been storing. I kept it together, though, didn't make a scene or anything, for Abs' sake. She was, as you would expect, in pretty rough shape. I spoke with her briefly, hugged her trembling body to mine, but I felt uncomfortable. I hadn't seen her for so long, and she looked different, as if something had been siphoned out of her.

而，葬礼却真的刺痛了我，那存储已久的歹意被激发了出来。其实，我一直怀揣这些歹意，只是因为阿布丝的缘故，我一直没有让它爆发。如你所料，她已经不成样子了。我和她简短说了几句，把她颤抖的身体抱入怀中；然而，我却感到了不舒服。我已经很久没见过她了，她看起来和以前不一样了，好像体内的某样东西被抽走了。

Strangely, though, after things started to settle down, Abs started to get more involved in my life. I was walking okay by now, so I had given up the Tai Chi. Abs was obviously not away any more, so she started teaching again, and eventually managed to drag me out to a class. I don't know if she needed someone familiar to hold onto, but she seemed to like having me there. There was some initial awkwardness, but eventually I started gaining strength. Abs seemed to be coming back to life, as well.

奇怪的是，当事情慢慢沉淀下来，阿布丝开始越来越多地介入我的生活。现在，走路对我而言已经不是什么问题，所以我放弃了太极。阿布丝显然不经常出门了。所以，她又开始教太极；而且最终设法劝我加入了她的一个班。我不知道她是否需要有熟人可以靠一靠，但她似乎喜欢有我在。最初有一点点尴尬，但最终我还是恢复了体力。阿布丝似乎也逐渐生活正常化。

Then, one night after class we were having a pint down at our local and Abs suggested that I get back on the bike again. I told her I thought

然而，有一天晚上，下课后，我们正在当地的一间酒吧里喝啤酒。阿布丝建议我再骑摩托。我告诉她这是个馊主

she was barmy. I mean, I could walk again, but one wrong twist of the knee still sent volcanic pains surging through me. Besides, I had no confidence. I knew my racing career was knackered and I didn't see any point trying to live in the past. Abs kept prodding me and eventually I had to admit that I was scared. I was scared of crashing, scared of the pain. But more importantly, I was scared of failing. I thought that I would look like a total wanker out there on the track, and that if I couldn't even keep the bike up, I would never ride again. I didn't want to face that. It was easier to do nothing. I was the guy who had the horrible crash and couldn't ride anymore. That was a role that other people understood, a role that I could play.

意。我的意思是，虽然我可以再走路了，但只要膝盖稍微扭一下，我的全身就会感到如火山岩浆般的灼痛。除此之外，我没有信心。我知道我的赛车生涯已严重受损，我也看不出试图生活在过去有任何意义。阿布丝不断激将我，最终我不得不承认，我很害怕。我害怕撞车、害怕疼痛，但更重要的是，我害怕失败。我觉得自己在跑道上看起来就是一个彻头彻尾的傻瓜；更有甚者，如果我连车都扶不正的话，我将永远不会再骑车了。我不想面对。什么都不做不是更容易吗？难道我不是那个被摔碎过、不能再骑车的人吗？扮演那个角色既能得到别人的理解，自己也好过些。

Well, Abs called bollocks on this. She actually got angry, telling me that I was giving up too easily. She told me that I should I try to get on a bike if for no other reason than to honour Paul's memory. She said that Paul wouldn't want me to quit, and as I sat silently listening to her, running my finger around the

阿布丝称我的想法是一派胡言。她真的生气了，说我太容易放弃。她告诉我说，不为别的，哪怕是为了向保罗的记忆致敬，我都应该努力再骑摩托。她说，保罗不希望我停滞不前。我坐在那儿，静静地听着，用手指搅着杯子里的啤酒泡沫。

sagging foam in my pint glass, I wondered if she was right. I mean, I had tried to bury Paul long before he was actually dead, and I had forgotten that he had once been a good mate. Still, it was hard to think of honouring Paul after what he had done to me. I said no to Abs that night, but she kept at me. Eventually I gave in, not for the sake of Paul's memory, but for Abs. I didn't want *her* to be disappointed in me.

So one sunny Monday I managed to borrow a bike and I gave it a run on an open track day at Donington. God I was slow. And in pain. But I made it around the track, finishing two laps. The second lap hurt more, but was a little faster. After I stumbled off my bike, Abs gave me a big hug as I tried to peel my sweat-soaked gloves off my hands. She said she was proud of me.

After that I practised more and more, and it got easier. It never felt as comfortable as it used to, but I didn't expect it to. I finally got to the point where I was able to get my knee down again, and I started thinking about racing. Not seriously,

我在掂量她说的话。我的意思是，在保罗死之前，我就已经努力埋葬了他；我已经忘了他曾是一个好伴侣。在他对我做了这么多之后，我很难对他再有敬意。那晚，我对阿布丝说了“不”，但她却一直缠着我。最后，我让步了，不是为了保罗的记忆，而是为了阿布丝。我不想让*她*对我失望。

在一个阳光明媚的星期一，我设法借到了一辆摩托车。在多宁顿的赛道开放日，我让自己试了一把。天哪！我太慢了，而且浑身疼痛。然而，我沿着赛道跑了两圈。第二圈时，我疼得更厉害，但速度却上来了。当我趔趔趄趄从车上下来，吃力地摘掉汗水湿透的手套时，阿布丝给了我一个大大的拥抱，说她为我感到骄傲。

在那之后，我练习得更多，骑摩托对我来说也变得越来越容易，但感觉总不如从前那样自在。当然，我也并不奢望。我的膝盖终于能弯曲到骑车转弯时需要的低度。我开始想赛车的事。当然，这想法还

of course. It was more like one of those daydreams where you stare out the window at the puffy clouds and say "what if?" I mean, I wasn't exactly old, but while I was on the track I would see these young lads, looking like they were barely out of nappies, come flying into the corners and I'd be gob-smacked. I'd swear they were heading for the gravel traps or maybe a big slide, but they always managed to gain just enough control to push their bikes through the corners, back wheels wobbling. Don't get me wrong, I was fast too, and I certainly held my own. But some of these guys didn't seem human, didn't seem to have any sense at all of their own mortality.

不成熟，更像是一个白日梦，那种凝视着窗外漂浮的白云说"如果……那么……"时所做的白日梦。我的意思是，虽然我还不算老，但在赛道上我见到的都是些年轻的家伙们。他们看起来像是刚刚摆脱了尿布，就飞一般地冲进了赛道的转弯处，让我目瞪口呆。我发誓，当他们冲向砾石坑或一个大滑坡时，他们总能设法掌控得恰到好处，顺利通过转弯——尽管后车轮会摇摆不定。别误会，我也快，我也能控制自己的车，但他们中的一些简直就不像凡人，好像他们也完全不知道自己是肉身、有生死。

Abs actually seemed more serious about my racing than I was. She came to watch me practise, always offering encouragement, hugs. We didn't talk of Paul any more, which suited me. Eventually, after a few months of her gentle encouragement, Abs convinced me to sign up for an amateur-night race.

对于我参赛与否，阿布丝似乎比我更认真。她来看我训练，总是鼓励、拥抱。我们再没提过保罗，这正是我需要的。经过几个月温柔的鼓励，阿布丝终于说服我报名参加一个"业余选手之夜"的比赛。

The race was just some of the locals, out for a bit of fun on a Tuesday night. None of them were

参赛的只是一些当地人，是周二晚上走出家门的一点乐趣。他们中没有一个是专业赛

professional racers as I had once been, but none had been smashed up either. I had to get special permission, but eventually I was let in.

I was utterly terrified as I lined up on the grid. Abs gave me a thumbs-up from the stands as I sat on my bike, the red lights burning my eyes through my visor. It was about to begin.

****

I've completed one lap and I've got him in my sights again. He is going fast, but my bike seems able to keep up. This doesn't make sense. I'm just riding a street bike, but he's got a MotoGP monster. This shouldn't be happening. The pack is still well ahead—I lost a lot of time in the gravel—but I seem to be gaining ground.

I go screaming into one of the high speed corners way too fast, and then it's almost like I've gone deaf. The wind whistle in my helmet is instantly gone and the engine's whine is just a muted drone. What the hell's going on? I push hard, desperately trying to carve the

车手，而我曾经是，但也没有谁像我那样被摧毁过。我必须得到特别许可。最终，他们还是允许我参赛了。

当我们列队站在赛车起跑线上时，我感到了恐惧。当我跨上车时，坐在看台上的阿布丝对我竖起大拇指。红灯闪烁，隔着眼罩灼痛着我的眼。比赛要开始了。

****

我已经完成了一圈，我的视线里再次出现了他。他跑得很快，但我的车似乎也能跟得上。这没道理。我骑的是街道上随便跑着的摩托，而他骑的却是参加世界摩托车锦标赛用的超级怪物。这种情况怎么可能发生！离前面的车群还有一段距离，我刚才在砾石堆里已经损失了不少时间——但我似乎正在赶上。

我尖叫着驶入高速上的一个转弯处，太快了，接着我好像是失去了听觉。吹进我头盔里鸣叫的风瞬间消失了，发动机的轰鸣声像是被消音的无人机发出的。到底是怎么回事？我拼命地推着把，膝盖刮着地面上的沥青，希望车轮能内

corner, knee scraping the asphalt, when Paul's voice suddenly starts flooding my brain. "Balance the forces." He used to tell me this when he tried to explain his "God at 300 km/h" theory. The idea was that when you approach a corner at suicidal speed, you know that in a few seconds there will be only a couple of very small patches of rubber contacting the pavement, keeping the forces in balance. It's hard to believe, but these few square centimetres of tyre are keeping the massive forces of momentum, centrifugal force and gravity all perfectly harmonized. Paul said that when once you overcome the terror of it and realize that such a small thing can balance such large forces and prevent mortal pain and agony, it was like seeing God.

切，卡着地面驶出弯道。这时，保罗的声音突然淹没了我的大脑。“平衡力量。”他说。这是他试图向我解释他的“上帝就在每小时 300 公里处”理论时说过的一句话。意思是，当你以自杀的速度接近一个转弯时，你应该知道，有几秒钟的时间里，车轮和路面的接触面只有小块补丁那么大，但却在平衡着各种力。很难想象，这几平方厘米的胎面能承受动态所产生的巨大离心力，并使之和地球引力保持和谐。保罗说，一旦你克服了它带来的恐惧，并意识到这样一个小小的接触面竟然能平衡各种巨力、阻止致命的伤和剧烈的痛，那种感觉就像见到了上帝。

I don't have time to think about God. The mantra repeats over and over as the bike wiggles, grips then pulls out of the corner. My senses are numbed, and I feel no fear, no pain. I've got to catch up to that baby-blue bastard. I start carving corners like they're butter, staying right on his tail, and we eventually

我没有时间去思考上帝。当我的摩托车颤抖着、挣扎着驶出转弯处时，这句话像咒语一样在重复着。我的感觉麻木了，没有恐惧、没有痛苦。我必须赶上这个淡蓝色的家伙。我的车轮开始像切黄油般地切入弯道，紧紧跟在他的后面。终于，我们赶上了车群。接

catch up to the pack. Then, his bike begins to glow like a comet, and he shoots through the middle of all those shrieking bikes, passing them like they're stuck in sheep shit. I lose sight of him as he blazes around the next corner, but I'm now positioned firmly in the middle of the mob. I smooth the bike through a few more corners and then with a burst, I manage pip a Kawasaki for second at the finish line.

着，他的车开始发光，就像一颗彗星，从中间穿过那群尖叫着的摩托，就像它们陷在羊屎堆里一般。在下一个转弯处，他从我的视线里消失了。我现在已经稳稳地处在车群中。我又顺利地驶过几个弯道；接着，我突然发力，在最后时刻扭转局面，超过了一辆川崎，第二个冲过了终点线。

Leather-drenched, leg-numbed, I coast the bike back to the pits. I don't understand what's just happened, don't know how I could have ridden so fast. It's as if I had suddenly become weightless. Abs is beaming. She shoots like a falling satellite across the oily asphalt and hugs me until I feel something again. "Paul would be proud," she says and I can't help but smile. She puts her arm around my waist as my knee suddenly catches fire and buckles. Her shoulders are strong.

我的皮衣已经湿透，腿也麻木了，我让摩托车滑行回到车圈里。我不明白刚刚发生了什么，也无法得知我怎么可能骑得那么快！就好像我突然变得没有重量。阿布丝眉开眼笑。她像一颗坠落的卫星，穿过油腻的柏油路朝我冲来，拥抱我，直到我又一次有了感觉。"保罗会感到骄傲的。"她说。除了微笑我还能怎样？我的膝盖突然像着了火直不起来，她用手搂着我的腰。她的肩膀很强壮。

Broken Symmetry

失衡

A less meticulous man probably wouldn't have noticed it. But Anthony John, controlled and precise Anthony John, picked out the fragment immediately, two words that jumped up from the page, beckoned to him from the hundreds of other words on the newspaper that he normally scanned on his morning Skytrain ride to work.

一个不细心的人可能根本注意不到它，但安东尼·约翰是一位有掌控力、做事缜密的人，他立即就挑出了那个片语——两个字，它们似从页面上几百个字里跳出来，向他招手。每天早晨，他乘坐空列去工作时都会快速扫读一份报纸。

...John Anthony...

……约翰·安东尼……

His head tilted slightly, leaning closer to the paper. His eyesight was perfect, uncorrected, but he still felt the need to examine this article more closely.

他的头微微前倾，更靠近报纸。他的视力很好，不是被矫正过的，但他还是觉得需要更仔细地查阅这篇文章。

...was seriously injured. Witnesses stated that the blue transporter entered the intersection on a red light and struck the Toyota on the passenger side, killing the 45 year-old nurse instantly...

……严重受伤。目击者称，蓝色运输车闯红灯进入十字路口，撞上一辆停靠在人行道边上的丰田牌小轿车，造成一位45岁的护士当场死亡……

He needed context. He traced back to the start of the sentence.

他需要上下文。他追溯到这个句子的开始。

Katrina Anthony, a health-care worker from Leith, died yesterday in a collision and her husband...

卡特里娜·安东尼，一位来自利思的卫生保健人员，昨天死于撞车事故，她的丈夫……

He quickly read the rest of the article. *Drunk driver...good driving conditions...historically dangerous intersection...survived by two adult children...long recovery expected...* Letting the newspaper settle on his lap, he looked out the window. The February sky was heavy, the colour of dull lead, droplets of rain crawling randomly across the glass as the Skytrain headed east, clacking on the rail joints. Anthony looked deep into the fog that had settled over the harbour, trying to find some sense in the article he had just read. His wife's name was Kathleen. She was a

他快速阅读文章的其余部分。*酒醉的司机……良好的驾驶条件……历史上危险的十字路口……身后留下两个已成年的孩子……预期需要长时间从打击中恢复……*他把报纸放在膝盖上，向窗外望去。2月的天空很沉闷，单调的铅色。空列向东行驶，轨道交接处发出咣当、咣当的声响，雨滴顺着车窗玻璃胡乱向下流淌。安东尼盯着笼罩着港口的雾霭深处，试图在他刚读过的那篇文章里找到某种意义。他妻子的名字是凯瑟琳。她是

nursing instructor, 54 years old, drove a Toyota.

How strange.

John Anthony was described as an engineer who worked for an Edinburgh software company. Anthony John worked for a Burnaby telecommunications company, managing customer accounts. Not much point of commonality there. But the wife, the wife…

Anthony folded the newspaper and slid it neatly into the side pocket of his briefcase. He normally enjoyed this morning ride to work, the Skytrain car only half full of passengers traveling against the flow, away from downtown. This more civilized commute allowed him time to relax as he reviewed the newspaper. The quiet contemplation, though, was displaced this morning by the odd article. Coincidence? Of all the billions of people in the world and random events that occurred every second of every day, was it not possible that occasionally some sets of circumstances would align themselves to create what appeared to be highly improbable connections? Pure chance could be the only possible explanation.

一个护理教师，54 岁，开一辆丰田小轿车。

多么奇怪。

据描述，约翰·安东尼是一位工程师，在爱丁堡的一家软件公司上班。安东尼·约翰为一家本拿比的电信公司工作，管理客户账目。没有什么共性。但是，这位妻子……，妻子……

安东尼把报纸折好，把它整齐地放入公文包的侧袋里。他早上通常喜欢坐这趟空列去上班，车内只有一半乘客，和进城的车流对开。这种更文明的乘车环境让他有时间放松，检阅报纸的内容。然而，今天早上，这种安静的沉思却被这篇奇怪的文章打破。是巧合吗？世界上有数十亿的人，每天、每时、每刻都会有偶然的事情发生。难道就没有一些组合环境会偶尔串联起来，形成一种看似非常不可能的关联吗？纯粹的巧合只可能是唯一的解释。那么到底是什么促使他看那页报纸呢？他并不是每

But what had caused him to look at that particular page? He didn't read every page of the paper; he only scanned, looking for items of interest. And what of the newspaper itself? This wasn't his regular paper. A shipping delay, the old man at the newsstand had told him that morning, scratching the back of his hand on grey chin stubble. Why don't you try this one, instead? The man had handed Anthony the thick, Scottish daily. He was pleasantly surprised by its weight, the density of the text. One of the best papers around, the old man had winked, his words fighting their way through his gravely phlegm. Anthony had been buying his newspapers from the old newsstand in downtown Vancouver for years, but had never learned the old man's name. The newsstand was a relic, an anachronistic wart among the smooth flesh of glass and steel and concrete. Anthony wondered how the old man stayed in business in the age of the internet, but there always seemed to be customers around the battered, graffiti-scarred metal kiosk. It was located in the corner of a small square a few blocks from the main business

页都读；他只是快速浏览，寻找那些他感兴趣的。那么，报纸本身有问题吗？这并不是他通常读的那份报。那天早晨，老人一边用手背蹭着自己灰色的短髭，一边对他说，报纸被延误了，你为什么不试试这个呢？他递给安东尼一份厚厚的苏格兰日报。他惊讶于它的重量和文本的密度，还不错！老人眨着眼睛，告诉他说，这是周围最出色的报纸之一了。老人喉咙里有浓痰，他说的话必须吃力地冲破浓痰才能被听清。多年来，安东尼一直在温哥华市中心的这个旧报亭买报纸，但从不知道老人的姓名。报亭是一个遗迹，就像一个由光滑玻璃、钢筋和混凝土构成的肌体上的一个疣，给人时空错位的感觉。安东尼一直想知道，老人在互联网时代如何能让生意一直继续。然而，在那个伤痕累累、遍体涂鸦的金属报亭周围总是有顾客。它位于一个小广场的角落，离主要商业

core, the type of square that attracted both men in suits and men in heavy, dirty jackets. The old man always knew what he wanted, always called him "sir", always gave him a three-tooth smile, his grey eyes lost in the folds of experienced flesh on his face. Although the old man sometimes talked to Anthony about current events, sports, weather, he never violated the unwritten contract prohibiting the exchange of personal information.

On his way home, Anthony decided to walk back through the square. He usually approached it from the west, in the morning, but now from the east, the newsstand appeared different. He had never seen it closed before, and was surprised by the colour of the corrugated metal doors across the entrance. The rest of the kiosk was grimy and grey, but the doors were bright, even in the low, filtered light of the setting sun. Anthony drew his hand across the smooth metal, wondering why the doors were free of the spray-painted profanity and art—the urban expressionism—that covered the sides of the metal shack.

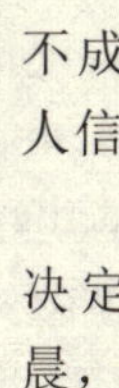

区只有几个街区远。这类广场既能吸引西装男，也能吸引穿着肮脏、沉重夹克的男人。这位老人总是知道他想要什么，总是称呼他"先生"，总是给他一个露着三颗牙齿的微笑。他灰色的眼睛几乎被脸上满是岁月沧桑的皱纹掩埋。尽管老人有时与安东尼讨论时事、体育、天气，但他从不触碰那不成文的协定——不交换个人信息。

在回家的路上，安东尼决定步行穿过广场。在早晨，他通常从西面接近它，但现在，他从东面向它走去。报亭看起来与平常有所不同——他以前从未见它关闭过，并且，在入口处有一道带有波纹形状的金属门，其颜色也让他惊异。报亭的其他部分肮脏、灰不溜秋的，只有这扇门在低沉的、落日的余晖中闪着亮光。安东尼用手在它光滑的金属表面划过，他想知道为什么门上没有被涂鸦或喷上艺术作品，即所谓的城市表现主义，而金属亭子的其他地方却都是。

Kathleen wasn't in their apartment when he got home. There was note on the kitchen table: one of her colleagues had called in sick and she had to go out to Port Coquitlam to cover a pre-natal class that evening. Anthony was glad. He wanted a quiet evening: a glass of Malbec, perhaps, and a crossword puzzle. Even if he closed the door to his study, Kathleen's presence—the buzzing murmur of the television, her loud laugh—could still irritate him. After thirty years together, they had each constructed their own spheres of exclusion. With her gone for the evening, he felt he could let his sphere expand a little.

他到家时，凯瑟琳不在房子里。他注意到厨房的桌子上有个条子：她的一个同事打电话，请了病假，她不得不在那天晚上去科奎特勒姆港替她上一节产前教育课。安东尼很高兴。他想要一个安静的夜晚：一杯马尔贝克，或许再玩一个纵横字谜。即使他关上了书房的门，凯瑟琳的存在——电视机的嗡嗡杂音、她的大笑——仍然能扰怒他。在一起生活 30 年了，他们各自都已经营建了只属于自己的排他性空间。今晚她不在，他觉得自己的领域可以扩大一些。

He was feeling quite relaxed, second glass of Malbec in hand, when the door buzzer rang.

他感觉很放松。当第二杯马尔贝克酒端在手上时，门上的蜂鸣器响了。

****

The funeral was well attended. Kathleen had made many friends over the years through her work, and they were all shocked and saddened by the accident. She had been on her way to her class when her Corolla was struck on the driver's side by a brown Suburban driven by a seventy-two

参加葬礼的人很多。在过去的几年里，由于工作关系，凯瑟琳已经结识了很多朋友。他们对这场交通事故感到震惊和悲哀。在她去上课的路上，她的科罗拉牌小汽车的驾驶位那侧被一辆棕色的雪佛兰撞上，司机是一

year old man who had not seen the stop sign. Paramedics were on the scene quickly, but she was already dead when they got there.

Anthony had no tears at the funeral. There had been a few in private—salty, bitter drops that slid down his cheek, collected at the corner of his mouth. He tried to feel anguish, grief, but found he was more consumed with a sense of injustice that somehow his meticulous control of his environment had been compromised. Their son, Patrick, had flown in from Calgary where he was working for an oil company. Anthony hadn't seen Patrick for two years. "Busy schedules" they both offered as an explanation, both knowing that this was only partly the reason.

Patrick decided to stay for a while after the funeral. Anthony was glad, but also hoped that he wouldn't stay too long. Although it was a comfort to see his son again, he felt that he really needed to be alone to process his feelings, to try to understand the significance of that strange reference in the newspaper. The parallels were uncanny, and although they could be attributed to

位 72 岁的老人，没有看到停车指示灯。医护人员迅速赶到现场。他们到达时，凯瑟琳已经死亡。

安东尼在葬礼上没有眼泪。但私下里他还是流了几滴——咸咸的、苦涩的，它们滑过脸颊，汇集在他的嘴角。他试图感受痛苦、悲伤，却发现他更多地被一种不公平感所控制，即他那种仔细掂量过的、对环境的控制被瓦解了。他们的儿子帕特里克已经乘飞机赶了回来。他在卡尔加里的一家石油公司工作。安东尼已经有两年没有见到帕特里克了。“忙”是他们各自提供的理由，但彼此都清楚这只是部分原因。

帕特里克决定在葬礼过后待一段时间，安东尼很高兴，但也希望他不会待太久。虽然再次见到儿子是一种安慰，但他真的觉得需要独处来处理自己的感情，来试图理解那份报纸上奇怪的所指及其重要性。不可思议的相似！尽管它们可能归因于简单的巧合，安东尼想知道是

simple coincidence, Anthony wondered if there was something else going on. Was someone, something trying to communicate with him? For what purpose? And why, in such a bizarre and cryptic manner? It didn't make any sense.

Anthony returned to work two weeks after the funeral. Patrick had gone back home, giving his dad a rare hug at the airport. As he sat on the Skytrain, he remembered the image of his son disappearing into the crowd at the airport security gate and wondered how many more years it would be until he saw him again. He unfolded the paper and scanned the front page. At the newsstand that morning, the old man had handed him his regular paper, but Anthony had instead pointed at the Scottish daily that sat behind the counter. He had never really looked that closely before, but the small kiosk contained newspapers from around the world, and he marveled at all these competing viewpoints, all these different cultural perspectives and languages lying together so peacefully and neatly ordered on a shelf. The old man had simply nodded when Anthony had

否还有别的事情在进行。难道是某人或某事想给他传递某种信息吗？为了什么目的？为什么用这样一个奇异的、隐晦的方式呢？他猜不透。

在葬礼后的第三个星期，安东尼回去工作了。帕特里克已经回家，在机场罕见地拥抱了他的父亲。他坐在空列上，还记得儿子消失在机场安检处人群中的模样，心想不知过多少年才能再次见到他。他展开那张报纸，扫了一眼头版。那天早晨，在报刊亭，老人把他通常读的报纸递给了他，但安东尼却指了指柜台后面的那份苏格兰日报。以前他从未如此近距离地观察这一切。小小的报亭里有来自世界各地的报纸。那些相互争执的观点、不同的文化视角和语言如此平静而又井然有序地躺在架子上，他不由地感叹。当安东尼要求买那份苏格兰报时，老人只是点了点头，但安东尼认为，他在那双

requested the Scottish paper, but he thought he saw a hint of a knowing look in the ancient, grey eyes. The old man hadn't said anything about his two-week absence. Anthony had wanted to ask him about the strange message he had uncovered two weeks previous, but what could he say? No, he decided he would just keep reading this paper, looking for other clues. In all probability it was just coincidence, but Anthony needed to be sure there wasn't some greater significance to the message.

古老的灰色眼睛中看到了理解之光。老人没有问及他为什么消失了两个星期。安东尼就两星期前他发现的那则奇怪信息向老人咨询一下，但他又能说什么呢？不，他决定继续阅读这份报纸，寻找其他线索。很可能只是巧合，但安东尼需要确定，在那则信息里没有更重要的暗示。

Most of the articles in the first few pages dealt with the usual topics: government incompetence, automobile accidents, violent occurrences, economic malaise. Anthony flipped to the sports section. Football, football, football—seemingly endless analyses of the inner workings of Celtic and Rangers. He had never liked soccer, and found the articles even duller than the game itself. He quickly thumbed to the end of the section and scanned the last page.

报纸头几页的文章大多是老生常谈的话题：政府无能、汽车事故、暴力事件、经济不振。安东尼快速翻到体育版。足球、足球、足球，似乎有无穷无尽针对凯尔特人队和流浪者队内部运作机制的分析。他从来就不喜欢足球，他发现文章比比赛本身更无聊。他迅速翻到这版的版尾，扫读了最后一页。

And then he saw it.

就在那儿！他看到了它。

John Patrick, a twenty-seven year old mountain climber from Glasgow had frozen to death in an attempt to

约翰·帕特里克，一位27岁、来自格拉斯哥的登山者，在试图翻越阿根廷的阿

scale Aconcagua in Argentina.

John Patrick.

The train lurched as it went around a bend, wheels squealing as they held on to the rails. Anthony's hands were suddenly slippery and they left dark smudges on the newsprint. A cold ache began spreading behind his eyes. He had to get off this train, had to think. He stood up, pulled himself toward the door. The train eased to a stop and as the prerecorded female voice announced "Royal Oak", Anthony staggered through the doors onto the platform. The damp air around him swallowed the electric echo of the departing train.

He waited until he was alone on the platform then sat down on a bench, his overcoat absorbing the damp that clung to the polished metal. The newspaper pages were heavy in his hand, pulled down by deceptive gravity. He flexed his wrist, testing the weight of the newsprint. The paper could be flipped onto his lap, could be opened. He let the anvil in his stomach settle then, with an abrupt flourish, opened the paper.

空加瓜山时被冻死。

约翰·帕特里克。

列车走过一个弯道时趔趄起来，轮子在抓住轨道时发出嘎嘎的响声。安东尼的手突然变得湿滑，在新闻纸上留下黑乎乎的污迹。一种冰冷的疼痛开始在他的眼底蔓延。他得离开这列火车，得去思考。他站起来，拖着身子向门口走去。火车在一个站台上停了下来，事先录好的女音在播报着“皇家橡树站”。安东尼步履蹒跚地穿过几道门下到站台上。电动火车离站时发出的回声被他周围潮湿的空气吞没。

他等待着，直到站台上只剩下他一人，然后他坐在一条长凳上。他的大衣吸干了敷在抛光金属表面上的潮气。那叠报纸在他的手上很沉，被骗人的地球引力向下扯着。他抖了抖自己的手腕，掂量了一下报纸的重量。报纸可以被放在膝盖上打开、翻页。他让胃里那块沉甸甸的铅坨落安稳了。接着哗啦一声，他打开了那份报纸。

He examined each word, parsing the letters. It confirmed what he had seen before. John Patrick. 27. Mountain climber. Dead. His son: Patrick John. 27. Mountain climber. Not dead…

Anthony fumbled with the inside pocket of his overcoat, found the phone. He punched the numbers with shaking hands. It rang once then directed him to Patrick's voice mail at work. Shit. His foot squelched an arrhythmic tattoo, smooth leather on wet cement. His voice cracked as he left his message. Five minutes later, the phone rang.

"Patrick."

"Dad?" Gravid silence. Then, "Are you okay?" Patrick's voice was distant, flat, a tinny facsimile of a voice he barely knew any more.

"Patrick. Are you…well?"

A pause. "Dad, I'm at work right now—"

"I know, I know. I just wanted to make sure that everything was okay."

"Yeah, I'm fine. Look dad, I know things are tough right now.

他分析每个单词，拆分着字母。之前他读到的那则信息被确认：约翰·帕特里克，27岁，登山者，死了。他的儿子：帕特里克·约翰，27岁，登山者，没死……

安东尼在他的大衣口袋里摸索，找到了电话。他用颤抖的手指敲打着每一个数字。电话响了一下，然后跳转到帕特里克的语音信箱。他妈的！他的一只脚胡乱地敲打着潮湿的水泥地面，皮面鞋底啪啪作响。他给帕特里克留言，声音嘶哑。五分钟后，电话响了。

“帕特里克。”

“爸爸？”重重的沉默。然后，“你没事吧？”帕特里克的声音遥远、平淡，像是有气无力地模仿一个他不甚记得的声音。

“帕特里克。你……好吗？”

一个短暂的停顿。“爸爸，我正在工作……”

“我知道，我知道。我只是想确保你一切都好。”

“是的，我很好。哎，爸爸，我知道日子不好过。

Could I call you tonight? I'm kind of busy—"

"Patrick, this is important," Anthony interrupted, suddenly energized. "Are you planning any trips to the mountains soon?"

"Yeah, actually this weekend. I'm going to Canmore."

"You can't! I mean, don't go." Anthony felt like he was hanging on to the edge of cliff, fingertips rubbed raw, flesh peeling away, blood slowly oozing from torn skin, hands slipping until gravity yanked him into the abyss. "Please don't."

"Look Dad, I'll be fine. I've done this route a million times. Don't worry. I'll talk to you tonight, okay?"

A few people were beginning to filter up the stairs, waiting for the next train. Anthony flipped the silent phone shut and began pacing the platform, staring down empty rails swallowed by grey concrete.

****

Patrick didn't phone that night, as Anthony had expected. He knew his son wouldn't be too concerned

今晚我给你打电话怎样？我现在有点儿忙……"

"帕特里克，这很重要，"安东尼打断了他的话。鼓了鼓劲，他问："你计划不久会去山里吗?"

"是的，实际上就在这个周末。我要去坎莫尔。"

"你不能去！我的意思是，不要去。"安东尼感觉就好像他正挂在悬崖的边缘，指尖磨烂了，皮磨掉了，血从撕裂的皮肤中慢慢渗出；他的手在滑动，直至地球引力把他拉进深渊。"请不要去。"

"哎，爸爸。我会没事的。这条线路我已经走过一百万次了。别担心。我今晚再和你聊，好吗?"

一些人开始稀稀拉拉走上台阶，等下一班火车。安东尼把已经挂断的手机关了，在站台上来回踱步，盯着空当当的铁轨在远处被灰色的混凝土吞噬。

****

正如安东尼所料，帕特里克那天晚上没有来电话。他知道儿子不会太关心父亲

about his father's anxieties. He thought about phoning him at home, but what could he tell him? A crazy premonition fueled by oblique clues in a Scottish newspaper didn't make sense. Patrick was practical, rational. He would dismiss his father's ideas as he had many times before—two cliffs on opposite sides of a chasm, blankly facing each other but never getting closer.

的焦虑。他想往他家里打，但他又能告诉他什么呢?那份苏格兰日报上一个没有意义的线索而导致的疯狂预感吗？没有任何理性而言。帕特里克既实际又理性，他会把父亲的想法像往常一样弃之不理——他们就像深谷两侧的悬崖，茫然地面对面，但彼此从未接近过。

The call came on Sunday morning. The temperatures had been warm in the Rockies that weekend. Patrick had been caught in a spring avalanche. He was an experienced hiker, but even experience doesn't always trump bad luck. Patrick's girlfriend sobbed out the news, her voice catching, hesitating, her lungs gulping air. Anthony had already numbed himself in anticipation, sent conscious commands to his nerve endings to stop feeling. When she hung up, Anthony grabbed his coat and keys. He knew the newsstand would be closed, but he was now drawn to it like a helpless iron filing pulled by a magnet across a sheet of polished metal. The clouds had begun breaking up; shafts of weak, buttery

星期天早上，电话打了过来。那个周末，落基山脉一直很温暖。帕特里克葬身于春天的雪崩。他是一个经验丰富的登山者，但经验并不总是胜过坏运气。帕特里克的女朋友哭着说出了这个消息。她的声音断断续续、充满了迟疑，肺部吃力地喘着气。安东尼已经在预期的等待中让自己麻木了。他命令自己的神经末梢停止感受。当她挂了电话，安东尼抓起了大衣和钥匙。他知道，报亭可能已经关了，但他现在就像一块无助的铁，被磁石吸引般地向着那扇抛光金属门走去。云层已经开始分离，一些微弱的、奶油色的光轴洒落在空荡荡的广

light played across the empty square. In this light the closed doors on the kiosk seemed even brighter, and as he stared at the polished metal, he could make out the ambiguous reflection of his own form, flattened and bloated by the slight curvature of the doors. His face was distorted by the grain of the metal, swirls of pink and blue and tan that didn't look human. This isn't me, he thought, I need to see behind the doors.

场上。在这种光线下，报亭关闭的门似乎显得更耀眼。他盯着抛光门看时，他能看到自己的形状被模糊反射在门上；由于其表面略呈弧形，他的形状略显扁平、臃肿；金属的小颗粒使他的脸变形；粉色的、蓝色的、褐色的漩涡状色彩让他的脸看起来不像是人脸。这不是我，他想，我需要看到门后的东西。

****

He didn't sleep that night, and was at the kiosk Monday morning at 4.30. He had to talk to the old newsagent, wanted to see him arrive at the kiosk, wanted to see where he came from. The front doors on which he had been leaning suddenly slid open, shushing as they disappeared into dark cavities in the walls. The old man was there, inside the kiosk, but Anthony had not seen him approach. Could he have been inside the whole time? Anthony's fatigued brain ached with this impossibility.

"Morning sir. You're quite early today." The old man's voice was less gravelly, fresher.

****

那晚他一夜没睡。周一早晨 4 点 30 分他已经站在了报亭跟前。他一定要跟这位卖报老人谈谈；他想看着他走到报亭，看他是从哪里来的。然而，他一直靠在其上的那两扇门突然滑开，嘘的一声消失在两边墙里黑暗的门槽里。老人就在那里，在报亭内，但安东尼并没有看到他从任何地方走进报亭。他整个时间都有可能在报亭里吗？安东尼疲惫的大脑被这种不可能性折磨着、痛着。

“早晨好，先生！你今天来得很早啊。”老人的声音不是那么沉重，比往常更清新。

"I…need to talk to you." Anthony stumbled on his words, his control slipping. He had felt such a strong need to come here, but he hadn't actually thought about what he would say. The old man simply gave a nod with his raw, swollen, spider-veined nose as he started stacking the day's newspapers.

"我…… 需要和你谈谈。"安东尼费力地说着，发现自控力在下滑。他感到如此强烈地需要来到这里，但实际上他从来没有想到过他想要说什么。老人只是点了点头，脸上那粗糙、臃肿、布满蜘蛛网状血管的鼻子格外醒目。他开始堆放当天的报纸。

"How…" Anthony stopped, squeezed the bridge of his nose, as if trying to funnel his scattered thoughts deeper into his brain, "…why did you give me that Scottish newspaper?"

"怎么……"安东尼停了下来，捏着自己的鼻梁，就好像要把分散的思想更深层地输入自己的大脑，"……你为什么给我那份苏格兰报？"

"Best there is sir." The old man kept stacking his papers.

"它是最好的，先生。"老人一直在堆放着他的报纸。

"But, you must have known…my wife, son…they died…it was in the paper…" Anthony's tongue felt like it was tripping on his teeth.

"但是，你一定早就知道……我妻子、儿子……他们死了……在报纸里……"安东尼的舌头像是被牙齿绊住了一样。

The man looked up, his deep eyes suddenly sympathetic, dark pools that seemed to conceal their own tragedies. "I'm sorry to hear that, sir. My condolences."

那男人抬起头来，刹那间，同情涌现在那双深陷的眼睛里；它们像两汪黑色的池水，似乎隐藏着属于自己的悲剧。"听到这个消息我很抱歉，先生。我深表哀悼。"

"But…it was in *there*!" Anthony slammed his hand down on the counter, frustrated by the old man's neutral response. He wanted answers, wanted to know why this grizzled newsagent had given him these newspapers, what his role was. He tried to articulate his questions, but his head felt as if it were encased in ice.

"Look sir, have this one on the house today." He extended a thick, grey roll towards Anthony. The strong scent of fresh newsprint stung his nostrils, tickled the back of his eyes.

"But…"

"Just take it sir. A great deal can be learned from reading the news. A great deal."

Anthony squeezed the Scottish paper, weighing it carefully in his hand. He looked at the old man and swallowed, words lodging in his throat.

"Just read it."

****

Anthony slowly unfolded the newspaper on his kitchen table. He had not looked at it on his walk home, his grip tight on the pages. It was

"但是…… 它就在*那儿*！"安东尼用手拍打着柜台，被老人不痛不痒的反应所激怒。他需要答案，想知道为什么这个头发斑白的老报商给了他那些报纸，他的角色是什么。他试图说清楚他的问题，但他的头就像是被放在了冰匣子里。

"先生。这份报纸今天免费。拿上吧。"他把一卷厚厚的、灰色的报纸递给安东尼。新鲜报纸那特有的强烈气味刺激着他的鼻孔，让他的眼睛深处不舒服。

"但是……"

"拿着，先生。阅读新闻可以让你学到很多。很多。"

安东尼把这份苏格兰日报压了压，用手仔细掂量了一下它的重量。他看着老人，把哽在喉咙里的话咽了回去。

"你读就是了。"

****

安东尼在厨房的桌子上把报纸慢慢展开。在回家的路上他没有看报纸，他只是紧紧攥着报纸的每一

dated the previous Sunday. There was a substantial weight to the paper with its various supplements—entertainment, real estate, book reviews, sports, special features. Anthony began scanning the front page, dreading how long it would take to review every page, knowing that he had no choice.

页。报纸的日期是上个星期日。因为有各种各样的补充读物——娱乐、房地产、书评、运动、特写等，这份报纸分量很重。安东尼开始扫视头版。他一方面害怕挨页审读会花很长时间，另一方面又深知他别无选择。

After finishing with the first section, he decided he needed coffee. He spread out the different sections on the table, hoping that freeing the pages would inspire the words he needed to leap off the newsprint. The kettle rumbled with agitated water. He filled the coffee press, then returned to the table and saw it. It was in the Books section: a name, *Antonio Giovanni*.

第一版块看完后，他决定要喝咖啡了。他把整个报纸的不同版块摊放在桌子上，希望通过释放每一页报纸，他需要的字会受到激励跳出页面。水开了，水壶隆隆作响。他把水冲进咖啡压力杯里，然后回到桌子跟前——他看到了它。就在“图书”版块里：一个名字，安东尼奥·乔凡尼。

He held the paper close to his eyes, as if looking for a splinter with tweezers. Giovanni was an Italian author. A translation of his latest novel, *Broken Symmetry*, was being reviewed. The reviewer was unquestionably a fan of this author, and his praise for this latest work was effusive. “A gripping read that explores the deep and complicated psychology of regret.” The story dealt

他把报纸举到眼前，就好像要用镊子从中找到一个小碎片。乔凡尼是一位意大利作家。他最新的一部小说《失衡》被翻译，对此有评论。评论人无疑是作者的粉丝，对这部作品的赞美之情溢于言表。“这部作品引人入胜，探讨了深层而复杂的悔恨心理。”这个故事讲

with a middle-aged physicist who was estranged from both his wife and son. Throughout his career, he had been obsessed with discovering the essential nature of matter through his research into particle physics. His obsession with discovering evidence of supersymmetry—a theory about relationships between elementary particles—and subsequent failure to do so had left him questioning his life and the relationships he had destroyed. The novel, according to the reviewer, was rich with deep metaphor, evocative writing and sustained and intense pathos. The shocking and surprising ending, the moment of self-realization, on the eve of the Nobel Prize ceremony where the protagonist's work was finally recognized made this one of the finest novels of the year.

述的是一位中年物理学家被妻子和儿子疏远；在他整个的职业生涯中，他一直痴迷于通过对粒子物理的研究发现物质的本质。小说描述了他对发现超对称证据的痴迷——一种关于基本粒子之间关系的理论。随后而来的失败导致他不停地质问自己的生活和已经被毁掉的关系。据评论家称，这部小说大量使用深刻的隐喻，文字激昂，产生的感伤持续而强烈。那令人震惊与惊讶的结局——那自我实现的时刻，即诺贝尔奖获奖典礼前夕主人公的作品得到认可的那一时刻——使得这部小说成为年度最优秀的小说之一。

Anthony's sweat-washed fingers started bleeding the ink on the page. He peeled the greasy newsprint away. Somehow this story of a self-absorbed physicist and his unsuccessful attempts to make sense of matter, resulting only in a theory of "broken symmetry" seemed too familiar. The reviewer's descriptions of "failed relationships", "emotional

安东尼已经被汗水湿透的手指开始使报纸上的油墨模糊、渗透。他把被油墨弄脏的那张撕去。这个故事情节太熟悉了——热衷于自己想法的物理学家试图用理论解释一切现象，失败了，其结果就是"失衡"理论的诞生。评论人的描述，如"失败

ambivalence and disinterest" rattled around in Anthony's head like dice in a cup. He needed to know more.

He ran into his study and flipped on the computer. Fingers drummed on the mouse through the agonizing boot-up routine. Then the internet, the search. First the author, then the book title. Nothing, nothing, nothing. He slammed his hand down on the desk. What was the "shocking and surprising ending"? He tried different search engines, different databases, different spellings. He went to the website of the publisher. Everywhere he looked, there was nothing. He even went to the online edition of the Scottish newspaper, but could not find the review again. The reviewer's name turned up no hits either. It was as if all evidence of the book, the author and the reviewer had been wiped clean from Anthony's gleaming, polished plane of reality. But the newspaper still existed, lying on his kitchen table, the smudged words teasing him, goading him onto—what?

He slammed the lid of his laptop down and grabbed his coat. The

的关系"、"情感矛盾和冷漠"等就像杯子里跳动的骰子那样，在安东尼的脑袋里嗡嗡作响。他需要知道更多。

他跑进书房，啪地打开电脑。手指不停地击打着鼠标，等着程序启动时那熬人的时间快点结束。然后他登陆互联网，进行搜索。先是作者名，没有结果；再试书名，还是没有结果。什么都查不到。他的手拍打着桌子。那"令人震惊和惊讶的结局"到底是什么？他试了不同的搜索引擎、不同的数据库、不同的拼写。他浏览了出版商网站。无论他查哪里，都是没有结果。他甚至查阅了那份苏格兰日报的网络版，却找不到那篇评论。输入评论家的名字，没有结果。就好像关于书的所有证据、作者、评论家都已经被从安东尼那发光的、打磨过的现实平面上抹去了。但那份报纸仍在，躺在厨房的桌子上。那污迹斑斑的字在逗弄着他、刺激他去——做什么？

他啪地合上了笔记本电脑的盖子，抓起了大衣。那

newsagent must know something. He had been so cryptic, yet so certain. Anthony was convinced he was the key.

The sun had risen higher now, and the streets were crowded with busy people on their way to work. He pushed his way through the mass of suits and ties, nylons and heels, his knees aching, his chest binding and cramping. He had to know.

Sweat drenched his back by the time he got to the square. The sun was bright in his face, and he had to squint into the skyscraper shadows. Something didn't look right. He ran across the square and stood where it should have been. His palms faced outward, a vain supplication to the indifferent crowd that moved around him. He fell to his knees, traced the rough concrete with his hands. There was no sign, no evidence of its existence. The newsstand was gone. He turned in circles, looking, searching, grinding the thin cloth of his pants into the grey cement, but all he could see around him was an empty void, a dirty, featureless plane

位老报刊经销商一定知道点什么。他一直那么神秘、那么肯定。安东尼确信他就是答案。

太阳现在升得更高，街上挤满了人，都忙着去上班。他在这些身着西装和领带、穿着尼龙长袜和高跟鞋的人群中急匆匆走着。他的膝盖疼痛；他的胸口绷得紧紧地，抽搐着。他必须知道答案。

等他走到广场时汗水湿透了他的背。太阳亮晃晃地照着他的脸，他不得不眯起眼睛看摩天大楼的阴影处。有些不对劲。他跑过广场，站在它原本矗立过的地方。他手掌向外，徒劳地恳求周围走动的、冷漠的人群。他跪倒在地，双手摸索着粗糙的水泥地面。没有迹象、没有证据表明它曾经存在过。报刊亭不见了。他转着圈子，看着、找着，单薄的裤子在灰色的水泥地上磨着；但他在周围能看到的就只是一个空当当的、肮脏的、毫无特色的平面。

Super Mail

When Kevin opened the mailbox that afternoon, he had been hoping for that one letter, the one that would finally change things. But, instead of that letter, he found a shovel handle. The plastic wasn't broken or cracked, so apparently someone had deliberately removed it from the end of a snow shovel and stuck it inside his mailbox. Was this a joke? Only the letter carrier had a key for the mailbox. And Jackie, his wife, of course. He looked around to see if someone was watching, laughing at him. But the street was empty, the sand-crusted piles of snow dribbling slowly into the gutter.

He slipped the grip into his coat

超级信件

那天下午，当凯文打开信箱时，他期盼着收到那封信，那封能让他生活改变的信。然而，没有那封信；相反，他收到了一把铲柄，是塑料的，没有碎、没有裂痕。显然，它是有意被从雪铲上拔下来，塞进了他的信箱。这是一个笑话吗？只有信差才有信箱的钥匙——当然，还有他的妻子杰茜。他环顾四周，看是否有人在观察他、嘲笑他。街上空空如也，融化的雪水从表面有一层沙土的雪堆里慢慢流进排水沟里。

他把铲柄放进他外套口

pocket as he walked back to his house, leafing through the letters. It was mostly junk — charitable solicitations, flyers for real estate agents. There were a couple of utility bills as well, but nothing he wanted. He should phone Canada Post, register a complaint against the letter carrier. He looked at his watch. It would have to wait until tomorrow.

袋里，走回家，快速翻阅信件。大多数是垃圾信件——慈善募捐、地产经纪人的小册子等。有一两个水电费账单，但没有他想要的。他应该给加拿大邮政打电话，对投递员进行投诉。他看一下表。这事得等到明天才能做了。

Jackie was in the kitchen, stirring something in a bowl. “Anything interesting in the mail?”

杰茜在厨房里，搅拌着碗里的东西。“有什么有趣的信件吗？”

“Um, no. Just the usual.” He hung his coat in the closet, leaving the grip in his pocket.

“嗯，没有。还是老样子。”他把外套挂在壁橱里，铲柄仍在那个口袋里。

He kissed her cheek. “So how was your day?”

他吻了她的脸颊。“今天过得怎样？”

“Pretty average. Although… I did find out something that you probably aren’t going to like.”

“就那样。但……有件事情定了下来。你或许并不喜欢。”

She pushed the bowl to the side. Her pale green eyes held his for a moment, as if she were challenging him. “I got my summer schedule today; I’m not going to be able to take my holidays when we planned.”

她把碗推到一边，淡绿色的眼睛有那么片刻盯着他的眼睛，好像是对他挑衅。“今天，我的暑期时间表出来了。我没办法在我们计划的时间段里休假。”

“Oh.” He knew she wanted some kind of response from him, an expression of disappointment perhaps. “That’s too bad.”

“哦。”他知道她想从他这儿得到什么样的反应——一个失望的表情，或许吧。“这太糟糕了。”

She turned back to her bowl stirring more vigorously than before. Kevin opened the newspaper and began scanning an article about a missing child. "Tragic," he murmured, "I hope they find —"

"You know," she interrupted, "I thought you might be more disappointed. About the holidays, I mean."

"I am disappointed."

Exasperation spread across her face. "I…just don't know, Kevin. Sometimes you seem so…so toneless. You're like a sheet of unpolished grey metal. Light hits you and it just dies."

"I don't know what you mean."

"That's the problem."

Kevin felt very tired when he had these talks with Jackie. She wanted more from him, but wouldn't say what. His strategy of waiting her out only seemed to frustrate her further. He looked into her eyes, green like the sea-foam of an ebbing tide, but she turned and ran up the stairs, her feet heavy on the creaking treads.

He took the shovel grip from

她回过身去，更激烈地搅拌着碗里的东西。凯文打开报纸，开始浏览一篇关于一个失踪孩子的文章。“悲剧。”他低声说道，“我希望他们找到——”

“你知道，”她打断了他，“我以为你会更失望些。我的意思是假期的事。”

“我的确失望。”

愤怒已经布满了她的整个脸。“我……就是不明白，凯文。有时候你的语调……如此无味。你就像一片毫无光泽的灰色金属。即便有光照射到你，它也得死。”

“我不明白你的意思。”

“这正是问题的所在。”

当凯文和杰茜这样谈话时，他感到很累。她想从他那儿要得更多，但却不说出来。他等着她说出来的策略似乎让她更恼怒。他看着她的眼睛，绿色的、像海水退潮时的泡沫。然而，她却转身跑上楼梯，重重的脚步使得台阶吱嘎作响。

他把铲柄从大衣口袋里

his coat pocket and retreated to his study in the basement. The fluorescent light hummed with sluggish electrons. There was still a chill in the basement at this time of year, and Kevin's skin mottled into crisp goose-pimples. A drafting table stood in one corner, covered with various sized pieces of paper, documents of his ideas, his inventions. Once per week, he mailed out summaries of his ideas to different intellectual property houses. He had a dream, that one day he would cash in, would become that brilliant and famous inventor everyone talked about. He had many ideas: kitchen utensils, automotive tools, consumer products. They were all useful, all important, the kind of items advertised on infomercials. But so far, he had sent out 276 enquiries and received 276 rejections. Jackie had at one time been encouraging, but now she didn't even ask about the letters that arrived each week. Kevin wasn't discouraged, though, as he knew that persistence was essential.

A large, heavy desk stood in the other corner of the room. Its old, oak

掏了出来，回到地下室的书房里。电子荧光灯嗡嗡作响，慢慢启动，亮了起来。在每年的这个时候，地下室里仍然有些寒意。凯文的皮肤上开始麻麻点点地起鸡皮疙瘩。书房的角落里有一个绘图桌，上面摆满了各种尺寸的纸张、记录他想法的文件，以及他的发明。每周一次，他把自己思想的结晶寄给不同的知识产权局。他有一个梦想：总有一天，一切都会兑现，他会成为一名杰出的、著名的发明家；人们知道他、谈论他。他有许多点子：厨房用具、汽车工具、消费产品。它们都是有用的、重要的，是那种在电视导购节目中被推销的产品。但到目前为止，他已经发出了 276 个询问，收到了 276 个拒绝。杰茜曾一度支持他，但现在，她甚至对每周到达的信件问都不问。然而，凯文没有气馁；他知道，坚持是必不可少的。

在房间的另一个角落里有一张沉重的大办公桌。橡

surface was a pale, honey colour, ink stained, discoloured with pieces of brittle cellophane tape speckled about randomly. The veneer was chipped and worn. He had bought it at the bankruptcy auction of a local lumberyard. Jackie thought it was ugly.

树的桌面年代已久，原来是淡淡的蜂黄色，现在上面已墨迹斑斑，很多地方被无意落在桌面上的透明胶带弄得失色，整个桌面看起来颜色斑驳。表层的装饰板已经起皮、磨破。这张桌子是在当地一家木材场破产、搞拍卖时买下的，杰茜认为它很丑。

Kevin placed the shovel grip on top of the desk. It looked almost alien lying on the warm wood. Its green moulded plastic, curvilinear shape contrasted sharply with the flat planes. The wood pulsed with an organic energy. The shovel grip, on the other hand, was an artifact made in some factory in China, a concoction of chemicals, cooked, cooled and stamped by metallic plates operated by a computer. He tapped the object lightly on his desk. There was no spirit, no life in the dull *thunk*.

凯文把铲柄放在书桌上。背衬温暖的木头，这铲柄看起来是那么异样。它绿色的模压塑料、弯曲的形状都与平平的桌面形成了鲜明对照。木质是有机的，有能量和脉冲，然而，铲柄却是中国某厂家制造的，是化工产品的混合物，在电脑控制的金属模子里被加热、冷却、打上标签。他用铲柄轻轻敲击桌面，毫无生机；在单调的*铛铛*声中没有任何生命。

He eased himself into his chair, turning the grip over and over in his hands. Was it just a joke? An early April Fool's prank? That seemed like the most obvious conclusion, yet not quite plausible. Every weekday at 5.00 p.m. he collected the mail

他坐进椅子里，让自己更舒服些，把铲柄握在手里来回翻看。这只是一个笑话吗？一个为时尚早的愚人节恶作剧？那似乎是最显然的结论了，然而却不太合情理。每个工作日下午 5 点，

from the communal box on the corner, but he never once saw it being delivered. He was certain the mail carrier must be a woman, however. There was something maternal, something in the way the letters were always neatly stacked in his box, largest on the bottom, smallest on the top, which suggested a feminine touch. Why would she play a joke on him? Jokes like that were only funny if the perpetrator could observe the result. Kevin was certain that nobody had been watching.

他都从街角的公共信箱里查收信件，但他从未见过它们是如何被放进去的。然而，他确信邮递员是个女人；他看到了母性，比如信箱里的信件总是摆放得很整齐，体积最大的放在最下面、个头最小的摆在最上面。这是女性的手法。那她为什么要开他的玩笑呢？笑话的乐趣在于制造恶作剧的人能够看到结果。凯文确定，当时并没人在看。

The sun was starting to go down and the room was now lit only by cold fluorescence. He pulled the chain on the banker's lamp. Under the more intense light, he could see that the grip was scratched and worn—it had obviously been well used. How had the letter carrier come to possess it? Was it from her shovel? Had she found it on the ground, discarded? That was certainly possible. Snow had been heavy over the winter and Kevin was already on his second shovel. Maybe she randomly chose a compartment in the box and placed the handle

太阳开始下沉，房间里只有冷冰冰的荧光。他拉了一下老式台灯上的链子，把灯打亮。在更强的聚光下，他看出这把铲柄有刮痕和磨损——显然被用过多次。邮递员是如何拥有它的呢？是从她的雪铲上卸下来的吗？或者是别人丢弃的被她捡着了？当然，这是有可能的。这里的冬天一直有积雪，他已经用坏了一把雪铲，开始用第二把了。或许她只是随意挑选了一个信箱、不假思索地把铲柄丢了进

inside in a moment of arbitrary silliness.

Kevin shivered in the cool basement air and pulled on the old cardigan he kept on the back of his chair. Could the handle have been a message? Maybe the letter carrier was trying to tell him to do a better job shoveling his sidewalk. A vague sense of guilt spidered through his veins as he thought of the thick snow pack still smothering the concrete path. He knew he was neglecting his suburban duty, but an immaculate sidewalk didn't seem important to him anymore. The snow would eventually melt.

No, that kind of message seemed too simplistic. The letter carrier didn't walk in front of his house anyway, as the SuperMailbox was on the other side of the street. He thought about codes, ciphers, rebuses, but nothing seemed to fit. Except —

Maybe, having seen all the rejection letters, the letter carrier knew that he was an inventor. Maybe she was trying to help, trying to give him an idea. But she wouldn't just tell him directly. She

去，属于一时的、任性的愚蠢行为。

凯文在地下室的冷空气里瑟瑟发抖，他把搭在椅背上的开襟毛衣穿上。难道这把铲柄要传递某种信息？或许是邮递员希望他干点好事，把他门前人行道上的雪铲除掉？当他想到厚厚的积雪仍然堆在水泥路面上时，一种模糊的羞愧感像蜘蛛网一样顺着他的静脉血管爬遍全身。他知道他忽略了郊区居民的责任，但对他而言，是否有一个完美的人行道似乎并不重要。雪最终会融化的。

不，那样的信息似乎太过简单。邮递员不可能从他门前走过，因为公共信箱在街的另一边。他思考着代码、密码、字谜，等等，但好像都不符合这种情况。除了——

也许，在看到所有那些拒绝信后，邮递员知道了他是一个发明家；也许她想帮忙，试图给他一个想法，但又不想直接告诉他。她想让他猜出来，看他是否在智力

wanted him to figure it out, wanted to see if he was intellectually worthy of her idea. The handle was the first piece of a puzzle. If he figured it out, maybe she would share her idea with him.

上配得上她的想法。铲柄只是整个谜局的第一块。如果他猜出来的话，也许她会和他分享她的想法。

He opened his desk drawer and began sifting through the haphazard pile of office supplies. He smiled when he found what he wanted, felt his cheeks flush. He slipped off the cardigan. *Maybe she'll understand, maybe she'll get it.*

他打开抽屉，开始浏览随意堆放在里面的办公用品。当他发现要找的东西时，他笑了，觉得自己的脸颊发烧。他脱掉开襟羊毛衫。*也许她会明白，也许她会心领神会。*

A knock at the door made his heart stumble. Jackie never came to his study. He swallowed. "Yes?"

敲门声使他的心一落千丈。杰茜从未来过他的书房。他稳住声音问："什么事？"

"I'm going out." Jackie's voice was distant. "I have to … see someone."

"我要出去。"杰茜的声音听起来很遥远。"我必须……见个人。"

Her footsteps quickly faded up the stairs before he could reply. He turned the object over in his hands, nodding as his heart slowly found its pace again.

在他能回答前，她的脚步声已迅速消失在上行的楼梯上。他把手里的东西翻了个个儿，点着头，心跳慢慢恢复常态。

****

6.02 a.m. Jackie was still asleep. He stepped lightly on the sloping driveway, trying not to crunch the packed snow, and crossed

****

早晨 6 点 02 分。杰茜还在熟睡。他轻轻走在车道的斜坡上，尽量不踩响上面的积雪，穿过了马路。防滑

the street, the tarmac glowing antiseptic orange under the sodium lamps. Carefully, almost tenderly, he placed a full roll of cellophane tape, complete with dispenser, into the empty compartment then shut the ribbed, dull metal door, double-checking the lock.

Jackie was standing in the living room when he got back, arms crossed, the belt of her robe drawn tightly around her bony waist. She didn't say anything.

"I…went for a walk. I felt restless."

She pulled the belt tighter. "You've never taken morning walks. Not once in twelve years."

He loosened his coat and let it fall to the floor. "I just needed some air."

Jackie's lips were like a thin scar on her face. He used to enjoy tracing the sharp angles and slim contours of her body with his fingers, but now those harsh features seemed to always challenge him, to question his inability to give her a child and be the man she wanted. The trip they were to take this summer was her idea, a relaxing

的沥青在钠光街灯下发出冷漠的橙色。小心翼翼地、几乎是温柔地，他把一整卷的透明胶带、连同它带切割齿的底座，放进了空空的信箱。然后，他把带小栅栏的、单调的金属门关上，检查了两遍，确保其锁上了。

等他回到家时，杰茜正站在客厅里等她；她胳膊交叉抱在胸前，睡袍的腰带紧紧系着，显出她瘦骨嶙峋的身材。她什么也没说。

“我……出去散步了。我感到烦躁。”

她把腰带系得更紧。“你早晨从没散过步。十二年来一次都没有过。”

他松开外套，让其自然滑落到地板上。“我只是需要一些空气。”

杰茜的嘴唇就像脸上的一道细疤。他过去喜欢用他的手指追寻她身体的棱角和纤细的轮廓，但现在这些棱角似乎总在挑战他、质疑他的无能——不能让她怀孕、不能成为她要的男人。这个夏天去旅行是她的主意，在海滨胜地度假，时机也恰到好处。她一直希

seaside resort, the perfect timing. She had hoped they could finally conceive, finally get the baby she needed.

望能怀上孩子，能有一个她需要的孩子。

"Do you think the air, the exercise…helped you?"

"你认为空气、晨练……对你有帮助吗?"

"Yes," Kevin replied, ignoring the implied criticism in her words, "I feel much better."

"是的，"凯文回答，对她话里隐含的批评置之不理，"我感觉好多了。"

****

With shaking hands, he fitted the irregular brass key into the lock, shut his eyes and turned. The lock clicked open smoothly, as it always did. The tape roll was gone. Kevin jammed his hand into the compartment. Three items: a bank statement and two pieces of junk mail. He stuck his face close to the opening, the metal edge of the compartment pressing into his brow and chin. He let out a short breath of disappointment, a muffled echo in the small box. The adrenaline that had surged in his veins as he opened the box now faded, his pulse slowing as a gust of wind fluttered the letters in his hand. He slammed the mailbox shut.

用颤抖的手，他把犬牙状的铜钥匙插进锁孔，闭上眼睛转动着。和往常一样，锁"咔嗒"一声顺利打开。胶带卷不见了。凯文把手严严实实地伸进信箱。里面有三样东西：银行账单和两封垃圾邮件。他把脸凑近信箱口，额头和下巴抵着周围的金属框往里看。他失望地出了口短气，那小小的信箱匣子发出低沉的回声。他开信箱时，肾上腺素在静脉血管里激增；现在，它消退了，脉搏也减慢下来。一阵狂风吹过，他手中的信呼啦啦作响。他砰地关上了信箱。

The letter carrier hadn't left

邮递员没有给他留下

anything for him, but the tape roll was gone. His message had been received, his gift accepted. Maybe she wasn't expecting a response to the initial communication and was unprepared. Now that he had completed the first exchange, she would understand that contact was successful. Tomorrow seemed more probable. She would be ready then, would be able to continue the process.

任何东西，但胶带卷不见了。他的信息已经被接收，他的礼物已经被接受。也许她并没有料想到，自己的主动出击竟会得到响应，因而毫无准备。现在，他已经完成了第一次交换。她会明白，那次联系是成功的。明天的可能性更大。那时，她会准备好，会让这个过程继续下去。

****

"We need to talk."

"我们需要谈谈。"

Kevin had just put a spoonful of cereal in his mouth. He chewed slowly and swallowed. "What?"

凯文刚把一勺麦片放进嘴里。他慢慢咀嚼着，然后咽下。"什么?"

She sat down at the far end of the table. "I don't want to do this anymore."

她在桌子的另一端坐下。"我不想再这样了。"

The spoon clattered on the side of the bowl. "What do you mean?"

勺子在碗边发出碰撞声。"你什么意思?"

Her palm slapped the table. "You are such a dickhead sometimes. Don't you get it? Don't you understand what's going on here?"

她的手掌拍打着桌子。"有时候你就是个真真切切的白痴。你不明白吗?你不明白这里正在发生什么吗?"

Kevin knew he needed to be attentive, but his mind seemed to be leaping around, fluttering like a fly

凯文知道他需要专心，但他的思想似乎到处跳跃，像一只苍蝇，呼扇着翅膀，

evading a rolled up newspaper. "Is this about our holidays? Because—"

"No, no. I'm just tired of everything. I'm tired of you. Tired of not talking. Tired of meaning nothing. Tired of… of no baby."

He could see her cheeks colouring, pale rose blotches spreading like a rash under her eyes. He wanted to reach out, to grab her hand, but her sideways comments, her barely veiled sarcasm cemented his hands to the table. "I see your point."

"What? My *point*? I'm not arguing with you, Kevin, I'm telling you it's over. Doesn't that mean anything to you?"

To Kevin, the angles were all wrong. Words seemed to be coming from obscure directions, ideas were oblique. He didn't want to have this conversation with Jackie right now. He groped for an answer to her question, but all he could find was the truth. "I don't know."

The blotches were slowly fading; her skin was becoming a nullity, a colour that wasn't white or

正在逃脱一份卷起的报纸。"是关于我们的假期吗?因为——"

"不，不。我厌倦了一切。厌倦了你，厌倦了没话说，厌倦了没有意义的话，厌倦了……厌倦了没有孩子。"

他可以看到她的脸颊在变色，眼底的淡玫瑰色斑点像皮疹似的在散开。他想伸出手去，去抓住她的手，但她的旁敲侧击、她几乎不加掩饰的挖苦像水泥般地把他的手固定在桌面上。"我明白你的意思。"

"什么?我的*意思*?我不想与你争论，凯文，我告诉你，我们完了。难道这对你不意味着什么吗？"

对于凯文而言，角度完全错了。话语似乎来自模糊的方向，想法也不够光明正大。眼下，他不想跟杰茜有这样的谈话。他寻找着应对她问题的答案，然而他所能找到的只有事实——"我不知道。"

斑点在她的眼底慢慢消退，她的皮肤渐渐失色，变成了一种既不白、

pale, a colour that simply wasn't there at all. Her lips quivered like butterfly wings for a moment then tightened over her teeth as she got up from the table. Kevin knew there was something he should be doing, something he should be saying, but gravity seemed to have suddenly become stronger under his chair, pulling him into the curves of the wooden seat, dragging the words back down his throat. He watched as Jackie grabbed her purse, her coat, keys jingling in her hand. She stopped at the front door. "Kevin, you always want to invent something. Why can't you just make things work instead?" She pulled the door shut, making sure the lock had engaged.

也不是苍白的颜色，确切地说是无色。她的嘴唇颤抖着，如同蝴蝶扇动着双翅；片刻之后，她把嘴唇抿紧在牙齿上站了起来。凯文知道他应该马上做什么、说什么，但椅子下的地球引力似乎突然变得超强，让他的屁股像粘在座位上一样，冲到嘴边的话也被生生拉回到喉咙里。他眼睁睁看着杰茜抓起她的钱包、外套和钥匙——钥匙在她的手上叮当作响。她停在前门口。"凯文，你总是想发明什么。为什么你就不能解决现有问题呢？"她拉上了门，确保门锁上了。

Kevin knew he should be feeling a burning or gurgling inside, but he was calm. He took his pulse. Perfectly normal. He finished his cereal and checked his watch, confirming the number of hours until the mail delivery.

凯文知道，他内心应该感到愤怒或汹涌澎湃，但他很平静。他把了下脉，超乎完美地正常。他吃完麦片粥，看了看表，确认时数，直到邮递员送信的时间到了。

****

5.07 p.m. He stood in front of the mailbox, looking at his hands.

****

下午 5 点 07 分。他站在信箱前，看着自己的手。

Steady. There was a calm, a confidence in his anticipation, a certainty there would be something inside the box. He took a deep breath and turned the key.

A pile of letters – more than usual. As he pulled the stack of mail out, he heard a metallic clunk. He stuck his hand into the box and pulled out—

A pair of scissors.

He slowly extracted them from the box, as if pulling a long, glinting sword from a scabbard. They were a standard pair of domestic scissors, with burgundy coloured, rubberized hand-grips. Kevin stuck his fingers into the handles and opened the blades. He drew his index finger slowly across the sharpened metal, flinching as the edge penetrated his soft skin. A droplet of blood oozed out of the tender flesh. He took a closer look at the blades. No signs of wear. The scissors must have come straight out of the package. He smiled. This was good—a sign of intent, a deliberate, positive action to continue the exchange. He handled the scissors more carefully now, placing them between two

稳住！在他的期盼中有一种冷静、自信和一种肯定：信箱里一定有某样东西。他深吸一口气，转动了钥匙。

有一堆信——比平时多。当他把那沓信掏出信箱时，他听到了金属的碰撞声。他把手伸到信箱深处，拉出来了——

一把剪刀。

他慢慢把剪刀从信箱里取出来，就像把长长的、闪着亮光的剑从鞘里拔出一样。它是一副标准的国产剪刀，酒红色的橡胶握柄。凯文把手指伸进握柄，撑开了剪刀。他用食指慢慢滑过锋利的刀片。他哆嗦了一下，刀刃割开了他柔软的皮肤，一滴血流了出来。他更仔细地看了看刀口。没有被用过的迹象。剪刀一定是刚被打开包装的。他笑了。这很好——这是一种意图的表示，一个深思熟虑的、积极的、想要继续交流的行动。他现在更小心地处理这把剪刀，把它夹在两个信封中间。

envelopes.

他回到地下室的办公室里，微微打开剪刀，放在靠墙的桌子上。然后，他伸手把铲柄从抽屉深处拿出来，在眼前举着。他一会儿把它拉近，一会儿把它推远，测量其比例。他把它放在桌子上，对其研究了片刻，然后把它旋转了大约 20 度。这一定要正确，角度和位置都要正确。

Back in his basement office, he opened the scissors slightly and placed them on a side-table. He then dug the shovel grip out of a desk drawer held it in front of his face, moving it closer and further from his eyes, measuring its proportions. He put it on the table, studied it for a moment then rotated it by approximately twenty degrees. This had to be right, the angles and positioning correct.

当他研究这两样东西时，他意识到缺了什么。他翻遍了另一个抽屉，找到了一支笔和一张纸。在纸的左上角，他用正楷写上“磁带”，然后从抽屉里拿出自己那把用钝了的剪刀，把这个词从纸上剪了下来。他把那四方形的小纸片放在桌上，在铲柄和剪刀之间。连续性很重要。他需要保持思维按正确的顺序流动。

As he studied the two objects, he realized there something missing. He rummaged through another desk drawer until he found a pen and a piece of paper. In block letters, he wrote TAPE in the upper corner of the paper. He then took his own, duller scissors from the drawer and cut the word from the page. He placed the small square on the table, between the grip and the scissors. Continuity was important. He needed to keep the flow of ideas correctly ordered.

他对自己的工作很满意，开始在房间里踱来踱去，寻找下一个交换物。目前还看不出任何模式，但他

Satisfied with his work, he began pacing the room, looking for the next object to exchange. There was no pattern yet, but he knew that somehow he would intuitively identify the correct item. There was some type of unspoken communication happening here, some meaning buried in the objects. The puzzle the letter carrier had set up was exciting for Kevin; his cells tingled, a reminder of something strong he felt long ago. He couldn't imagine what sort of invention she might have come up with that would justify this game, but he knew their exchanges were important.

His hand was deep inside a tightly packed drawer when his fingers brushed over a coarse surface. A ball of twine. He turned it over, stray strands of fibre sticking out haphazardly, catching the light from behind in a way that made them look darker, thicker. This was perfect. Kevin wanted to immediately place it in the mailbox, but he knew he had to stick to the routine. Hopefully she was ready for him this time. He went to bed and slept deeply, dreaming of the peace of endless, quiet caves.

****

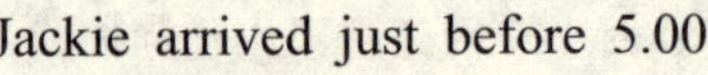

Jackie arrived just before 5.00

知道，他能够本能地判定出哪些物件是合适的。这期间有一种无言的交流，一种意义深藏在物件中。邮递员设的谜让凯文激动万分；他的每个细胞都在颤抖，有一种强烈的感觉，这种感觉已经在他身上死去多年。他无法想象她还会出什么花样，让这个游戏值得继续，但他知道，他们之间的交换很重要。

他的手在装得满满的抽屉深处摸着，手指滑过一个粗糙的表面。一个绒线球。他把它反转过来，看到一些凌乱的布条随意地从球里迸出来，袒露在从背后射过来的光里，使它们看起来颜色更深、体积更大。这简直太好了。凯文想立即把它放在信箱里，但他知道他必须按程序走。希望这次她为他准备好了。他上床睡觉，睡得很沉，梦见了安静的、无边无际的洞穴——那样的和平。

****

时针刚指向下午 5 点

p.m., interrupting his vigil. She was already like a pencil outline to him, a tracing on thin paper. He knew she would come back, as she hadn't taken anything with her when she left, but he had thought that she might dissipate like a vapour.

钟，杰茜回来了，打断了他对时钟的守候。对他而言，她早已经变成了一幅铅笔画、一种在薄薄的纸上留下的痕迹。他知道她会回来，因为她离开时没带任何东西，但他也曾想过，她或许会像水汽一样蒸发。

She went to the bedroom without saying a word and began packing. He hoped she wouldn't take too long. When she came back down with her suitcase she paused, arms at her sides. "Is there anything you want to say?"

她一句话也没说，径直走向卧室，开始打包收拾行李。他希望她不会花太长时间。当她拿着行李箱再回到地下室时，她停顿了一下，双手放在身体两边。她说："你想说点什么吗?"

"No. Not really."

"没有。真的没有。"

"So that's it then? Twelve years gone, just like that?"

"那么就这样了？12年，就这样完了？"

He looked at his watch. "Well, this is your decision. I didn't tell you to leave."

他看了看手表。"嗯，这是你自己的决定。我没有让你离开。"

"You didn't ask me to stay, either."

"你也没有让我留下来。"

"I'm sorry."

"我很抱歉。"

"Doesn't this bother you? Don't you feel anything?" Her voice was both pleading and angry. Kevin always had difficulty interpreting her simultaneous contradictions.

"难道这对你无所谓吗?难道你没有任何感觉?"她的声音既有恳求又有愤怒。凯文总是很难理解她同时拥有的矛盾情感或想法。

"I can't say what you want to hear." He blinked, his eyes taking a

"我说不出你想听的话。"他眨了眨眼睛，扫了

glance at his wrist. 5.15 now. He wished she would leave.

"Why do you keep looking at your watch? Do you have some secret rendezvous planned?" Her voice was sharp like an icicle tip.

Kevin was surprised. It had never occurred to him that she might interpret his indifference this way. "No, it's nothing like that."

She smiled, a sarcastic turn of the lip that she always reserved for him. "No, I suppose not." She threw her house key and mail key on the end table.

He turned toward his office. "You better go now."

The door slammed, the wheels of her suitcase rumbling and clicking as she manoeuvered the compressed contents of her life to her car. When the echo of her squealing tires faded, he hurried to the mailbox. There was no mail today, not even a flyer, but Kevin smiled as he reached in and grabbed the object. It looked like a pair of small pliers. He examined the series of semi-circular indentations marked with numbers on each side of the blades. Electrical wire-stripper. He opened and closed it

一眼腕上的手表。5 点 15 分。他希望她离开。

“为什么你不停地看你的手表?你有什么秘密的、计划好了的约会吗?”她的声音锋利得像一条冰柱子。

凯文很惊讶。他从来没有想到过，她竟会以这种方式理解他的冷漠。“没有，没那样的事。”

她笑了笑，嘴唇上表现出了时刻为他准备好了的挖苦。“当然，我猜也不会有。”她把她房间的钥匙和信箱的钥匙扔在了茶几上。

他转向他的办公室。“你最好现在就走。”

门砰的一声关上了。接着是手提箱轮子滚动的隆隆声和她设法把箱子搬上车时的碰撞声，那箱子里压缩了她全部的生活内容。当车轮呼啸着走远时，他向信箱奔去。今天没有信件，甚至连广告册子都没有。然而，当凯文伸进手去摸到一样东西时，他笑了。它看起来像一把小钳子。他仔细端详着它。钳口的每一边都有一系列半圆形的压痕，标有数字。是电动剥线器。他把它压开、合上、合上、压开，来回

several times, mimicking the motion of pulling the vinyl coating off a wire, exposing the bare metal below.

做了几次，模仿着把电线表层的乙烯基材料剥掉的动作，让藏在下面的金属裸露出来。

****

Two weeks had passed since the first exchange, and the initial exhilaration was beginning to wear off. Every morning he had placed an object in the box and every afternoon he had retrieved the one placed there by the letter carrier. He was still excited to see each day's new arrival, but he found that the pounding pulse and shaky, moist hands had been replaced by a more calm routine. He knew that there would be something there each day, as long as he waited until after 5.00 p.m. to collect it. He briefly considered varying the routine, but he knew that consistency and repetition were the keys to this communication.

****

从第一次交换东西到现在，两个星期过去了。最初的兴奋开始消退。每天早晨，他在信箱里放样东西；每天下午，从信箱里收到邮递员放在那里的某样东西。他仍然期盼着每天有新花样到来。然而，那种脉搏怦怦跳动和手掌颤抖、出汗的紧张与兴奋被常规带来的平静所取代。他知道，每天那里都会有一样东西在等着他收，只要他等到下午 5 点以后。他曾一度考虑是否改变程序，但他知道，一致性和重复是这种交流的关键。

Weekends were trying. With no mail delivery on Saturday or Sunday, the long hours stretched into a vast, featureless plane, a desert of fused, flawless glass. To fill the time, Kevin worked on arranging and rearranging the artifacts on the

周末很熬人。周六和周日都不发送邮件。漫长的时间拉伸成一个巨大的、毫无特色的平面，像一望无际的沙漠、毫无瑕疵的玻璃。为了消磨时间，凯文摆弄着桌子上的

table. There were now eight objects separated by eight pieces of paper. After trying several different arrangements, he had reverted to alternating the scraps of paper identifying his offerings with the gifts received. He had tried keeping all of the letter carrier's gifts together — arranged first alphabetically, then by size, then by colour, then by date received—but no arrangement seemed to suggest any meaning. He finally decided to close his eyes and randomly select objects and scraps of paper, arranging them in a circle on the table. Something about the unity and continuity of the circle appealed to his eye, and he was certain that a pattern would eventually coalesce. To spur the cognitive gelling, he made lists as he rearranged the items, records of the progression of his thought process.

物件，把它们这样排列或那样排列。现在有八样东西，被八张纸片分隔开。在尝试了几种不同的排列后，他决定返回到他试过的一种模式：用收到的礼物来间隔排列那些标着他送出的礼物的纸片。他试过把所有邮递员的礼物放在一起——先是按字母顺序排列，然后是按大小、颜色和接受日期。然而，没有任何排列能显示出任何意义。最后，他决定闭上眼睛，胡乱选择收到的物件和纸片，在桌子上把它们排成一圈。那个圆的一致性和连续性吸引了他的眼睛，他确信某种模式终将显现。为了让自己的认知更清晰，当他重新排列这些东西时，他列了个单子，记录下自己的思维过程。

My Items	*Her Items*
Tape	*Shovel Handle*
Twine	*Scissors*
Glue	*Wire stripper*
Staples	*Small jar of solvent*
Pencil	*Staple remover*

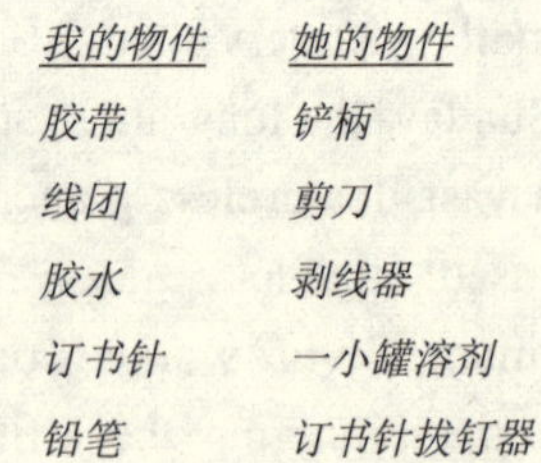

我的物件	*她的物件*
胶带	*铲柄*
线团	*剪刀*
胶水	*剥线器*
订书针	*一小罐溶剂*
铅笔	*订书针拔钉器*

Pen	*Eraser*	*钢笔*	*橡皮擦*
Paper clip	*Hole punch*	*纸夹*	*打洞器*
Rubber band	*Utility knife*	*橡皮筋*	*工具刀*

He repeated the names of the objects over and over, out loud and in his head, but he wasn't satisfied. There was something here – connections, disconnections – but he couldn't quite figure out what the letter carrier's intent was. More items were needed to define the pattern, to provide the freedom he craved.

他一遍又一遍重复这些东西的名字，或是大声喊出来，或是在脑子里默念，但他不满足——一定会有什么暗示的。关联在哪里？无关联又在哪里？但他仍然不能完全弄明白邮递员的意图。他需要更多的物件使迷局明朗化。那一刻是他渴望的自由。

On the Monday of the third week, he placed a package of page reinforcements in the mailbox. So far, all the items he had used had been office supplies. The letter carrier was less consistent—the shovel handle and wire stripper were particularly troubling. He opened the mailbox that afternoon and discovered the package exactly where he had left it, now sitting in front of the mail. He grabbed the reinforcements, stroking the box, confirming its existence. He wondered about temporal displacement. Perhaps the letter carrier hadn't seen the package

第三周的星期一，他把一包纸张加固页放在信箱里。到目前为止，他用的所有物件都是办公用品。邮递员的东西不太一致——铲柄和剥线器特别让人费解。那天下午他打开信箱，发现自己放在那儿的东西还在，只不过，它现在的位置是在信箱的最前面。他抓起那包纸张加固页，击打着信箱，证实它的存在。一时间，他恍惚是否时间错位：或许邮递员没有看到这个包，因为时间对它做了手脚；也许她已经厌倦了这个过

because time had warped around it. Perhaps she had just grown tired of the process. Maybe she was no longer amused with the game. These thoughts kindled a deep ache in Kevin. He was close to understanding the puzzle, but just needed a few more clues.

程；也许她不再对这个游戏感到有趣。这些想法在凯文体内酝酿，让他有切肤之痛。他已经接近谜底，只是还需要再多一点线索。

On Tuesday, the reinforcements were still there. Kevin slammed the mailbox door, his keys jangling against the cool metal. He had to take several deep breaths to calm himself.

周二，纸张加固页仍然在那儿。凯文啪地关上了信箱门，钥匙在冰冷的信箱门上晃荡着。他不得不做几个深呼吸，让自己冷静。

On Wednesday and Thursday, the reinforcements had not changed position. Mail had come both days, so Kevin now knew that she was ignoring him. Why? Had his gifts offended her? He thought over his list again, but could not see how. Had he signaled something he hadn't intended? He couldn't be sure, as he didn't really understand his own intentions. What then? A cruel joke with a silent punch-line?

周三和周四，那包纸张加固页仍原封不动地躺在那儿。其他信件照常来。凯文现在意识到，她是在故意不理他了。为什么呢？他的礼物冒犯了她吗?他再一次把他的单子在脑海中仔仔细细过了一遍，但看不出什么。难道他无意中发出了某种信号？他无法确定，因为他并不真正理解自己的意图是什么。那么，接下来呢？在最关键处用沉默来证明这是一个残酷的玩笑？

The sheets twisted around him, damp with his sweat. He couldn't get to sleep. He was feverish, the

他出汗了，身上缠着的床单湿透了。他无法入睡。他发烧，悬而未决的

unanswered questions spreading like a mutating virus. He couldn't continue like this; he had to do something, had to act on Friday. The weekend would be intolerable if the situation stayed the same. He yanked the sheets back, friction burns blossoming on his bare flesh, and lay staring at the ceiling, ideas uncoiling in his brain like snakes released from a basket.

问题像变异病毒在蔓延。他不能继续这样；他必须做点什么，必须在周五采取行动。如果这种情况继续，周末将是无法忍受的。他猛地把床单撩开，皮肉被扯得火辣辣地疼。他盯着天花板，思想乱窜，像无数条蛇从篮子里被放了出来。

****

Three hours he had been sitting in his car, parked in front of the SuperMailbox, keeping an eye on it in his rearview mirror. A whisper of an April breeze feathered his skin through the open window, faint relief for the fever that simmered within him, despite the coolness of the false spring. He swallowed and popped another piece of gum into his mouth. He didn't dare drink anything, couldn't afford to be away from his stakeout for even five minutes. He looked at his watch. 1.57. Soon, soon.

A low rumbling from behind, bits of gravel popping under tire treads. In the mirror he could see a

****

他已经在车里坐了三个小时了。车就泊在信箱前。他的眼睛一直盯着后视镜里的信箱。车窗开着。尽管春天还没真正到来，凉意盎然，他体内还是暗火酝酿。一阵 4 月的微风吹来，像耳语、像羽毛轻拂他的皮肤，他稍感轻松了些。他咽了口口水，往嘴里又扔了一块口香糖。他什么也没敢喝，因为无法容忍哪怕是 5 分钟的时间离开后视镜。他看了看手表。1 点 57 分。快了，快了。

车后传来隆隆声，很低，是砾石被车轮碾压的声音。从后视镜里，他可以看

dark grey mini-van pull up to the SuperMailbox. He waited, his palms clammy. Eventually the driver's door opened and a short woman with dark, curly hair hopped out, a large canvas bag slung over her shoulder. Her cheeks were full, her hips rounded, nothing like Jackie. He wanted to see her eyes, wanted to gauge her intelligence, but she wore wrap-around sunglasses. She jabbed a key into the main lock and swung the entire front panel open, surprising Kevin. He had always assumed that each box opened separately. What the letter carrier was now doing made much more sense, but there was something unnerving about all the open, exposed slots. She worked quickly, clinically, grabbing the rubber-banded packages from her canvas bag and slotting them into the correct compartments.

She was nearing his slot. He opened the car door and eased himself out, consciously slowing his breath, wiping his hands on his pants. He drew air deep into his nostrils as he tried to detect her fragrance. There was no scent except

到一辆深灰色的客货两用车在信箱前停了下来。他等着，手掌湿漉漉的。终于，门开了，一个矮个子女人从车里跳了出来；她有着黑色的卷发，肩膀上挂着一个大帆布袋。她脸颊饱满，臀部滚圆，和杰茜没有共同之处。他想看到她的眼睛，衡量她的智慧，但她戴着包边太阳镜。她把钥匙猛地插进主锁，掀开一块板架，上面是一扇扇信箱门。这让凯文吃惊。他一直以为，每个信箱的门是单独打开的。邮递员用的这种开门方式更有道理，但也有一些令人不安的因素，因为所有的门都开着，里面的东西暴露着。她手脚麻利、动作准确，把扎着皮筋的一捆捆信从帆布袋里掏出来，丢进正确的信箱里。

她马上就要接近他的信箱了。他打开车门，从车里下来，舒缓自己，有意识地放慢呼吸，把手在裤子上擦了擦。他用鼻子深深吸气，试图找到她身上的气味，然而，没有。到处弥漫的是春

the spring smells of decaying and thawing leaves and grass. He jangled his keys.

天里解冻的腐草、烂叶的味道。他拿出信箱钥匙。

"You'll have to wait until I'm finished." She continued slotting the mail, flipping the packages like a casino dealer with a fresh set of cards.

“你得等我弄完。”她继续往邮箱里扔着邮件；她翻阅、分发手上的一包包信件，就像赌场工作人员摆弄手里的一副新牌似的。

"I'm Box C7." Kevin's voice sounded postcard-thin.

“我的信箱是 C7。”凯文的声音听起来就像明信片那样薄。

"Just give me another minute." Her tone was sharper now.

“再给我一分钟。”她的语气变得更尖锐。

Kevin moved around the open door and stood behind her. "No, you don't understand. I'm box C7." He pointed.

凯文在开着的信箱门前转悠，站在她的身后。“不，你没明白我的意思。我的信箱是 C7。”他指着。

She finally turned and looked at him, pushing her sunglasses up on her forehead. Her dark brown eyes were wide, conveying a mixture of annoyance and suspicion as she regarded Kevin. She followed his pointing finger then shrugged.

她终于转过身来，看着他，把她的太阳镜推到前额上。她深棕色的眼睛大大的，在看着凯文时里面有恼怒和猜疑。她顺着他的手指看了一下，然后耸耸肩。

Kevin felt his fever boiling over. He thrust his finger at the box. "There! There! The box with the reinforcements."

凯文觉得火冒三丈。他手指戳着信箱。“那儿！在那儿！里面有一包书本加固页的那个信箱。”

She looked again, then reached in and pulled out the package. "You

她又看了一下，伸手把里面的书本加固页拉了出

mean these? I was wondering why these were left here." She handed them to Kevin.

He took the reinforcements from her, the skin on the back of her knuckles cool on his sweaty palm. The neurons in his brain were firing blanks, his nerve endings numb. "The others…you didn't… I mean, you didn't leave the other…gifts… in my mailbox?"

"Gifts? No, I've only been on this route since Monday."

"Only…Monday…" He felt as if his blood flow were changing direction in his arteries. "Do you…do you know the letter carrier who was here before?"

"No, I have no idea who ran this route. We're subcontractors, you see." Her tone had softened. "Why do you need to know? Was there some kind of problem?"

Kevin wandered away from her, sound slapping his eardrums as he stumbled across the street. He fumbled for his keys, but eventually got the front door open.

Inside, he lay on the ceramic

来。"你的意思是这包纸?我还想知道它为什么被留在这儿呢。"她把那包纸递给了凯文。

他从她手上接过书本加固页。她手背关节处的皮肤冰凉，触碰到了他出汗的手掌。他大脑中的神经元在燃烧，一片空白，他的神经末梢麻木了。"其他的……你没有……我的意思是，你没有留下其他礼物吗……在我的信箱里?"

"礼物?不，我星期一才开始跑这条线路。"

"星期一才开始……"他觉得他动脉里的血流正在改变方向。"你……你认识以前跑这条线路的邮递员吗？"

"不，我不知道以前谁跑这条线路。你知道，我们是二级承包商。"她的语气已经变软。"你为什么要知道?有什么问题吗?"

凯文从她身边走开。当他跌跌撞撞走过街道时，他的耳鼓鼓膜嗡嗡作响。他慌忙翻出钥匙，最终打开了自己家的前门。

走进屋里，他在瓷砖地

tile for several minutes, bile churning inside his cheeks. He swallowed the bitter fluid, keeping everything down, letting the smooth, cool tiles slow his pulse. After several minutes he was able to get up.

He moved carefully through the hallways to his office. He stared at the artifacts on the table, memorizing their positions. He shut and locked the door to the office and wandered through the empty rooms of his house. On the walls were photographs of a couple. Strangers. On the kitchen table lay mail for Jackie, unopened.

上躺了几分钟，胆汁在他的脸颊内搅拌着；他吞下苦涩的液体，让一切冷却，让光滑、冰凉的瓷砖使脉搏的跳动慢下来。几分钟后，他能够站起来了。

他小心翼翼地穿过走廊，回到他的办公室。他盯着桌子上的物件，记忆它们的位置。他把办公室的门关上、锁上。整幢屋子里的每个房间都空荡荡的，他漫步其中。所有的墙上都挂着一对夫妻的照片。陌生人。厨房的餐桌上放着杰茜的私人信件，从未被开启过。

Cold Memory

He is walking in a forest. The air is scented with pine. He is not running but he feels the urgency of the quarry. He knows he must get somewhere, quickly. His steps quicken on the frozen ground. He doesn't know who his pursuer is, but he can sense that he, or it, is near. He can feel his pulse pounding in his ears. His breath clouds in the heavy air. He holds his arms close to his body, trying to shake the chill.

Suddenly, the ground begins to change. His feet begin sinking. His steps slow. The ground is no longer frozen; the icy ooze begins creeping up his legs. His heart pounds in his chest. He knows the pursuer is getting closer, but he can't move.

冰冷的记忆

他在丛林中走着，脚下是冻土，空气中弥漫着松香。他没有跑，却能感到被追猎的紧迫。他知道他必须快速到达某地。他的脚步在加快。他不知道谁在追他，但能感到就在附近。他的耳朵能听到脉搏跳动的声音。他的呼吸在沉重的空气中形成雾团。他双臂紧抱、贴在胸前，驱赶寒冷。

突然，脚下的大地有所变化，他的脚开始下沉。他放慢了脚步。脚下不再是冻土；冰冷的泥开始顺着他的腿往上蔓延。他的心怦怦乱跳。他知道追赶者在迫近，但他却动也动不了。冰川沼

The glacial swamp has a firm grip on him now. He must break free. He must...

泽现在已经牢牢地抓住了他。他必须挣脱，他必须……

Theodor Molnar woke with a start. He blinked and looked around the darkened room, trying to find a reference point in the pitch-like gloom.

西奥多·莫纳尔突然惊醒。他眨了眨眼，看着四周漆黑一片的房间，试图在沥青一般的阴暗中找到一个参照点。

Where am I?

我在哪儿？

He shook as an icy hand seized his bowels. His feet were frigid, as if he had just walked through a mountain stream. His eyes, now adjusted to the darkness, picked out a familiar, pale orange glow behind the curtains.

他颤抖起来，就像有一只冰冷的手抓住了他的肠子。他的脚是冰冷的，就好像刚刚在一条山涧小溪里走过。他的眼睛现在已经适应了黑暗，锁定在窗帘后一个熟悉的、浅橙色的光点。

He sighed. *I wish Marion wouldn't leave the window open. It's still too early in the year.*

他叹了口气。*我真希望玛丽昂关上了那扇窗户，时节还太早。*

He rolled out of bed, sliding into his comfortable slippers. He padded silently to the window and pulled the curtain aside. He stared for a moment at the tall, Victorian streetlight that stood in the middle of the island that centred Cambridge Court. He always thought that the streetlight, with its graceful, ornate

他翻身下床，双脚塞进舒适的拖鞋里。他悄悄移步到窗前，把窗帘拉到一边。有那么片刻的时间，他凝视着那盏维多利亚风格的街灯，高高矗立在小岛的中央——剑桥法庭的所在地。他总认为，这盏线条优雅、装饰华丽的街灯在这个现代郊

lines, looked out of place on this modern suburban cul-de-sac. Too European, he thought. Who are they trying to fool?

区的死胡同里显得那么不合时宜。太欧洲化了，他想。他们想唬弄谁呀！

He reached to slide the window shut, but it was firmly latched.

他伸手去把窗户合上，但插销却把它牢牢固定住了。

Why am I so cold?

我为什么这么冷？

He put his robe on over his pajamas and slid back into bed. Marion was breathing deeply, slowly. She stirred slightly as he put his arm around her. As he stared at the back of her neck, he tried to remember the details of the dream that had woken him. He pushed his head deeper into the pillow, trying to bury his troubled thoughts, trying to shake the chill that still gripped him.

他在睡衣外又披上了睡袍，缩回到床里。玛丽昂呼吸沉重、缓慢。当他用手臂揽住她时，她微微翻了个身。他盯着她的后脖子，试图记起梦里的细节——那让他惊醒的细节。他把头更深地埋进枕头，试图埋葬受困的思绪，摆脱缠绕他的寒冷。

****

****

"More coffee, Ted?"

Theodor looked up from his newspaper. His wife's smiling face was patterned with strips of brilliant, spring sunshine. The warm rays cascaded through the kitchen window, falling on his wrinkled hands, taking some of the edge off the chill that he still felt.

"还要咖啡吗，泰德?"

西奥多从报纸上抬起头。妻子的笑脸上是一条条春日灿烂的阳光。温暖的光线透过厨房的窗户蔓延进来，落在他布满皱纹的手上。虽然他仍感到寒冷，但其边角现在被驱走了一些。

"Thanks," he mumbled, holding out his cup.

Marion poured Theodor's coffee, studying his face as the warm liquid gurgled in the cup.

"You look tired."

"Mmm. I didn't sleep well again."

"Really?" She didn't try to mask the concern in her voice. "That's the third time this week. Are you still having bad dreams?"

"I guess so. It's the same one; I'm being chased, I'm cold..." Theodor's voice trailed off as he took a sip of his coffee.

Marion sat down beside Theodor and put her hand on his arm. "Maybe a hobby..."

Theodor pulled his arm out of her grip. "Oh I suppose you think I'm losing my mind, now that I'm retired. I still read my scientific journals, you know. I keep up with news," he said, flipping his newspaper. "I don't think my mind is any less active."

Marion tried to mask the hurt look on her face. "Honey, don't

"谢谢。"他咕哝着，伸出杯子。

玛丽昂一边倒咖啡，让温暖的液体汩汩流入西奥多的杯子，一边观察着他的脸。

"你看起来很累。"

"嗯。我又没睡好。"

"真的吗？"她并不想掩饰声音里的担忧。"这是本周第三次了。你还做噩梦吗？"

"我想是这样的。相同的梦。我被追逐，我冷……"西奥多呷了口咖啡，声音小了下去。

玛丽昂在西奥多的身旁坐了下来，把手放在他的胳膊上。"也许有个爱好……"

西奥多把胳膊挣脱出来。"哦，我猜想你一定是认为我退休了有些失神落魄。但我仍在读科学期刊，这，你是知道的。我每天都读新闻。"他说着，抖动着手上的报纸。"我并不认为我的大脑不像以前那么活跃。"

玛丽昂极力掩盖受到伤害后脸上可能会出现的表

misunderstand me. I'm not saying there's anything wrong with you. I just think that if you were busier maybe…I don't know…maybe the dreams would stop. I mean, you never had these dreams when you were working."

Theodor sighed, swirled his coffee slowly in the cup. "Maybe it's just the change. Maybe I'll have to just wait this out until it gets better."

"Um, well you could do that." Marion grabbed both of Theodor's hands and squeezed them. "I'm worried about you Ted. I hate to see you suffer. I was thinking that if these bad dreams continue, you could try talking to someone about it, you know, maybe a counselor or somebody like that."

Theodor was going to object, but Marion's soft, beautiful eyes silenced him, made him realize just how lucky he was. He could still not believe that having escaped his shattered country to arrive in a strange land with nothing, he could somehow have wound up with such a wonderful, caring wife, a fulfilling and interesting career, two

情。"亲爱的，别误解我的意思。我并不是说你有什么问题。我只是觉得，如果你忙起来的话，或许……谁知道呢……或许梦就会停止。我的意思是，你还上班的时候，从来没有做过这些梦。"

西奥多叹了口气，慢慢转动着杯子里的咖啡。"或许这只是一种变化。或许我不得不等待熬过这个阶段，直至一切都变得好起来。"

"嗯，你当然可以那样做。"玛丽昂抓起西奥多的双手，揉搓着它们。"我有点担心你，泰德。我讨厌看到你受苦。我在想，如果这些恶梦继续的话，你可以试着跟别人谈谈；你知道的，像心理咨询师之类的人。"

西奥多本想反对，但玛丽昂温柔、美丽的眼睛让他沉默了下来。他意识到，他是多么幸运。他仍然无法相信，在他逃离了破碎的祖国、只身来到一个陌生的国度、一无所有之时，最终还能拥有一位关爱他的娇妻、一份充实而有趣的职业、两个出色的孩子和一座美丽的

wonderful children, a beautiful house. He still found it overwhelming at times.

房子。有时，他仍然感到这简直不可思议。

He released her hands and wiped the hint of a tear from his eye. “Don’t worry, honey, it’s going to be okay. I’ll be alright.”

他松开了她的手，擦了擦眼睛里隐约的一滴泪，说：“别担心，亲爱的，一切都会好起来的。我会好起来的。”

She hugged him, and whispered, “I just want to make sure you’re happy.”

她拥抱了他，小声说，“我只想确保，你是快乐的。”

“I am,” he whispered back, almost believing his own words.

“我是。”他小声回应，几乎相信了自己说的话。

****

In the month since he had retired, Theodor had found it difficult to find ways to occupy his time. He had always applied a back-breaking work ethic to any endeavour he was involved with, a trait which had served him well in his career in astrophysics research. Now, he was overwhelmed with a sensation of aimlessness. Each day stretched out in front of him like a vast desert, seamless, with no reference points. Each morning, when he had finished his coffee and newspaper, he would attempt to venture into that desert. Like a lost

****

在退休后的头一个月里，西奥多发现很难打发时间。长期以来，他一直奉守干活不遗余力这一职业道德。无论干什么，他都如此。这一特性使他在天体物理学研究领域卓有成效。现在，他被一种无所事事的感觉击垮。每一天，他的眼前都好像是一望无际的沙漠，没有缝隙、没有参考点。每天早晨，他喝完了咖啡，读完了报纸，就想尝试着进入那个沙漠冒险。像一个迷路的流浪者，他开始感到

wanderer, he began to feel the edges of his sanity being nibbled away by confusion and despair.

自己的理智一点点地被疑惑和绝望蚕食。

The first thing he tried to do was to help Marion around the house. Marion expressed appreciation for his efforts, but he could tell she was not sincere. Marion had always exercised total control of the household, striving to maintain a normal family life while her husband dwelled in the abstract world of planetary motion, the world of late nights at the campus lab or observatory. Marion had difficulty giving up control of her universe, but she tried, understanding that Theodor's transition was going to be as difficult as hers was when their youngest son left home.

他试图要做的第一件事是帮玛丽昂打理家务。虽然玛丽昂对他的努力表示了欣赏，但他能感觉到，她并不是真心的。长期以来，一直是玛丽昂在照顾家务，确保家庭生活正常运转，老公能沉浸在行星运动的抽象世界里，或在校园实验室、观测室里忙到深夜。要让玛丽昂放弃对她的宇宙的控制很难，但她还是努力去做。她能理解，这个过渡期对西奥多而言是多么的艰难，就像当初小儿子长大、离开家去独立生活时她所经历过的那样。

After three weeks of fumbled domestic efforts, Theodor finally considered Marion's suggestion of a hobby. He had never had a hobby before. His work had always occupied him completely. He really had no idea how to relax. Still, after only four weeks of retirement, Theodor knew that he was starting to annoy his wife. He knew he had to find something to do.

经过三周的努力，西奥多终于放弃了不擅长的家务，开始采纳玛丽昂的建议去培养一种爱好。他以前从未有过任何爱好，工作一直完全占据了他的时间和精力。他真的不知道如何放松。退休生活刚刚过了四周，西奥多就知道他开始让妻子感到了烦。他知道他必须找点事去做。

He immediately ruled out any of the traditional manly pursuits such as woodworking or automotives. He had no interest or skill in these areas. Although he appreciated his wife's efforts with their beautifully landscaped yard, he knew that gardening would not hold his interest. Golf just seemed pointless to him. Finally, after several days of considered deliberations, he found something that piqued his interest.

他立即排除了任何传统意义上能显示男子气概的追求，如木工或汽车。他在这些领域既没有兴趣，也没有技能。虽然他欣赏妻子的努力，把院子的景观搞得错落有致、像模像样，他知道，园艺不会是他长久的兴趣。高尔夫在他看来毫无意义。最后，经过几天的考虑，他发现了能激发他兴趣的事。

"History?" Marion seemed perplexed.

"历史?"玛丽昂感到迷惑不解。

"No, not history in the general sense. My history, my people's history."

"不，不是一般意义上的历史；是我的历史，我的民族的历史。"

Marion, patient as always, simply looked at him over the kitchen table, her face an unspoken question.

玛丽昂像往常一样耐心。她隔着餐桌直直地看着他，脸上写着一个大大的问号。

"Don't you see? When my mother and I fled Hungary in '56, I lost all contact with my past, my roots. I really know very little about my family history, my country's history. I want to find out where I come from, who I am."

"你不明白吗?当我的妈妈和我在 1956 年逃离匈牙利时，我的过去就中断了，我失去了根。我对家族、对祖国的历史知之甚少。我想知道我来自哪里，我是谁。"

"Well Ted, I think that's wonderful," Marion said in a tone of

"好吧，泰德。我认为这好极了。"玛丽昂的语气

cautious compassion. "I'm just curious, though, why you've suddenly developed this interest. The few times that I've suggested you go back to Hungary for a visit, you were opposed to the idea."

里不无谨慎和同情。"我只是好奇，你怎么突然对这个感兴趣了。有几次，我建议你回匈牙利访问，你总是反对。"

Theodor stared at his wife and blinked twice. "I don't really know why. It just seems like…like now is the right time."

西奥多盯着他的妻子，眨了两次眼睛。"我真的不知道为什么。现在看起来像是……像是合适的时间。"

Marion smiled, unsure of why she felt uneasy.

玛丽昂笑了笑。不知道为什么她感到了不安。

****

He is running. He sucks in the frigid air, burning his lungs. A full moon illuminates the late-autumn snow. His feet pound rhythmically on the slippery ground. He knows he must get somewhere, soon. But where?

他在跑，吸着寒冷的空气，肺部像在燃烧一样。满月照亮了深秋的雪。他的脚在湿滑的地面上有节奏地敲击着。他知道，他必须到达某个地方，要快；但那个地方在哪里？

Up ahead he can see the dim outlines of two people. Is one a child? He can't tell; his vision of the twisting path is obscured by the thick, knotted forest. I must stay with them, protect them, he thinks. He coughs, icy daggers piercing his throat. He doesn't slow.

他能看到，前面模糊有两个人的轮廓。其中一个是孩子吗?他无法判定。他看不清那崎岖的小路，视线被浓密的树木遮住。我必须和他们待在一起、保护他们，他想。他咳嗽，像有冰冷的匕首刺穿他的喉咙。他没有放慢脚步。

There! Up ahead! He can see

在那里！就在前面！他

something. The trees are thinning. The moon is shining brighter down the path. This must be what he is looking for. His legs pump furiously. He must keep up with the shadowy forms ahead.

Suddenly, his feet shoot out from under him, his left knee bending at an unnatural angle. He hits the ground hard, winding himself. He lies on his back, his knee on fire. He looks up. He can see a narrow window of stars, framed by the dark crowns of the spinning trees. The stars are beautiful tonight, he thinks, wondering why he hasn't stopped to look at them yet. Then he remembers. He struggles to get up, but the pain is fierce. As he fights, he begins to feel frigid tendrils looping around his body. The frosty grip is firm, pulling him slowly, steadily down. He thrashes as the cold penetrates his bones. He looks up as a dark form looms over him.

Theodor screamed. Marion stroked his hair gently and rocked him, as if rocking a baby.

"It's okay, it's okay, it was only

能看到些什么。树木正变得稀疏起来，月光把小路也照得更清晰。这一定是他正在寻找的。他的腿立即像被打了气一样。他必须跟上前面的黑影。

突然间，他的两只脚在身下滑了出去，左膝盖扭了一下；他仰面倒在地上，摔得几乎岔了气。他躺在那儿，膝盖像着火一般。他向上看，树似乎在旋转。透过浓密的树冠，他能看到小块的天空繁星闪烁，就像透过窄窄的窗棂看夜空一样。今晚的繁星真好看，他想。我为什么不停下来好好看看它们呢！继而，他记起身在何处。他挣扎着要站起来，但疼痛难忍。他努力着，开始感到寒冷的触角在全身环绕。他被寒冷牢牢控制，身体似被往下沉沉地拽着。当寒冷刺穿他的骨头，他开始抽搐。他向上看着。这时，一片黑暗向他压过来。

西奥多尖叫起来。玛丽昂温柔地抚摩着他的头发，摇晃他，就好像他是一个婴儿一样。

“没事，没事。这只是

a dream."

Theodor looked at his wife, his eyes confused, pleading. As he shivered in her arms, he could form only one coherent thought.

What the hell is wrong with me?

****

As Theodor sat at the study carrel, he reflected that he had always loved the smell of books, especially old books. He turned in his chair and looked at the endless shelves in the Centennial University Library. How much knowledge, how much effort had gone into creating those wonderful, leather-bound tomes, he wondered as he inhaled the musty air.

After a moment, he turned back to the weighty publication opened in front of him, A Brief History of Hungary. Yet another bit of marketing dishonesty, he muttered, as he fingered the edges of the dry pages that numbered well over eight hundred.

He sighed and focused his tired eyes on the page. The detailed analysis of the Austria-Hungary dual

一个梦。"

西奥多看着妻子，眼睛里充满了困惑、恳求。当他在她的怀抱里颤抖时，他只有一个想法还能连贯起来：

我到底怎么啦?

****

西奥多坐在读书格子间里。他回想着，自己一直就喜欢书的味道，尤其是旧书。他在椅子上转过头去，望着纪念大学图书馆那一排排、望不到头的书架。吸着那有霉味的空气，他在想，要制作那些精美的、皮面装订的书籍得需要多少的知识、花费多少的努力啊！

过了一会儿，他转过身来，看着面前打开的厚重出版物——《匈牙利简史》。又是另一个不诚实的市场运作，他咕哝着说道，手指快速划过干巴巴的书页，总共有800多页。

他叹了口气，疲惫的眼睛注视着书页。对奥匈帝国二元君主制的详细分析不是

monarchy was not holding his interest. He had already waded through the initial Magyar period, the Tartar invasion, the Ottoman period, but nothing had yet captured his imagination. Somehow he had imagined that this process was going to be more invigorating, more stimulating. He had believed that the history of his people would leap off the page at him, challenging him to dig deeper, exciting his senses. Yet after four hours in this dimly lit, dank bunker, he only felt a sense of fatigue.

他的兴趣所在。他已经快速浏览过了最初的匈牙利人时期、鞑靼人的入侵时期、奥斯曼时期，但还没有任何信息能激发他的想象力。不知何故，他曾想象，这个过程应该更有活力、更刺激。他曾相信，他的民族历史会从书页里跳出来迎接他，挑战他去更深刻地阅读，让感官都活跃起来。但四个小时过去了，在这个昏暗、潮湿的读书格子间里，他能感觉到的就只有疲劳。

He took his glasses off and rubbed his burning eyes. As he massaged his right eyelid, kaleidoscopic bursts of colour infiltrated his field of vision. He thought the colourful patterns were a welcome contrast to the ubiquitous grey concrete of the campus. He continued kneading his right eye while his left eye looked vaguely at the open book.

他摘下眼镜，揉了揉灼疼的眼睛。当他按摩右眼睑时，眼前出现了万花筒般的色彩，和校园无处不在的混凝土灰色形成鲜明的对比。这倒不坏，他想。缤纷的图案是一个欢迎的表示。他继续揉搓着右眼，左眼模糊地看着打开的书。

Something on the page made him stop. A word, a name, what was it? He felt a vague tingling sensation in the back of his head. He stopped rubbing his eye and searched the

书页上的某样东西让他停了下来。一个字，一个名字，到底是什么？他感到后脑勺微微萌动。他停了下来，揉搓眼睛，开始在那一

page frantically.

There! He read the sentence again. It described the 1848 revolt, led by Lajos Kossuth.

Kossuth!

A sharp pain dug into his temples. He shut his eyes tightly. Kossuth? That name was familiar. Why? He concentrated, trying to remember why he should know that name. After a moment, he opened his eyes and let out a deep breath.

He couldn't remember.

But he knew, someday, he would.

****

Marion poured Theodor a cup of herbal tea. Although Theodor liked strong, ebony coffee in the morning, he preferred herbal tea in the afternoon.

"So how did it go? Did you find out anything interesting?"

Theodor watched as his wife tipped the teapot back, a small drip falling silently on the table. He wondered how much he should tell

页书上疯狂搜寻。

就在那儿！他把那整个句子又读了一遍。它描述的是拉约什·科苏特在 1848 年领导的叛乱。

科苏特!

他的太阳穴突然刺痛起来。他紧紧闭上了眼睛。科苏特？这个名字很熟悉。为什么？他集中精力，试图记起他为什么会知道这个名字。过了一会儿，他睁开了眼睛，长出了一口气。

他记不起来了。

但他知道，总有一天，他会的。

****

玛丽昂给西奥多倒了一杯花草茶。西奥多虽然在早上喜欢喝浓浓的、乌木色的咖啡，但下午他喜欢喝花草茶。

“进展如何？你发现什么有趣的东西了吗?”

西奥多看着他的妻子倒完茶把茶壶微微后倾，还是有一小滴静静滑落在桌面上。他不知道应该告诉她多

her. He knew she was worried about the state of his mental health. Unnecessarily worried, he thought.

少。他清楚，她担心他的心理健康。不必要的担心，他想。

"Oh, it was somewhat interesting. I covered a great deal of the more distant history; invasions, wars, political intrigue. You know. The usual things you find in the history of any country."

"哦，还算有趣。我读了大量较远的历史——入侵、战争、政治阴谋。你是知道的，那些在国史中经常能读到的东西。"

Marion wiped the spilled tea drop with a dainty hand. "Did you find anything that was, uh, more personal?"

玛丽昂用小巧的手把那滴溅出来的茶抹掉。"你找到任何……呃，任何和你有关的东西了吗?"

Theodor put his teacup to his lips, trying to read his wife's expression. She was a master of reading his moods. "No, not really. It was pretty dry. Almost dull, actually."

西奥多把茶杯放在嘴边，极力揣测妻子想要表达的意思。在阅读他的情绪方面，她是一个专家。"不，还没有。很无趣。实际上，可以说是很无聊。"

She put the cozy back on the teapot and sat down. "Oh, that's too bad. I know you were hoping to find some clues about your family."

她把茶壶套放回到茶壶上，坐了下来。"哦，那太糟了。我知道，你一直希望找到一些有关你家庭的线索。"

Theodor grunted, trying not to give her any clue about the agitation he experienced in the library, not wanting to worry her.

西奥多哼了一声，尽量不让她察觉出他在图书馆里经历的悸动，免得她担心。

Marion continued to study his face. "You know, we've been married a long time..."

玛丽昂继续研究他的脸。"你知道，我们结婚已经很长一段时间了……"

"Yes, I know."

Marion continued, not even acknowledging his sarcasm, "… and although we've done many things together, you really haven't told me much about your early life."

"是的，我知道。"

玛丽昂继续说话，甚至不理会他话里的挖苦意味，"……虽然我们一起做过很多事情，但对于你的早期生活，你却没告诉过我什么。"

He ran his finger around the rim of his cup. Marion had asked him this question a number of times when they were younger, but he had never given her much information. Eventually, she stopped asking. Now, as he tried to construct a response, his concentration was upset by a sudden whooping noise from outside.

他的手指沿杯口划着。在他们年轻的时候，玛丽昂已经不止一次问过这个问题，但他从未给过她太多的信息。最后，她不再问了。现在，他试图做出一个回应。然而，外面一个突然的噪音扰乱了他的注意力。

He turned his head to the window, and muttered, "Must be Richard's car alarm again. I don't know why he bothers with it anyway. Every time the wind rocks that little sports car of his, it sets off that ridiculous thing."

他转过头看着窗外，喃喃自语，"一定又是理查的汽车防盗器。真不知他为何多此一举。每次风晃动他那个小跑车，这怪东西就会叫起来。"

Theodor turned back to Marion, who looked at him expectantly. "Well, there really isn't much to tell. I fled with my mother after the revolution in '56, and we wound up in London. She died soon after we arrived. You've heard most of the

西奥多转过身来，发现玛丽昂仍然期待地看着他。"嗯，确实没什么可谈的。我和母亲在 1956 年的革命后就逃亡了，最终在伦敦落脚。不久，她死了。那之后的许多事情你都听过啦。"

story since then."

"But what about before you fled? You've never really said much about that?"

"Quite frankly, I really don't remember anything. I was only eleven, after all, when we fled." Theodor turned his head and cringed at the blaring siren.

Marion looked like she was going to say something, but then she stopped.

"Anyway, that's what all this research is all about. I'm hoping that something will look familiar to me, trigger a memory perhaps."

Marion got up and stood behind Theodor. She massaged his shoulders, hoping that he hadn't seen the concern creasing her face. "Well if there's anything I can do to help, just let me know. Okay?"

"Okay," he replied, relaxing a little as the car alarm finally stopped.

"那在你逃亡之前呢？你对此好像从未真正谈过多少吧？"

"坦率地说，我真的什么都不记得了。当我们逃离时，我毕竟只有 11 岁。"西奥多转过头去，刺耳的报警声使他不安。

玛丽昂似乎想说点什么，但最后还是什么也没说。

"不管怎样，这就是为什么我现在要做这个研究。希望能找到点熟悉的东西，触动我的记忆。"

玛丽昂站起身来，踱到西奥多的身后。她按摩他的肩部，希望他没有看到她脸上露出的担忧。"好吧。如果我能帮上任何忙，让我知道。好吗?"

"好的。"他回答。小车的报警声终于停了下来，他略感轻松。

****

The damp air chills him. As he runs, clouds of his breath tumble and spin, trailing off behind him, reflecting the pale moonlight. He is

潮湿的空气让他感到寒冷。他跑着，呼出的气团翻滚、旋转，在他身后逐渐消失，映射出苍白的月光。他

sweating under his wool coat. The sweat feels like it is congealing in the cool air. His armpits feel stuck to his torso. He flails his arms as he runs, trying to shake the chill in his bones.

Faint outlines of naked branches spider the sky, but he doesn't see them. He is focused on the path. He knows he is going the right direction, although he doesn't know his destination. The urgent, rhythmic pounding of his legs keeps him alert. He's almost there. He can feel it.

He bursts into a clearing, and before he can stop, he slides into a murky bog. His boots are immediately filled with sludgy liquid, creating a numbing ache in his feet. He tries to walk, but he can't move his feet. He struggles and pulls, but just sinks deeper. He is desperate, knowing that he must keep up with them. He wants to call out, but he bites his tongue, knowing he can't. He continues to fight the mire, tasting thickening blood in his mouth.

Behind him, a tall form approaches, momentarily casting a

穿着羊毛外套，浑身是汗。汗水给他的感觉像是在凉爽的空气中凝固。他的腋窝像是和身体粘在了一起。他边跑边挥动双臂，试图摆脱骨头里的寒意。

赤裸的树枝像蜘蛛网一样隐约勾画着天空。但他看不到这些。他正集中精力盯着小路。他知道，他正朝着正确的方向跑，但他不清楚目的地在哪里。他的双腿急促而有节奏地摆动着，这让他保持警觉。他几乎到那儿了。他能感觉到。

他闯进了一片空地。在能停步之前，他已经陷入一个阴暗的沼泽。他的靴子里立即灌满了泥泞的液体，双脚感到令人麻木的疼痛。他试着要走，但脚却无法移动。他挣扎着把脚往上拔，却陷得更深。他绝望。他知道，他必须能让双脚听他使唤。他想喊叫，却咬住自己的舌头，因为他知道他不能喊叫。他继续在泥潭里挣扎，嘴里品尝着越来越稠的血。

在他身后，一个高大的形体在接近；片刻间，其阴

shadow on him. He stops straining, and turns toward the form. In the darkness, he cannot distinguish any features, but he can tell it is a man in a uniform. The man slowly, calmly raises a weapon, a gun. He cannot see the man's face as he hears the hammer click into the place.

影笼罩了他。他不再紧张，向那个形体转过身来。黑暗中，他无法辨别其任何特征，但他可以肯定，这是一个穿着制服的男人。这个男人慢慢地、平静地举起了武器，一把枪。他看不清那人的脸，他听到了撞针的声音。

"Marion!"

"玛丽昂！"

Explosion.

爆炸。

Blackness.

黑暗。

Theodor felt his body shuddering as his wife held him. She didn't say anything, didn't have to say anything. He knew now that she was right, that he needed help.

妻子抱着他，西奥多感到自己的身体在发抖。她没说什么，也没必要。现在，他意识到，她是对的。他需要帮助。

****

Theodor flipped the pages of the encyclopedia briskly, looking for a particular entry. He had about an hour to kill before his appointment with the psychologist, so he decided to continue his research in the library.

西奥多快速翻阅着那本百科全书，寻找一个特定的词条。在见心理医生之前，他大约还有一个小时的时间可消磨；因此，他决定在图书馆继续他的研究。

After his third dream in four days, he didn't need much encouragement from Marion. He had, of course, had nightmares before. But they always seemed

四天里，竟然做了三个梦，他用不着从玛丽昂那儿再得到更多的鼓励。当然，他以前也做过噩梦，但它们总是显得抽

abstract, distant. The dreams he had been having the past few weeks, although indistinct in details, were very real in sensation. He woke up, his heart pounding, his body clammy, certain that he had actually just experienced the terrifying scenario. The vividness and consistency of the sensation, along with the exhaustion he was beginning to feel, convinced him that he needed some professional help.

象、遥远。在过去几周里的梦却不同，尽管在细节上不甚分明，但它们给人的感觉是真实的。他醒来时，心怦怦乱跳、身体湿漉漉的。他确信，他刚刚经历过可怕的场景。那种生动而持续的感觉，加上他开始感到的疲惫，都让他深信，他需要一些专业的帮助。

He continued flipping the pages, reflecting on the vague sense of shame he felt. He always prided himself on his mental discipline, at his ability to problem-solve. He never imagined that he would need psychological counseling. He sighed and wondered if this was just another sign of the slow, inevitable breakdown of his body, the trudging procession to death. He felt like he had aged ten years in the last month.

他继续翻着书页，反思着自己微微感到的一种羞耻。他总是对自己训练有素的智力感到骄傲，对自己解决问题的能力感到自豪。他从来没有想到，他会需要心理咨询。他叹了口气，不知道这是否只是另一个症兆，表明他的身体正在缓慢地、不可避免地衰老，踯躅走向死亡。他觉得在上个月里他老了十岁。

Finally, he stopped flipping the pages, as he found the entry he was looking for: Kossuth, Lajos.

终于，他停止了翻页。他找到了那个词条：拉约什·科苏特。

He read with interest about the man who was sometimes known as the Hungarian George Washington.

他满怀兴致地读着对这人的介绍——史称匈牙利的乔治·华盛顿。他读到了

He read about the 1848 rebellion, the valiant struggle for independence. It sounded very noble, admirable. Then he dug further into the article and discovered that, although Kossuth sought independence for Hungary, he would not grant independence to minorities within the empire. This apparent contradiction in values led to his ultimate defeat.

1848 年的反叛，为争取独立而进行的英勇斗争。听起来非常高贵、令人钦佩。接着，他进一步深读这篇文章。他发现，虽然科苏特为匈牙利的独立而战，但他却不愿意让帝国里的少数民族独立。这种明显的、矛盾的价值观导致了他最终的失败。

Theodor sat back in his chair and considered what he had read. "Nothing ever changes," he muttered to himself, wondering if most or all of the apparently great leaders had these moral inconsistencies.

西奥多让自己靠在椅背上，思考着他读过的东西。"从未改变过。"他自言自语道。他想知道，是否大部分或全部看似伟大的领导人都会有着道德上的不一致性。

He shook his head and continued reading. Although interesting, the article had not provided any of the hints he was looking for.

他摇了摇头，继续阅读。文章虽然有趣，却没有提供任何他要找的线索。

Near the end of the article, however, he discovered that Kossuth had been born in Monok. Theodor recognized this name. He closed his eyes, trying to remember something about the town. He pressed clenched fists to his temples, as if he could squeeze the memory out of his skull.

然而，在文章的最后，他发现，科苏特出生在芒诺克。西奥多知道这个名字。他闭上眼睛，试图记起任何关于这个小镇的事情。他把握紧的拳头压住太阳穴，好像这样，他就可以把记忆从头盖骨里挤压出来一样。

He sighed. He was at a

他叹了口气，一筹莫

complete loss. He could not recall any detail of the small town in northeastern Hungary at all.

展。对于这个位于匈牙利东北部的小镇，他已经记不起任何细节了。

Yet the name was familiar. There was an echo of something…

然而，这个名字是熟悉的。似乎有种回声……

****

"So why, exactly, are you here?"

"那么，说说看，你到底为什么来这儿？"

Theodor looked at Erich's face. The kind, neutral eyes had the look of a psychologist's, although the exaggerated roundness of his face and receding hairline gave Erich a slightly menacing appearance.

西奥多看着埃里克的脸。那双眼睛中立、善良，是心理学家常有的。然而，那夸张的圆脸和后退的发际又让埃里克看起来有些威慑力。

"Well, I…I'm mostly here because my wife asked me to come."

"嗯，我……我来这里主要是我的妻子要我这样做。"

Erich smiled slightly. "And why did she do that?"

埃里克微微笑了笑。"那她为什么要这样做呢?"

"Well, I've been having some rather troubling dreams lately, and she's concerned about me, I suppose."

"嗯，我最近一直被一些梦困扰。我想，她是关心我。"

"And are you concerned?"

"那你关心自己吗？"

"I guess so. I mean, I haven't been sleeping well lately, and the dreams seem to be more frequent than they used to be."

"我想是吧。我的意思是，我最近睡不好觉，比以前做梦更频繁。"

"And how long have you been

"你做这些梦有多长时

having these dreams?"

Theodor shifted in the plush chair. The room, with its gentle colours and soft furniture, was certainly designed to put its occupants at ease. Nevertheless, he was still uncomfortable being here. He always thought counseling was for people who were weak. He never considered himself weak, before. "Well, I guess it's been a little over a month." He paused then added, "Ever since I retired."

Erich simply nodded and wrote something quickly on a notepad. "And what was your job before you retired?"

"I was a professor at Centennial University; astrophysics research, to be precise."

"Well that's a very demanding profession. It must have occupied much of your time."

"Indeed it did."

Erich wrote something else on the lined notepad, and then sat back in his chair, a friendly smile creasing his face. "So how have you found retirement, so far?"

"Well, other than the dreams, I

间了？"

西奥多在舒适的椅子上移动着身体。房间里的颜色柔和、家具柔软，其设计就是要让人感到放松。尽管如此，他在那儿还是感到不舒服。他总是认为，咨询是那些弱者们干的事。他从不认为自己弱。"嗯，我想有一个多月了吧。"他停顿了一下，接着说，"自从我退休以后。"

埃里克只是点点头，迅速地在一个记事本上写着什么。"你退休前是干什么的？"

"我是纪念大学的教授；准确地说，是搞天体物理研究的。"

"哇，这是一个要求很高的职业。它一定占据了你的大部分时间。"

"的确如此。"

埃里克又在有包边的记事本上写了些什么。然后，他仰身靠在椅背上，脸上绽出一个友好的微笑。"那么，到目前为止，你觉得退休怎么样？"

"嗯，除了这些梦，我

suppose it's been alright. I've had a little trouble adjusting to all the free time now. But generally, it's been fine."

觉得还可以吧。现在，一下子有了这么多空闲时间，要适应，还真有点困难。但整体而言，还不错。”

Erich appeared thoughtful for a moment, and then said, "Well, let's talk about these dreams a little more. What can you tell me about them?"

埃里克沉思片刻，然后说：“好吧，让我们再来谈谈这些梦。你能告诉我点什么吗？”

Theodor took a deep breath. "Unfortunately, I can't tell you too much. The problem is I have difficulty remembering the dreams after I wake up." He paused and looked out the window at the traffic below, pondering the patterns of the ebbing and flowing cars. Erich didn't say anything.

西奥多深吸了口气。“不幸的是，我没法告诉你太多。问题是，我醒来后就记不起梦了。”他停顿了一下，眼睛望着窗外和楼下的交通，思量着车来车往的规律。埃里克没吭声。

Finally, when it became clear that Erich wasn't going to lead him, Theodor continued. "I guess…well I don't exactly remember, but the dreams always seem to involve pursuit. I think I'm in a forest, at night. I think I'm being chased, but I'm also chasing someone else. I definitely have a sensation of anxiety, anticipation. The dreams always seem quite dark and cold. Yes cold. I always wake up shivering." Theodor closed his eyes tight. "And although I can't

最后，当他确定埃里克不打算引导他时，西奥多继续说道：“我想……我是不能准确记得。那些梦似乎总是和追寻有关。我想，我是在一片森林里，在夜里。有人在追我，但我也在追别人。我肯定有一种焦虑、有一种期待。梦里似乎总是很黑暗、很寒冷。是的，很冷。我醒来时，总是在颤抖。”西奥多紧紧闭上了眼睛。“尽管我无法记清那到底是什么，但就在我醒来之

remember what it is, there is always something quite traumatic immediately before I wake up, like I'm stuck, and am going to be captured by whatever is chasing me. My heart is always pounding right after I wake up."

前，总是有一些非常痛苦的事情。比如说，我陷在什么地方了、我马上要被追上了，等等。醒来时，我的心总是怦怦乱跳。"

Theodor took a couple of breaths then opened his eyes. Erich still sat silent, passively observing his patient. "I…I can't remember anything else."

西奥多深吸一两口气，然后睁开了眼睛。埃里克仍然沉默地坐着，被动地观察着他的病人。"我……我记不得别的事情了。"

Erich looked at his notepad, absently tapping his teeth with his pen. "Do you have any idea what these dreams might be about?"

埃里克看着自己的记事本，用钢笔心不在焉地敲着自己的门牙。"你知道这些梦可能是关于什么的吗?"

Theodor looked surprised. "Well, no. I thought that you might be able to tell me. Isn't that your job?"

西奥多显得有些吃惊。"嗯，不知道。我想你或许能告诉我吧。那不正是你的工作吗?"

Erich looked up. "My job is to help you find the answers to whatever is troubling you. The answers you come up with will be far better than anything I can provide."

埃里克抬起头来说，"我的工作是帮你找到解决困扰的答案。你能想出的答案会好于任何我能提供给你的答案。"

Theodor was going to give a sarcastic reply, but decided to keep his thoughts to himself. Erich, seeing that he wasn't going to get any further on the discussion of the

西奥多本想讽刺地回敬一句，但决定还是先把想法保留一下。埃里克看出，他再也无法把关于梦的讨论继续下去，就决定

dreams, decided to continue with general questions about Theodor's family and his life's activities. The conversation ambled on pleasantly, but seemed to lack focus. Theodor was starting to get tired of the meeting, and was about to end the session when they began discussing his childhood. Theodor related an abbreviated version of the events that occurred in London so long ago: his mother's death, his placement into foster care, his early jobs that he eventually gave up for university. It all seemed so distant now, almost like someone else's life. He had difficulty describing the events.

和西奥多唠唠家常，比如他的家庭、每天的活动内容等。谈话进行得缓慢、愉快，但似乎没有中心。西奥多开始厌倦这次会面。就在他们预约的时间段即将结束时，他们开始谈论他的童年。西奥多简洁地叙述了很久以前发生在伦敦的事件：母亲的死，他被寄养，他早期的工作，他最终放弃工作上大学。现在，这一切看起来都那么遥远，就像是别人的生活。他连描述起这些事件都感到困难。

"And what about what happened before you left Hungary. Can you tell me anything about that?"

“你离开匈牙利之前发生了什么。你能告诉我点什么吗?”

"No." There was no hesitation in his voice. "That was too long ago. I really don't remember anything about those times."

“不能。”他的声音里没有任何迟疑。“那是很久以前的事。我真的什么都不记得了。”

"And you were how old when you left?"

“你离开时几岁?”

Theodor bit the inside of his cheek to mask his impatience. "Eleven."

西奥多咬着脸颊的内侧，以掩盖自己的不耐烦。“11岁。”

Erich resumed tapping his teeth

埃里克快速翻看着那几

with the pen, as he flipped through several pages of notes. Finally, he opened the door of the walnut credenza that sat beside him, and calmly searched through the contents of the drawer. He found what he was looking for, and extracted a business card with a precise movement.

页笔记，又开始用笔敲击着自己的牙齿。最后，他打开了身边一个胡桃木书柜的门，在抽屉里平静地查找着。他发现了要找的东西，准确无误地抽出了一张名片。

He extended the business card to Theodor. “I think you might find this gentleman’s services quite useful…”

他把名片递给了西奥多，说：“我想，你或许会发现，这位先生的服务很有用……”

****

“Listen to my voice. Listen to my voice. Concentrate only on my voice. You are feeling relaxed. My voice is relaxing you…”

“听我的声音。听我的声音。只专注我的声音。你正感到放松。我的声音正在让你放松……”

Theodor was sitting in his favourite chair in his living room. He still was having difficulty believing that he actually let himself be talked into this. He always thought that stage hypnotists employed tricks, that the subjects were just plants in the audience. He never seriously believed that people could be made to involuntarily perform the ridiculous stunts had that popularized these stage shows.

西奥多正坐在自己的客厅里——在他最喜欢的那把椅子上。他还是难以置信，自己会被人用话语牵引着做事。他总是认为舞台上的催眠大师用了骗术，受试者是事先被安插在观众中的。他从来就不真的相信，人们可以不自觉地做那些荒谬的特技。他认为，那些不过是让舞台表演受欢迎的把戏。

“…keep listening to my

“……继续听我的声

voice…"

Still, when Erich had explained it to him, it sounded somewhat plausible. Erich felt that there was a memory of something that was blocked in Theodor's subconscious. He felt that hypnosis would be the quickest and easiest way to reveal the memory, and perhaps uncover the source of his disturbing dreams.

"…you are feeling very relaxed…"

Marion had been very supportive of the idea. Her gentle concern had finally tipped the balance, worn down his skepticism until he agreed to proceed with the hypnosis. He was vaguely aware of her in the darkened room, but he tried not to think of her, as he listened to the hypnotist's requests to empty his mind.

"…you are in a quiet place, a calm place…"

He knew that emptying his mind wouldn't be easy. He was thinker, a planner. His mind was always active. He found it difficult to think about nothing. Still, he knew he had to try. He didn't want to

音……"

尽管如此，当埃里克向他解释此术时，听起来却似乎有理。埃里克认为，西奥多记忆里的某样东西在其潜意识里受阻；他建议，催眠或许是揭示此记忆最快、最容易的方法，甚至可能帮他找到那些噩梦的源头。

"……你正感到非常放松……"

玛丽昂一直很支持这个想法。她的温柔与关心终于打破僵局，让他放下怀疑，直至同意进行催眠治疗。他模模糊糊地意识到，她就在那个被弄暗的房间里，但他试着不去想她，因为他听到催眠师要求他清空大脑。

"……你在一个安静的地方，一个平静的地方……"

他知道，要清空大脑不容易。他是一个思想家，善于做计划。他的思想总是活跃。他发现，什么都不想对他来说很难。不过，他知道，他必须试一试。他不想

continue having the dreams; continue worrying Marion.

"…keep listening to my voice…"

He felt his eyelids getting heavier. His limbs began sinking into the chair cushions.

"…my voice…"

The room seemed to be getting darker.

"…relaxed…"

The details of the walls, the furniture, were melting into vagueness.

"…listening…"

Nothing.

再继续做那种梦、继续让玛丽昂担忧。

"……继续听我的声音……"

他觉得眼皮越来越沉。他的四肢开始沉入椅子的坐垫里。

"……我的声音……"

房间里似乎越来越暗。

"放松……"

墙上的东西、家具都变得模糊。

"……听……"

什么都没了。

****

I hurry along the path. The dead pine needles are slick with the evening frost. I try to run as quickly as I can, but I know I must be careful. I cannot afford to slip, to lose time.

I pull my coat tighter. Despite my exertions, I feel the chill of the evening penetrating, infiltrating the thin wool.

"Theodor! Hurry," a voice from ahead hisses. I quicken my stride as much as I dare.

****

我在小路上急匆匆往前赶。脚下的松针上有一层晚霜。我尽可能地跑快，但知道我必须小心。我不能滑倒，那会浪费时间。

我把外套裹得更紧。不管我怎么努力，夜晚的寒意透过薄薄的羊毛衫渗进骨髓。

"西奥多！快。"一个声音压得很低，从前面传来。我尽可能大胆地加

As I turn the corner on the path, I can see two figures ahead, hurrying: Momma, Maria. At least the three of us are still together, I think bitterly. The memory of poppa's bullet-ridden body, lying on the cobbled Budapest street, still stings my eyes. I swipe at my cheek, unwilling to let the memory get the advantage of me.

I run faster and catch up to my mother and sister. As we continue winding our way through the forest, I whisper, "Momma, are we almost there?"

"Soon...Theodor...soon..." Her breath is ragged with the exertion.

Suddenly, my mother grabs both Maria and me by our shoulders and we veer crazily off the path. We crouch in the thick brush, the snow chilling our soles through the meagre leather. Momma puts her finger to her mouth, imploring us to be silent.

We watch the path. Wispy winter clouds partially obscure the full moon, but the light is still strong. We can see the path clearly, as two

快步伐。

当我在小路上转弯时，我看到前面有两个身形在疾走——是妈妈和玛利亚。至少我们三个还在一起，我苦涩地想。父亲弹痕累累的尸体，躺在布达佩斯鹅卵石街道上，那一幕仍然让我的眼睛刺痛。我猛击自己的脸颊，不让记忆控制了我。

我跑得更快，赶上了母亲和姐姐。当我们继续在森林里蜿蜒疾走时，我轻声问：“妈妈，我们快到了吗？”

“快了……西奥多……快了……”她每用力一下，就会上气不接下气。

突然，妈妈抓住了玛丽亚和我的肩膀。我们急速闪离小路，蹲在路边厚厚的灌木丛里。雪透过薄薄的皮鞋底，使我们的脚底冰冷。妈妈把手压在嘴上，恳求我们别出声。

我们盯着小路。冬日的薄云使一轮满月看着有点怪，但月光仍然很强。我们可以清楚地看见小路。两名

soldiers approach from the direction of their destination. The soldiers' boots crunch rhythmically on the snow, a patient, unhurried cadence to their steps. They seem to know what they are looking for.

士兵从他们住所的方向走来，战靴在雪地里发出有节奏的响声，不紧不慢、从容不迫。他们似乎知道在寻找什么。

We crouch a little lower as the soldiers pass, holding their breath. The soldiers continue, unaware of our presence. We can hear the soldiers' Russian profanity echoing as they disappear down the path.

当士兵走过我们时，我们蹲得更低，屏住了呼吸。士兵们继续前行，没有察觉到我们的存在。当他们在小路尽头消失时，我们可以听到俄语脏话在空中回荡。

"Okay, now," mother whispers, pulling us up from the snow. She turns and starts off through the trees.

"现在可以了。"妈妈低声说着，把我们从雪地里拉起来。她转过身，钻进了树林。

"But Momma, what about the path?" I am confused.

"妈妈，为什么不走小路了呢？"我搞糊涂了。

She turns, her eyes intense. "Quickly, Theodor. We are too close to the canal now. The Russians have blown up the bridge. We will have to find a way across further downstream." She reaches out her hand, "Hurry."

她转过身来，眼睛炯炯有神。"快，西奥多。我们现在离运河太近。俄国人已经把桥炸了。我们必须在下游找到过河的法子。"她伸出手来，说"快点"。

We fight our way through the dense forest, our shoes heavy with clotted ice. We try to move quickly, but are impeded by the heavy branches and slippery earth. Maria has been silent for most of the

我们在茂密的森林里艰难穿行，鞋子上沾满了冰疙瘩，很重。我们试图快点，但沉重的树枝阻碍着我们，脚下的雪地也很滑。一路上，玛丽亚都不怎么吭声。

journey. I wonder if my older sister is scared. Just as I am beginning to feel that I cannot go on, mother signals for us to stop. We crouch low, and I notice for the first time that the sky is brighter up ahead.

"There," Momma is pointing. "The canal is just ahead. Once we get across, we'll be in Austria. They won't follow us across the canal."

I squint, trying to make out details in the vague greyness. "But how will we get across, Momma?"

"Near the edge of the canal, there should be some dead trees. If we can find one that is long enough, we can make our own bridge." My mother stands up, and we begin moving carefully to the edge of the forest.

We crouch again, our eyes adjusting to the brightness of the clearing. The canal is just below us. The icy water is moving slowly, not quite frozen. We can see the other side! Freedom is less than a hundred feet away!

We look carefully in all directions. There are no signs of

我猜想，她是不是被吓坏了。就在我开始感到再也走不动时，母亲打手势让我们停下来。我们蹲坐着，我第一次注意到，前方、头顶上的天空更亮些。

"那儿，"妈妈用手指着，"前面就是运河了。一旦我们渡过去，我们就已经踏上奥地利的土地了。他们是不会追过河去的。"

我眯着眼睛，试图在一片灰蒙蒙中辨出细节来。"但是我们怎么过河呢，妈妈?"

"在运河边，应该有一些死木。如果我们能找到一根够长的，我们就可以搭个桥过去。"母亲站起身来，我们开始小心翼翼地往森林的边缘移动。

我们再次蹲坐着，让眼睛适应空旷地带的明亮。运河就在我们下面。冰冷的水正慢慢地移动，没有完全结冰。我们可以看到对岸！自由就在不到一百英尺远的地方！

我们小心翼翼地环顾四周，没有任何动静，没有俄

movement, no flashes of Russian uniforms.

"Okay children, hurry." Momma is still whispering. She guides us down the slope to the edge. She spots the trunk of a dead tree, lying near the canal. "This should do." There is urgency in her voice. "Theodor, help me with this. We'll take the heavy end and drag it to the canal. Maria, you guide the top end. Make sure the branches don't snag on the shrubs."

Working silently, we wrestle with large pine trunk, dragging it through the snow. We only have to move it about thirty feet, but the bulk is awkward. The branches snag once, but Maria manages to free them.

We are almost to the edge of the canal when a sharp CRACK splits the frigid air.

"Maria!" Momma drops the trunk and runs to where Maria has fallen. She sees almost simultaneously the uniform emerging from the trees and the spreading crimson pool under Maria. "Theodor, run, quickly, into

国军服配饰的反光。

"好吧，孩子们，快点。"妈妈的声音仍然压得很低。她引导着我们走下斜坡，来到河边。她看到了一棵死树的树干，躺在运河附近。"这个应该可以。"她的话音紧迫，"西奥多，来帮我一把。我们把重的这一头抬起来，把木头拖到运河边。玛丽亚，你把着轻的那一头，别让树枝被灌木丛挂住。"

我们悄无声息地干着，和巨大的松树树干较着劲，把它从雪地里往河边拖。我们只需把它移动大约 30 英尺，但其体积庞大、难以掌控。树枝曾被卡住了一次，但玛丽亚设法解决了问题。

我们几乎到了运河边，这时一声清脆的枪响刺破了寒冷的空气。

"玛丽亚！"母亲放下手中的树干，向着倒地的玛丽亚飞奔过去。她几乎同时看到了树丛中出现的军服和玛丽亚身下蔓延的深红色液体。"西奥多，快跑，跑到树林里去。"

the trees!"

"But Momma..."

"RUN!"

I am scared, more scared than I have ever been. I sprint up the slope, my ears pounding. I dive behind a bush, and then turn my eyes back to the canal. I can see the lone soldier beginning to descend the slope. The soldier slips, and begins sliding on his knees. I see Momma kneeling in the snow, cradling Maria's head. The crimson pool has grown larger.

The soldier has stopped sliding. He is searching for his rifle, which has fallen further down the slope. Momma is not even looking at the soldier. She is stroking Maria's hair.

The soldier finally spots his gun, and continues his descent. I am struck with the horrible realization about what is going to happen next. I am momentarily paralyzed, until I see the soldier moving closer to his gun. I am suddenly overcome with rage, a burning anger that I have never felt before.

I leap from behind the shrub and slide down the slope. A filmy

"但是妈妈…"

"快跑!"

我吓坏了，比以往任何时候都害怕。我冲刺般跑上斜坡，耳朵嗡嗡作响。我跳到一丛灌木后，扭头往回看着运河边。我能看到，那个孤零零的士兵开始下坡；他滑倒了，双膝着地在雪地里滑着。我看到妈妈跪在雪地里，抱着玛丽亚的头。那滩深红色的液体蔓延得更大。

士兵已经停止滑动，他正在找他的步枪。他摔倒时，枪顺着斜坡滑落到了更远的地方。妈妈甚至连看都没有看那个士兵，她正在抚摸着玛丽亚的头发。

士兵终于看到了他的枪。他继续顺着山坡往下行。我突然惊恐地意识到接下来可能发生的事。瞬时间，我吓瘫了，动也动不了。我看着士兵离他的枪越来越近。突然，我被一种愤怒控制，一种燃烧的、以前从未感受过的愤怒。

我从灌木丛后跳了出来，滑下斜坡。雪顺势灌进

layer of snow rides up under my shirt, but I don't notice. My animal mind is focused on only one thing now.

The soldier has his gun now. He shakes the snow off it. He carefully raises it to his shoulder.

Momma still hasn't looked at the soldier. She sees only Maria.

The gun is aimed. The finger is on the trigger.

A scream pierces the air, and the soldier turns just in time to see a vague shape flying through the darkness. Even in my rage, my aim is true, and I feel the soldier's knee buckle under my weight.

We both collapse onto the ground. The soldier has dropped his gun again. He holds his leg with one hand, grimacing in pain. The other hand is searching frantically in the snow for the rifle. I am shaking. I see the gun: it is half-buried in the snow, only about five feet from the soldier's groping hand. I am not thinking now, only reacting.

I leap up and dive for the rifle. I scoop it out of the snow, and before the soldier realizes what has

我的衬衣里，我根本就注意不到这些。我那野性的脑子里现在只专注一件事。

士兵现在已经拿回了他的枪。他把上面的雪晃掉，小心翼翼地把它举向肩膀。

妈妈还是没有看那个士兵。她的眼里只有玛丽亚。

子弹已经上膛，手指放到了扳机上。

一声尖叫在空中划过。士兵转过头来，还没弄清怎么回事，一个模糊的影子从黑暗中飞了出来。即使我愤怒到了极点，我的目标还是明确的。我能感到那个士兵的膝盖在我身体的重压下弯曲。

我俩都摔倒在地上。士兵的枪再次脱手。他一只手抱着腿，疼得呲牙咧嘴；另一只手疯狂地在雪地里找着枪。我在颤抖，我看到了枪：半埋在雪地里，离士兵摸索的手只有五英尺远。现在，我没有思维，只有反应。

我跳起来，扑向了步枪。我把它从雪地里掏出来。在士兵还没有缓过神来

happened, a second explosion fractures the icy air.

I am breathing hard. I look at the gun in my quivering hands. I then look over to the soldier. The soldier is lying in the snow, his legs twisted at a strange angle. I can see that under the soldier's helmet where his face used to be, there is now only a pulpy, oozing red and grey mass.

I drop the gun. I am shaking violently now, my breath coming in gasps. I fall to the ground and am barely aware of my mother, now awakened, as she wrestles the tree trunk the remaining few feet into the water. She grunts as she swings it through the placid fluid. It just reaches the other side.

My mother grabs me under the arms and starts dragging me to the canal. I can feel nothing. I barely notice the two bodies staining the quiet snow. My mother heaves me up, and then we both splash into frigid water. Momma gasps, but I do not notice the cold.

My mother keeps a firm grip under my armpits with one hand while seizing the log with the other.

之前，第二声枪响在冰冷的空气中炸开。

我呼吸困难，看着手中的枪，抖个不停。我再去看那士兵。他躺在雪地里，双腿以一种奇怪的角度扭曲着。我能看到，在头盔下原本有张脸的地方，现在只有一堆肉酱，往外流淌着红色的、灰色的东西。

我丢下枪，浑身剧烈颤抖，大口喘着气。我倒在地上，几乎感觉不到回过神来的母亲，她正拼命地把树干剩余的几英尺拖进水里。她低声哼着，用力把树干甩过平静的水流。树干刚够达到河的另一岸。

妈妈把我拽在她的胳膊下，拖向运河。我什么都感觉不到，我只是看到两具尸体正染红静静的白雪。妈妈把我向上撑着，我们都蹚入寒冷的水中。妈妈大口喘着气，而我根本就没感觉到冷。

妈妈一只手牢牢抓住我的腋窝，另一只手抓着那根木头。她在水中一英寸、一

She inches her hand along the tree trunk, pulling us through the water. Our progress is slow, and once, I feel my mother's grip slip. Her scrabbling, desperate fingers keep us from going under.

英寸地沿着树干移动。我们的进展缓慢；有一次，我感到母亲抓我的手滑了一下。她那摸索的、不顾一切的手指让我们没有下沉。

I have lost all sense of time and place. I don't know how long it has been. Eventually, we reach the far shore. My mother flops us out of the water, and then drags me to the trees.

我已经丧失了时间、地点概念。我不知道过了多久。最终，我们到达了遥远的彼岸。妈妈把我们俩从水里笨重地弄上岸，然后把我拖进树林。

I have still not felt the cold, not said a word. Momma is breathing heavily, and begins to cough. Her coughing is violent, rasping.

我仍然感觉不到冷，没说过一句话。妈妈喘着粗气，开始咳嗽。她咳得很厉害，声音刺耳。

Finally, she stops coughing and puts her hand on my head. "Theodor Kossuth..." she whispers, "...my baby. We've..." she begins coughing again, this time not as violently, "...made it."

最后，她停止了咳嗽，把手放在我的头上。"西奥多·科苏特……"她耳语道，"……我的宝贝。我们……"她又开始咳嗽，这次不是那么猛烈，"……成功了。"

I finally look up, a vague awareness in my eyes. My mother strokes my cheek. "We're free now," she continues. "We're going to start over..."

我终于抬起头，一种模糊的意识出现在我的眼中。母亲抚摩着我的脸颊，说："我们现在自由了。"她继续说，"我们要重新开始……"

I look at my mother. My eyes are glistening, and I feel like I want

我看着母亲。我的眼睛闪闪发光，我觉得我想说点

to say something.

She puts a finger to my lips. "Shh, my baby. Everything is going to be all right. You'll see. We are going to start a new life, and we are going to forget about this horror. Forget..." her words drift off as she looks at the far shore of the canal.

I begin to feel the cold; begin feeling the need for sleep. As my eyes get heavy, I hear my mother cough again, an icy rattle echoing in her chest.

什么。

她把一根手指压在我的嘴唇上。"嘘，我的宝贝。一切都会好的。你会看到的。我们要开始新的生活，我们要忘记这场噩梦。忘记……"她的话音渐渐消失。她遥望着运河的远处。

我开始感到冷，开始觉得需要睡眠。当我的眼皮变得沉重，我听到母亲又咳嗽起来，冰冷的咳声在她的胸腔里回荡。

****

Marion sat on the arm of the chair, her arms around Theodor. His body shook, his face buried in his hands. His quiet sobs were the only sound in the room. The hypnotist stood on the other side of the room, knowing it wasn't time to say anything yet.

Marion stroked Theodor's hair. She had never seen him cry before, and she was overcome with a sense of relief. Finally, she thought, finally it is over.

She continued rocking him slowly, until eventually he stopped shaking.

****

玛丽昂坐在椅子的扶手上，胳膊楼着西奥多。他身体颤抖，用手捂着脸。他轻轻的抽泣是房里唯一的声音。催眠师站在房间的另一边，知道还不是说话的时候。

玛丽昂抚摸着西奥多的头发。她以前从未见他哭过，她有一种如释重负的感觉。终于，她想，终于结束了。

她继续慢慢地摇晃着他，直到最后他停止颤抖。

Finally, she thought, brushing aside a stray hair on his forehead, finally a beginning.

终于，她想着，把他额头上的一缕散发理到一边，终于有了一个开端。

Reconstruction

重构

The muffled knocking at the door was still polite, but seemed more insistent now. It had taken Naat a few minutes to get out of bed and orient himself. He was still brain-fogged, exhausted from the arrhythmic concussions of the previous night's shelling, and it didn't occur to him to be cautious. He shuffled across the rough planks, clad only in his underwear, and pulled the door open.

低沉的敲门声仍然彬彬有礼，但比之前似乎更坚持了。纳特用了好几分钟才从床上爬起来，弄清身在何处。他脑子还是懵懵懂懂的。昨天晚上时不时的炮击让他十分疲惫，而他丝毫未想到要谨慎对待。他只穿了条内裤，踉跄地走过那些破木板子，把门拉开了。

He stood all but naked, arms limp at his sides, staring at the small woman who stood on his step. She had short, curly hair that glistened like anthracite. Her chin tapered to a point, her lips tightly confined by her small jaw. Her chestnut eyes

他站在那儿，几乎全身赤裸着，双手耷拉在身边，呆呆地盯着台阶上站着的矮小女人。她短短的卷发，像无烟煤那样铮亮。下巴尖尖的，嘴不大，双唇紧紧嵌在小小的颌骨上。她的眼睛是

were steady, unblinking.

"Naat," she said.

His bare skin tingled in the cool morning air, his nostrils tickled by the crisp, smoky aroma. Words were frozen, glacial in his sticky mouth. A pale light was just starting to brighten the Wall. Naat looked over the woman's shoulder at the street, trying to locate any new bomb craters. "You…better come in…"

She glanced at his body, and he was suddenly self conscious, aware of how exposed he was. She stepped hesitantly over the threshold, but then moved with confidence into Naat's front room. As she passed, Naat caught that familiar fragrance of cinnamon drifting up from her coal-curls, stirring memories. He hoped his face hadn't betrayed any reaction to the scent. He nodded toward the worn couch in the middle of the room.

She didn't show any sign of disapproval, no lip curl, no tightness in the eyes, as she sat on the stained fabric. Her face was as flat as the Wall. But where the Wall had

栗色的，看人时目光稳定，眼睛一眨也不眨。

“纳特。”她说。

他裸露的皮肤在清晨的冷空气中感到刺痛，鼻孔因空气中焦躁的烟味发痒。话被冻住了，在他发黏的嘴里冰凉。外面刚刚开始有一束苍白的光照亮那堵墙。纳特越过那女人的肩膀看了看街道，试图寻找任何新的弹坑。“你……最好是……进来……”

她瞥了一眼他的身体，他立即意识到自己几乎是光溜溜的。她迟疑地跨过门槛，接着便自信地走进纳特的前屋。当她从身边走过时，纳特闻到了熟悉的肉桂香味从她那乌黑的卷发中散发出来，搅动他的记忆。他希望脸上没有泄露任何那香味带给他的反应。他向屋子中央的一个破沙发点了点头。

她在那张脏沙发上坐了下来，没有显示任何不同意的迹象，没有撅嘴，没有嗔怒的眼神。她的脸平板一块，就像那堵墙。然而墙上

graffiti, there was nothing to read on her.

"I've got to…you know…" he pointed at the bedroom.

"Of course." It had been seven years since she had last seen his body, and it had grown thin, worn and pale. He found a faded, ruby coloured robe in the bedroom and slid it around his thin shoulders. He tied the belt tightly as he sat in the chair opposite her, covering a hole in the material with his hand.

The woman clasped her hands in her lap. She looks well, he thought, like she's been looked after, like the War hasn't touched her. She shifted slightly on the couch, trying to find some comfort on the broken spring, and then spoke quietly. "You must be wondering why I am here."

"Well, yes. I mean, I'm shocked…"

"I know, and I'm sorry I had to show up like this. I…I felt that I needed to see you again."

Naat felt several emotions—excitement, fear, suspicion—all

还可能有涂鸦呢，但她的脸上却什么内容都读不出来。

“我得……你知道……”他指着卧室。

“当然。”她最后一次看到他的身体是七年前。现在，它已经变得单薄、疲惫、苍白。他在卧室里找到一件褪色的、宝石红色的睡袍，把它披在自己瘦削的肩膀上。他在她对面的椅子上坐下来，束紧腰带，用手把袍子上的一个小洞盖住。

那女人把紧握的双手放在腿上。她看起来不错，他想。就好像有人一直照顾她，战争没有在她身上留下任何痕迹似的。她在沙发上微微移动身子，试图在破弹簧上找到一个较舒服的位置。然后，她静静地说：“你一定想知道我为什么来这里。”

“嗯，是的。我的意思是，我感到惊讶……”

“我知道。对不起，我不得不以这种方式出现。我……我觉得我需要再见到你。”

纳特百感交集——兴奋、恐惧、怀疑，全在他胸

muddle and tumble together under his rib cage, competing for his attention. Eventually they dissipated, drifting away like the lazy smoke of distant bombs against a pallid sky, and all he was left with was curiosity.

腔内搅在一起、跌宕起伏，争抢他的注意力。最终，它们渐渐消散，就像远处炮弹发出的懒洋洋的烟雾依稀消失在苍白的天空中。剩下的就只有好奇了。

"Why?" The word hung in the air like a leaden rain cloud until he added, "I mean, you left seven years ago, got remarried…" He stopped, suddenly aware of her hands, hands that had once given him such pleasure, but were now twisting in her lap, knuckles squeezed white. "What is it?"

"为什么？"这个词挂在空中，就像是一片沉闷的雨云。接着他补充说，"我的意思是，你七年前离开，结婚……"他停下来，突然意识到她的手、那曾经给他如此快乐的手，正在她的大腿上攥着、拧着，指关节处都压白了。"怎么回事？"

"We're…not married anymore. He's dead."

"我们……没有婚姻了。他死了。"

The words came out of her mouth flat, smooth like finished cement. Naat was surprised that her statement seemed to numb him. He had once been jealous of her affairs, angry at her eventual betrayal, but this news didn't make his stomach tremble, didn't make his heart quiver. He wondered if he was really awake yet. "So, what happened?"

话从她嘴里说出来平平的，光滑得就像打磨过的水泥地面。纳特很惊讶，她的话似乎对他有麻木功能。他曾经嫉妒她和别的男人有染、愤怒她最终的背叛，但这个消息并没有让他的胃抽搐、并没有让他的心颤抖。他想知道他是不是真的醒着。"那么，发生了什么事？"

"It was one of the Wester bombs. Middle of the night. We

"是一枚威斯特人的炸弹。半夜里。我们还没睡；

were still up; we were…arguing. Part of the roof caved in. Somehow, all the pieces missed me, but he was…crushed." She had relaxed her fingers. Colour was returning.

我们还在……争论。屋顶的一部分坍塌下来。不知何故，我没有被砸着，但他却被压碎了。”她松开了手，关节处的颜色恢复正常。

He knew he should express sympathy for her loss, give her the kind of reassurance that had once come so easily, but his tongue was deadened, his brain still anesthetised by the wailing klaxons announcing the early morning bomb-raid, his thoughts scrambled after spending the better part of two hours huddled in the dark of the cellar. Eventually he asked, "What were you arguing about?"

他知道，他应该对她的失去表达同情、给她宽慰，那是他以前轻而易举就能做到的，但他的舌头像死了一样，大脑像是被一大早尖叫的炸弹报警喇叭震得失去了知觉。虽然在黑暗的地窖里蜷缩了两小时还不赖，但思想还是一片混乱。最终，他问道：“你们争论什么？”

Teea turned toward the window, the emerging sun beginning to swallow the night shadows on the Wall. "He really hated the Westers."

提娅转头看着窗外。太阳正在升起，慢慢吞噬着那堵墙上夜的阴影。“他真的恨威斯特人。”

"I suppose it's normal to hate the people who are lobbing bombs at us."

“我想这很正常。他们正在向我们丢炸弹。”

She turned toward Naat, her face striated, tense. "You don't understand. He didn't just hate them as enemies. He hated them as people. He wanted to hurt them, make them suffer. He talked endlessly about ways he would

她转向纳特，脸上开始出现皱褶、表情紧张。“你不明白。他恨的是那个民族，而不仅仅因为他们是敌人。他想要伤害他们，让他们遭受损失。他没完没了地谈论一些折磨威斯特人的方

inflict pain on any Wester he could ever get his hands on. His thoughts were sick, sadistic. I had never seen this in him before. It scared me. We were talking about splitting up."

法，只要他能上手。他的思想是病态的、虐待狂式的。以前我从未在他身上见过这一点。这让我害怕。我们在谈分手。"

Naat wasn't surprised by this. He had met Teea's second husband many years ago and had immediately felt that the man was too confident in his opinions, too inflexible in his arguments. He didn't feel triumphant, though, now that she understood this.

纳特并不惊讶。多年前他遇到提娅的第二任丈夫，立即觉得那男人狂妄、固执己见、言论偏执。现在，尽管她认识到了这一点，他却并没有胜利的感觉。

"Has it been tough around here?" she asked. "I mean the bombings?"

"住这儿不容易吧？"她问道，"我指的是炸弹。"

"Five houses down, they got hit. A couple of kids killed, I think. That was the closest. I've had to replace windows a few times. It shakes the dust in the rafters loose as well. It's hard to…to keep the place clean."

"从这儿往下数五家房屋，第六家被击中。有两三个孩子死了，我想。那是最近一处的。我已经不得不换了几次窗户了。它把椽子上的灰尘都震松散了；很难……让这地方保持干净。"

Her eyes were softer than he remembered, almost sympathetic. He wanted to take her hand, but instead he asked "Why come to me now?"

她的眼睛比他记得的要柔和得多，几近同情。他想握住她的手，然而，他只是问道："为什么现在来找我？"

She looked disappointed, but not surprised, a look he had seen too many times when they were married.

她看上去是失望而不是惊讶。这种表情在他们还是夫妻时他见过多次。"我原

"I thought you might have been happier to see me. I've changed, and I can see you have as well."

以为，见到我时你会更快乐些。我变了。我能看出来，你也变了。"

He wondered if she was being sarcastic with her last comment, wondered if she had really been that untouched by the War. "I'm just…surprised, that's all. After what happened, what you said, I never expected to see you again."

他不确定她最后那句话里是否有讽刺的意味，想知道她是否真的没有受到战争的影响。"我只是……惊讶，仅此而已。发生了那事之后，在你说过那些话之后，我从没想过再见到你。"

"I know, and I'm sorry. I came here because…because, I don't know..." Her voice faded for a moment, and then she talked of the uncertainty of the raids, the need to live in the present. A sense of disbelief, like the glow of a warming lamp, seemed to grow in Naat as he listened to her words. He couldn't help but think that she was desperate, that she just needed someone to look after her and he was convenient.

"我知道，我很抱歉。我来到这里是因为……因为，我也不知道……"她的声音消失了片刻。接着，她谈论突袭的不确定性、需要活在当下，等等。听着她说话，一种难以置信的感觉像一束暖人的灯光，似乎开始在纳特心中滋长。他禁不住想，也许她太绝望了；她只是需要有人来照顾她，而他又很现成。

"So, are you asking if you can stay here?"

"那么，你是在问你是否可以留下来吗？"

"Yes, I guess that's what I want. At least for a while."

"是的，我想这就是我想要的，至少一小段时间吧。"

He thought about throwing her out. But there was something in her manner, the way her eyelids drooped

他想把她扔出去，但她举止里的某些东西让他相信她是真诚的：她的眼

at the corners, the tremble in her lips as she tried to smile, which made him believe in the sincerity of her wish.

脸低垂在眼角，她强笑时嘴唇在颤抖。

She gave a sudden gasp, covering her mouth with her small hand. "I never even thought. Are you with someone right now?"

她突然大吸一口气，用小手捂着嘴，说:"我甚至从来没有想过。你现在又有人了吗？"

He looked around the room, at the shamble of broken furniture covered with dust that had been shaken loose by the bombs. "No, there's no one now."

他四下看了看房间，看着落满灰尘的破家具，已经被炸弹震得松散、摇晃。"不，目前还没人。"

"Oh, I'm sorry, I didn't mean to…"

"哦，对不起，我不是故意的……"

"It's okay," he said, louder than he had intended. Then, more softly, "You can stay."

"没关系。"他说，声音比他想象的要大。接着，他用更柔和的声音说:"你可以留下来。"

She went to Naat and put her arms around him, squeezing his rigid, bony frame. He kept his arms at his sides. She rested her head on his shoulder and whispered "Thank you."

她走向纳特，伸手抱住了他，挤压着他僵硬的、瘦骨嶙峋的身子。他胳膊没动、一直垂在身体两边。她把头放在他的肩膀上, 轻声说道"谢谢你"。

Later that day, they went to the market. Teea carried the small cloth bag as he examined the meagre offerings of fruit. Naat noticed that she didn't offer any advice on what to buy, letting him make all the

那天晚些时候, 他们去了市场。纳特查看着市面上很少的水果供应，提娅手里拿着一个小布袋。他注意到她没有提任何建议，而是让他做决定买什么。

decisions.

At the house, Naat wondered how he would accommodate her. She certainly couldn't sleep with him, and she didn't even hint at this possibility. Still, a part of him wanted to feel her body next to his again, despite the pain she had caused him. A decent man would offer her the bed while he slept on the couch, but something about that solution seemed forced and unnatural to Naat. Fortunately, she saved him the angst of the decision by insisting on using the couch.

"It's not very comfortable," he told her, pushing on the strained springs.

"Don't worry." She smiled at him, stirring an ancient memory. "I really have no right to be here, no right to expect anything from you. The couch will be just fine."

He retrieved an armload of mismatched, multi-coloured bed linens. She gratefully took the sheets and began tucking them into the soft cushions. He watched her small hands move quickly and efficiently, flattening and creasing the bed into shape. Her hair was shorter now, the

在屋里，纳特拿不定主意怎么安置她。她当然不能和他睡，她甚至连这种可能性都没有暗示过。然而，尽管她使他痛苦过，他身体的某一部分还是想要她躺在身边的感觉。一个体面的男人应该把床让出来，自己睡沙发，但那种解决方案里似乎多了种强迫性的、而非自然的东西。最后，多亏她帮他解了围，坚持要睡沙发。

“这不是很舒服，”他告诉她，用手压着紧绷绷的弹簧。

“别担心。”她对他微笑，激起他远古的记忆。“我真的无权待在这里，无权从你这儿期待什么。沙发就很好。”

他搜到了一整怀不配套的、各种颜色的床上用品。她感激地接过床单，开始把它们塞进柔软的沙发垫子里。他看着她的小手快速、有效地移动，把床铺压扁、弄成形。她的头发现在更短，发卷比他

curls tighter than they had been when they were married, and he could see the mole on the back of her neck. He thought about the many times his tongue had traced, tasted that little bit of excess flesh.

Sleep never came easily to Naat, but he found he was even more restless than usual. A thin strip of moonlight leaked through a tear in his bedroom curtain, a reminder of a bombing that had blown out his windows last year. His eyes traced the irregular, blue-white shape on the wall. It reminded him of an iridescent moth that Teea and he had seen many years ago at a zoo, when the world still had time for zoos. He had wanted to brush the creature away after it landed on his hair, but she had held his hands tightly, smiled while she observed the slow, rhythmic pulsation of the shimmering wings. She had laughed as he briefly struggled and then shook his head violently, sending the moth away in a glittering flutter.

His consciousness was just starting to collapse into sleep when the air-raid siren came to life. The slowly building howl was pitched at

们结婚那时更紧，他能看到她脖子后面的痣。他想到，曾多少次他的舌尖舔过那多余的一点肉、品尝它的味道。

纳特一直睡眠不好。现在，他发现自己比以往更焦躁不安。一条细细的月光穿过他卧室窗帘的一个口子泄进来，让他想起去年的一个爆炸。他的窗户都被炸飞了。他的眼睛追随着墙上那条不规则的、蓝白色的光影，它让他想起了多年前他和提娅在动物园里见过的一只蛾子，是彩虹色的。那时，人们还有时间去动物园。它落在了他的头发上，他本想把它拂掉，但她紧紧抓住了他的手，笑着，观察它闪光的翅膀缓慢、有节奏地扇动。他简短地挣扎了一下，接着便使劲摇晃脑袋，蛾子振翅飞走了，她一直大笑着。

当空袭警报响起时，他的意识正开始陷入睡眠。由低渐高，空袭警报的吼叫规律、频繁，叫人无法无视它

the perfect frequency; there was no way to ignore it. He stumbled out of bed and grabbed the thin robe. The house was dark, but he could see a vague shadow in the living room. Teea was sitting up on the couch, staring at the window.

的作用。他跌跌撞撞地从床上爬起来，抓起薄薄的睡袍。房子很黑，但是他可以看到一个模糊的影子在客厅里。提娅正坐在沙发上，盯着窗外。

"C'mon, hurry," Naat grunted as he lifted the iron clasp of the cellar door.

"到这儿来！快！"纳特边说边拉起地窖门上的铁环。

Teea didn't move. As the cellar door thumped onto the floor, the air was fractured by a nearby concussion. Plates and glasses rattled and jumped on the shelves. Naat grabbed Teea's shoulders and steered her toward the cellar. She moved tentatively, but a second blast seemed to shake her out of her stupour. She started climbing down the ladder, with Naat behind her, urging her to hurry. He was just closing the cellar door when the third explosion came, this time very close. Glass shattered above them as the force of the explosion knocked Naat off the ladder. Although he was only three rungs from the floor, he landed awkwardly on Teea's foot.

提娅没有动。当地窖的门被掀起、翻过来落在地板上时，空气被附近的一起爆炸震裂，架子上的盘子和玻璃杯乱跳，颤动个不停。纳特抓住提娅的肩膀，带她往地窖口走。她迟疑地移动着，但第二起爆炸似乎让她从迷糊状态中醒来。她开始顺着梯子往下爬，纳特紧随其后，催促她动作快点。当第三起爆炸发生时，他刚好关上地窖的门。这一次非常近。当爆破的力量把纳特从梯子上掀下来时，玻璃在他们上面散落。虽然他离地面只有三个阶梯了，他还是笨重地落在了提娅的脚上。

She yelped, like a dog in pain. Naat's ankle twisted, shooting

她叫喊起来，像疼痛中的狗那样。纳特的脚踝扭了，

electrical jolts up through his thigh. He stumbled and fell to the hard earth, his neck snapping back, slamming his head into the ground. Dazed, he lay on his back, his leg twisted under him. Kaleidoscopic explosions of colour filled his vision, speckling the darkness.

电击一样的疼痛通过他的大腿向上传。他脚下一绊，跌倒在坚硬的地上。他的脖子是向后仰的，头重重摔在地上。他头晕目眩，仰面躺着，腿在身下扭着。似有万花筒般的颜色在他眼前炸开，在黑暗中一闪一闪的。

"Te—" He began coughing violently. He eventually got his throat cleared and carefully straightened his leg, ankle throbbing. He rolled over on his side and started groping in the dark.

"提——"他开始剧烈地咳嗽。最后，喉咙总算被清理干净了，他小心翼翼地把腿伸直。脚踝刺疼。他翻身侧躺着，开始在黑暗中摸索。

"Teea!"

"提娅！"

He found her face with his hand, felt the warm slipperiness on her cheek. He dragged himself closer and put his ear to her mouth. Her breath was warm in the damp cellar air. He felt her eyelids flutter.

他用手摸到了她的脸，脸颊上有一种温暖的、滑溜溜的感觉。他把自己向她拖得更近些，把耳朵放到了她的嘴上。在地窖潮湿的空气里，她的呼吸很温暖。他能感到她的眼睑在颤动。

"Wha..." She made a few groaning attempts, but couldn't form any words.

"唔……"她试图说点什么，但却连不成句子。

"Shh, shh." He stroked her face, his fingers sticking together. He probed gently, looking for the source of the blood, but there was no obvious flow.

"嘘，嘘。"他抚摸她的脸，手指却粘在了一起。他轻轻摸索，寻找血的源头，却无从得知。

They stayed immobile, in the

他们就这样在黑暗中一

dark for several minutes, Naat stroking her cheek. The earthen floor vibrated with more explosive thumps, but the bombardment seemed to be moving away.

动不动地待了几分钟，纳特一直抚摸着她的脸颊。由于更多的爆炸冲击，身下的大地一直在抖动。然而，轰炸似乎正渐渐离去。

Eventually she started squirming, trying to push herself up. Naat tried to help her, but he couldn't get any leverage.

最终，她开始蠕动，试图让自己站起来。纳特试图帮她，但他自己都找不到一个支撑点。

"Your head. I felt blood..."

"你的头。我摸到了血……"

Naat heard some shuffling, some scraping. "It's okay. It's okay. I just bumped it on the ladder. It doesn't seem to be bleeding now." Her voice sounded distant. "What about you?"

纳特听到了一些窸窸窣窣移动、刮擦的声音。"没关系，没关系。我只是撞在梯子上了。现在似乎不流血了。"她的声音听起来很遥远。"你怎样?"

"I'm...I'm okay. I think my ankle, it hurts..." The adrenaline ebbed and the pain took over, muddling his words. "I...it's hard to move."

"我……我很好。我想，我的脚踝受伤了……"肾上腺减退、疼痛占据了上风。他连话都说不清楚。"我……很难移动。"

He heard more shuffling, and then felt her hands under his back. "Can you sit up?"

他听到更多窸窸窣窣的声音，然后感觉到她的手伸到了他的身下。"你能坐起来吗?"

She grunted and heaved. His body was light, and she was able get his torso vertical, his back resting against the cellar wall. He suddenly felt chilled, the damp earth of the

她使着劲，喘着粗气。他的身体轻，她设法让他坐直了，背靠着地窖的墙。他突然觉得冷，潮湿的墙面直接把飕飕的凉气送进他的脊

wall sending cold creepers into his spine. His breathing began to slow.

"I think it's finally stopped." Teea's voice sounded closer now.

"We should try to get back out."

"One of those hits sounded close. I think there may be damage to the house."

"I don't know if I can make it up the ladder."

Naat's brain swam with this exchange. Their words seemed to swirl in a nebula of confusion, never finding a common focus, as if they were having two different conversations, the way it had been when they were married.

"Can you go up first? My ankle…"

He heard Teea breathing in the dark, fast but regular. His nostrils filled with the musty air of the cellar. He knew she was scared, knew that she must be remembering the bombing of her own house. He wanted to comfort her, but instead stayed silent.

A deep inhalation. "Okay, I'll go."

椎骨里。他的呼吸开始慢下来。

"我想，它终于停了。"提娅的声音现在听起来近多了。

"我们应该回到上面去。"

"其中的一个爆炸听起来很近。我想，房子一定被毁坏了。"

"我不知道自己是否还能爬上梯子。"

这种对话在纳特的大脑里游离着。那些字眼似在令人费解的星云里打着旋，永远找不到一个共同的焦点。他们似在进行两场不同的谈话。他们结婚以后的谈话方式历来如此。

"你能先上吗？我的脚踝……"

他听到提娅在黑暗中呼吸，很快但也均匀。他鼻孔里满是地窖发霉的味道。他知道她被吓坏了，也知道她一定正回忆起她自己的房子遭轰炸的情景。他想安慰她，但却保持了沉默。

在深吸气后，她说："好吧，我先上。"

He could feel her moving near him, hear the sound of her naked feet carefully searching for the rungs, followed by slow steady creaks from each step as she worked her way up the ladder. Then, an exasperated gasp as she pushed on the door.

"It's stuck. I can't get it open."

"Here, okay, let me try to…"

Naat put his knuckles down in the packed earth, and pushed as hard as he could. As he lifted himself up, he tried to keep his weight on the uninjured foot, but he had to push a little on the damaged ankle. The pain squeezed his sinuses, made his eyes water, as if the blood in his head had been pressurized. He clamped his teeth together and, with a couple of murderously painful hops, made it to the ladder. Despite the cold, sweat was now coalescing on his forehead.

"Naat. Are you okay?"

"Yeah, yeah. I'm going to try to get up this ladder so I can help you."

He grabbed the rails of the ladder, scraping his palms on the rough wood. He shifted his grip to the rungs, which were a little

他能感觉到她在附近移动，听到她光脚小心搜寻梯阶的声音；随后是缓慢的、稳定的咯吱声。她正顺着梯阶一个一个地往上爬。然后，当她向上推门的时候，她大口喘着粗气。

"门卡住了。我打不开。"

"我来了，好吧，让我试试……"

纳特把双手握起来、伸向落满物什的地面，用拳头的指关节面抵着地面把自己用力往上撑。当他设法让自己站起来时，他试图把身体的重量集中在那只未受伤的脚上，但那只受伤的脚踝还是会轻轻受力。疼痛挤压他的鼻窦，让他眼泪迸流，仿佛大脑里的血液被增压。他咬紧牙关，做了一两次单腿跳，经历了撕心裂肺般的疼痛，蹭到了梯子跟前。尽管寒冷，他额头上仍满是汗水。

"纳特。你没事吧？"

"是的，是的。我正在往上爬，这样可以帮你。"

他抓住梯子的扶手，手掌在粗糙的木头上蹭破了皮。他改抓一节节稍微顺滑一点儿的梯阶。尽管他手臂

smoother. Despite his thin arms, he was able to heave himself up the first two rungs with a combination of pulling and hopping on his good leg.

纤弱，他还是通过把身体往上提和单腿跳设法让自己上了两个梯阶。

"Just…move over a bit…I'm going to try to get up there beside you." His throat burned.

"我只是……挪了一点儿……我正向上往你那儿爬。"他的喉咙在燃烧。

Globules of sweat dripped off his face as he struggled up beside Teea. He managed to get himself into somewhat stable position: his good leg on the rung, his injured one off to the side, and one hand gripping the top rung. Teea had manoeuvred herself into a similar position. Their shoulders grazed each other as they swayed in the gloom.

当他挣扎着爬到提娅身边时，大滴的汗水从他的脸上滴落下来。他设法让自己稳住：那只好腿踩在梯阶上；那只受伤的腿吊在梯子的一边；一只手紧紧抓住最上面的那层梯阶。提娅设法让自己的姿势和他的差不多。他们就这样，在黑暗中摇晃着，彼此的肩膀相互摩挲着。

Naat pushed on the trapdoor. It moved slightly, but wouldn't open.

纳特推活动门。它稍稍有点动，但却不愿打开。

"There's something on top of it. It's not too heavy, though. I think if we can both push…"

"门板上面可能有东西，不过不会太重。我想，如果我们两人同时推的话……"

They each placed a flat palm on the rough wood and heaved. The door cracked open, but the weight on top held it down. Together they tried again, straining, with tickling drops of perspiration running like rivers on their faces. The lid began to creep up

他们每人伸出一只手，手掌平放在粗糙的木板上，一起憋足劲向上推。门吱吱嘎嘎开了，但上面的重量仍让它翻开不过去。他们又一起使劲，拼命挣着，脸上的汗像小溪一样往下淌。盖子

a few centimetres. Teea took her other hand off the top rung and jammed it against the trapdoor, hoping the forces between her arms and legs were balanced. Slowly, the door began to open.

开始慢慢上升几厘米。提娅把另一只手从最上面的梯阶上拿开，撑在开启的活页板下面，希望她的胳膊和腿之间的力量是平衡的。慢慢地，门开始打开。

With a shriek, Teea slipped off the rung, her foot thumping onto the one below. Naat reached out, grasping desperately at her flailing arms. He grabbed her wrist, but her momentum almost pulled him off the ladder. As she swayed outwards, he was barely able to hang on, splinters digging into the rough skin on his hand.

一声尖叫，提娅从梯阶上滑落，她的脚落在了下一节的梯阶上。纳特伸出手，拼命抓住她挥动的手臂。他抓着她的手腕，但她下沉的重量几乎把他从梯子上拽下去。在她向外后仰的时候，他几乎无法抓紧梯子，木屑扎进他手上粗糙的皮肉里。

"Okay, okay I've got a grip now." The strain on Naat's shoulder lessened as Teea's free hand gripped the ladder. "Let's get down for a minute."

"好了，好了。我现在抓住了。"当提娅一只空出来的手抓住梯子时，纳特顿感肩上的压力减小。"我们先下去待一会儿吧。"

They sat at the base of the ladder, breathing heavily. Naat directed Teea to some candles on a shelf. Some tentative fumbling, the scratch of a match, and then a sudden intrusion of light. Teea stood in front of him, a small amber candle glowing in her hand. "Okay, let's rethink this."

他们坐在梯子的底部，喘着粗气。纳特领着提娅，找到了货架上的几只蜡烛。一阵试探性的摸索后，火柴被划亮。突然间，一束光出现。提娅站在他面前，手里的蜡烛发出琥珀色的光亮。"好吧，让我们再想想怎么办。"

He looked at her flickering

看着她闪烁的身影，他

form, and was struck with a vision, a sensation, that he had seen an image like this before, an old picture perhaps of a nurse in a dimly lit ward of a war hospital. As the shadows danced around Teea, Naat felt the air get slightly warmer.

"We need a lever, something to push with, something to give us more force."

Teea turned and started searching the shelves behind her. "How about this?" She held an old axe handle in her palms, cradling it as if she were presenting an offering at an altar.

They struggled back up the ladder and repositioned themselves. They eventually shifted the door enough to jam the axe handle underneath it. Naat's muscles were screaming with exertion, his injured ankle complaining angrily. Teea managed to get her narrow shoulder under the door as she moved up a rung, coiling her compact body like a spring. Naat counted, and she pushed as he pulled on the handle. The door groaned, and then with a sharp thump, flung open. Naat swayed and started to tip backwards

被一种幻觉控制，激动不已。他以前曾见过类似的情景。好像是一张旧照片——一个护士，在战地医院灯光昏暗的病房里。随着影子在提娅周围晃动，纳特感觉到空气稍稍温暖起来。

"我们需要一个杠杆，一个使得上劲儿帮我们向上推的东西。"

提娅转身开始搜索她身后的货架。"这个怎么样?"她手掌里握着一把旧斧头的手柄，抱着它就好像在祭坛献贡一样。

他们挣扎着返回，再顺着梯子往上爬。在梯子上再次找稳了位置。他们终于把门盖掀开得足以把斧柄塞在它的下面。纳特的肌肉由于用力发出咔咔的响声，受伤的脚踝愤怒地抱怨着。提娅设法再上一个梯阶，把她瘦削的肩膀塞进门板下，身体像弹簧一样蜷缩起来。纳特扳着斧柄，当他数到三时，提娅就用力。门呻吟着。随着一声巨响，门被砰然掀开。纳特身子晃悠起来，开始向后倾。这时，提娅一把

until Teea grabbed his soaked shirt.

They stood on the ladder, swaying, holding on to each other as they poked their heads into the open air above. A thin, dawn light filtered into the room. The air seemed coarse, thick with motes of dust that had been stirred up by the trapdoor.

"Oh..." Teea's voice trailed off. The living room was a jumbled mess of splintered lumber, splayed books, overturned lamps, strewn pillow stuffing and crystalline shards. On the far wall, where the window had been, there was now just a jagged hole, plastered edges ripped into dusty points. A piece of the window frame hung down from the top of the hole, groaning as it swayed in the cool morning breeze.

Teea pulled herself up first, and then grabbed Naat's shoulders, helping him through the portal. They were silent as they surveyed the destruction. Naat could feel the energy that he had marshalled slowly ebbing away.

Teea tipped a chair back onto its legs and brushed the broken glass off with a chunk of wood. Naat hopped through the debris and sat

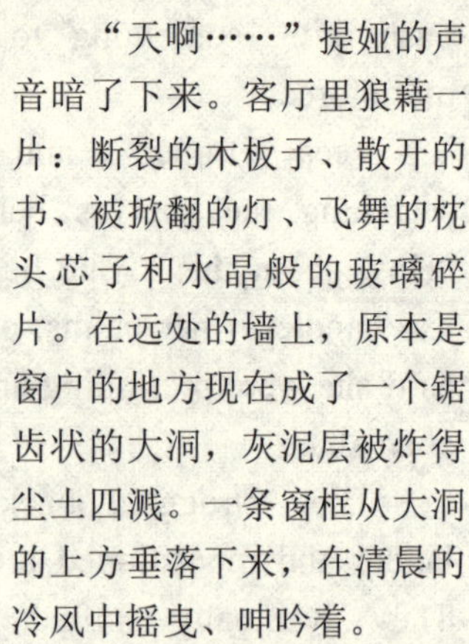

抓住了他湿透的衬衫。

他们站在梯子上，晃悠着，彼此搀扶着把头伸到地面上，感受上面的空气。一丝薄薄的曙光射进房屋。空气里似乎有粗糙的颗粒，是活页门板被掀翻在地时激起的尘埃。

"天啊……"提娅的声音暗了下来。客厅里狼藉一片：断裂的木板子、散开的书、被掀翻的灯、飞舞的枕头芯子和水晶般的玻璃碎片。在远处的墙上，原本是窗户的地方现在成了一个锯齿状的大洞，灰泥层被炸得尘土四溅。一条窗框从大洞的上方垂落下来，在清晨的冷风中摇曳、呻吟着。

提娅先把自己弄了上去，然后抓着纳特的肩膀帮他从那个洞口钻了出去。他们查看被毁坏的状况时，沉默无语。纳特能够感觉到他那集聚起来的能量正渐渐消失。

提娅扶正了一把被掀翻在地的椅子，用一块木板把落在上面的玻璃碎片扫掉。纳特单腿跳过废墟，在椅子

down. She knelt down beside him, her eyes soft and malleable in the growing light. "Now what?" The tone of her voice made him think of a time when they sat under bright pinpoints in the sky, talking about the movements of time and space, but that thought dissipated like a wisp of vapour on the fringe of a nebula

上坐了下来。她跪在他身边。在渐亮的曙光中，她的眼睛柔和、波动。"现在怎么办?"她的语气让他回想起从前他们坐在繁星闪烁的天空下谈论时间和空间运动的情景，但这样的想法很快就消失了，就像星云边际的一缕水蒸气。

"I…I guess I'll have to repair it. Fix it."

"我……我猜我得把它修补、修好了。"

"You mean we will. I will help you."

"你的意思是我们吧。我会帮你。"

Naat looked at the detritus left by the blast, his purple, bulging ankle, and realized that he had no choice but to accept Teea's help.

看着爆炸留下的碎片，看着他那黑紫色肿起来的脚踝，纳特意识到他别无选择，他只能接受提娅的帮助。

****

They spent most of that day trying to clear out the mess scattered by the blast. Teea had iced and wrapped his ankle, then found a piece of broken lumber that could serve as a cane. He felt a little better after this, and found that it wasn't too difficult to get around with the stick. He had watched her carefully as she wrapped his ankle, waiting for a subtle pressure on the tender flesh

那天的大部分时间都花在清除被炸得乱七八糟的东西上。提娅用冰处理过他的脚踝，把它包了起来。她找到了一条断木条，可以当作拐杖用。在这之后，他感到好多了。手里有个棍子帮忙，他发现到处走走也不是那么艰难了。当她包扎他的脚踝时，他一直仔细注视着她，等待她轻压他柔软的皮

or an aggressive twist of the bandage, but she was gentle to a fault.

肉或用力缠裹绷带。可惜，她只是一味地温柔，没有别的表示。

It was slow work, but they were able to right all the tipped furniture. The couch was a problem, but Teea carried the bulk of the burden, flipping the couch over by herself - though with little help from him. Naat wondered where she had found this strength. The splinters and shards of glass that littered the floor had to be swept up carefully. Teea did most of the sweeping while Naat brandished the dustpan. He found it easier to kneel down on the floor, as he could put some of his weight on his knees. Together, after a couple of hours, they were able to clear enough of the sharp debris to move around safely.

这是个慢活，但他们还是把所有被掀翻的家具归了位。沙发是个难题，但提娅抓住最重的部分，独自把它掀翻了过来。当然，他也帮了一点点小忙。纳特想不明白，她哪来的这个力气。散落在地板上的玻璃碎片和渣子被小心翼翼扫在一起。在大部分时间里，是提娅在清扫，纳特拿着簸箕。他发现跪在地板上更容易些，那样他可以把身体重量的一部分放在膝盖上。一起干了一两个小时后，他们已经把一些尖锐的碎片清理出去，有足够的空间可以安全走动了。

Naat eased himself into his chair. “We seem to be acting quite civilized for a change.”

纳特放松自己，坐进自己的椅子里。“我们似乎正以文明的方式进行改变。”

Teea sat on the couch, wiping her hands on her pants. “Isn’t that the way it should be?”

提娅坐在沙发上，双手在裤子上擦着。“难道那不是应有的方式?”

Naat nodded. “But it hasn’t been that way for a long time.”

纳特点点头。“但是已经很长时间没用这种方式了。”

“I know, I know.” Teea looked

“我知道，我知道。”

over to the gaping hole in the wall. "So what happened to us? How did we get to this?"

提娅看着墙上的大洞。"那么，我们之间到底发生了什么？我们为什么到了这步田地？"

"This?"

"这步田地?"

She turned toward him. "Well, you know. How did we get to the point where we have to force ourselves to be reasonable to each other? It was really natural once to just like each other."

她转向他。"嗯，你是知道的。我们什么时候变得必须用如此理性的方式对待彼此？以前，我们只是简单地喜欢对方。"

"That was a long time ago."

"那是很久以前的事了。"

"Yes, yes." Her words hinted at an impatience that Naat had grown to loathe over the years, a dissatisfaction with his plodding, methodical thought process. "But don't you believe that there is something that persists, something that always remains true between two people, even through the layers of armour that they put on?"

"是的，是的。"她的话里暗示着不耐烦，对此纳特已经深恶痛绝。这是对他多年以来缜密、有条不紊进行思维的不满。"难道你不相信有样东西可以坚持——那种即便是两人披上层层盔甲后，还能真实相待的东西？"

Naat's shoulders seeped back into the soft cushions. The adrenaline had started to drain from his body and he was suddenly very tired. "I don't know. How can we overlook all the words that have been said, all the things that have been done?"

纳特的肩膀向后深深嵌入软软的靠垫。体内的肾上腺素开始流失，他忽然很累。"我不知道。我们怎能忽视所有说过的话、做过的事？"

Teea's eyes turned to stone. She was silent for several moments. "You don't think it's possible for people to redeem themselves, to get better, to grow up?"

He sat motionless, breathing deeply, the weight of the inhaled air pushing him farther down. "I…don't know. I guess people can make themselves better. I just don't know if that makes any difference."

Teea's cheeks slouched slightly. Naat recognized the look on her face, knew that he had hurt her. He felt a flutter, a gripping sensation in his stomach, a stirring of a conditioned response. His fingers twitched, as if they wanted to reach out to her, but they didn't move. They were inert as bricks mortared into a wall.

After a moment, she got up, a few tight, but soft words bouncing through the silence of the rubble: "I think it can make a difference."

After supper, Naat decided to tackle the front window. Although the wall of the house was still intact, the window frame had been twisted by the force of the explosion,

提娅的眼睛变成了石头。她沉默了几分钟。"你不认为人们可以自我救赎吗？你不认为他们可以变好、可以成长吗？"

他一动不动地坐着，深呼吸。然而，吸入的空气重量让他更往下沉。"我……不知道。我猜想，人们是可以变得更好。我只是不知道，变好以后又能怎样。"

提娅的脸颊微微下沉。纳特能辨认出她脸上的表情，知道她受到了伤害。纳特感到胃里一阵悸动，被揪起来的感觉，这是一种条件反射。他的手指痉挛着，像是要伸出去触摸她，然而，它们却没有动。它们待在那儿，就像砌进墙里的砖头。

过了一会儿，她站了起来，有几分僵硬，但柔和的话语穿透废墟的沉默在空气中跳跃："我认为那会使事情有所不同。"

晚饭后，纳特决定把前面的窗户弄好。虽然房子的墙仍然完好无损，但窗框被爆炸的力量扭曲了，断开的木头像烂牙一

splintered wood that protruded like rotten teeth. As he stared through the gaping maw, he could see the Wall in the distance, with its slogans and profanity colouring the lower third of its face, the upper portion a smooth, flat realm of grey, almost invisible against the bruise-purple sky above. He wondered if more missiles would be coming over the top again tonight.

He turned and grabbed the largest piece of lumber that hung down. Although it looked like it was loose, it was difficult to dislodge. He yanked and twisted it, but found he couldn't move it. He then braced himself as best he could, adjusted his hands to the point where he thought he could achieve the greatest leverage, and pulled. His thin hands lost their grip and he tumbled onto his back. He lay on the floor, gasping, staring at the ceiling. Teea got up from the chair where she had been sitting and stood over him for a moment. Naat tried to read her face. It seemed to display a mixture of pity and amusement, but there was something else he couldn't quite identify: despair, or at least a

样杵着。当他从那张开的口子向外凝望时，他可以看到远处的那堵墙。墙面离地三分之一的地方写满了口号和脏话；上面的部分是光滑、平坦的灰色，背衬着淤紫的天空，几乎看不分明。他不知道今晚是否会有更多的炸弹越过那堵墙扔过来。

他转过身，把吊在那儿的最大一块木板条抓住。尽管它看起来松了，却很难拔掉。他又拽又拧，无济于事。接着，他让自己全身绷紧，把手调整到某一个他认为可以利用杠杆效力的位置上，然后用力拉。不幸的是，他瘦弱的手没抓紧，他仰面跌倒在地板上。他躺在地板上喘着粗气，盯着天花板。提娅这期间一直坐着。现在，她从椅子上站了起来，走过来，俯视着他。纳特想读出她脸上的表情：好像有同情、逗乐的表情混在一起，但还有一样东西他不是太确定——绝望，或至少是一种充满忧郁的渴望。

melancholic kind of longing.

She reached out a hand. When he grasped it, she pulled him back up, steadying him by placing her other hand on his waist. Without a word, she shifted and grabbed his makeshift cane, keeping her one hand on his waist. She handed him his cane, then went directly to the window and grabbed the dangling frame. With one crisp tug, the board came loose, cracking the air with the scream of nails released from their prison. She tossed the board through the open window and then proceeded to remove all the remaining loose pieces of frame, tossing each of them through the glassless void.

"Do you have a tarpaulin?" The shadows outside were deepening now. She had last spoken when the sun still flooded the front yard.

"Yes. It's in the cellar. You'll need a candle."

Teea quickly disappeared down the ladder into the earth. She emerged a few minutes later with a dusty, yellowish bundle under one arm and a hammer and small paper bag in her hand. She grabbed a chair

她伸出一只手。他抓住了它，她把他拉了起来，另一只手放在他的腰部，把他稳住。她一句话也没说。她稍稍移动了一下，伸手抓起他的临时拐杖；另一只手一直没有离开过他的腰。她把拐杖递给他，接着径直走到窗口，抓住那晃来晃去的木框条。随着干脆利索的一拽，木板松了。空气中有噼啪声、钉子摆脱牢笼的尖叫声。她把那条木板从开着的窗洞扔了出去，然后把所有剩在窗框上松动的木板条一一拆下，把它们从那个没有玻璃的洞口扔出去。

“你有防潮布吗？”外面的阴影越来越深。她最后一次说话时，阳光还洒满前院。

“是的。在地窖里。你需要一根蜡烛。”

提娅顺着梯子下行，很快消失在地下。几分钟后，她又出现，一只胳膊下面夹着一捆落满灰尘、泛黄的东西，另一只手上拿着一把榔头和一个小纸袋。她抓过一

and started tacking the tarp over the hole in the wall.

把椅子，站到上面，开始把那块防潮布钉到墙面上，堵住那个洞。

Naat lit the oil lamp he had retrieved from the kitchen. Electricity was intermittent during the day but always off in the evenings. The flickering flame made Teea's shadow jump energetically across the walls as she smoothly pounded the nails. When she was finished, she stepped off the chair, and carefully checked the edges of the tarp.

纳特点亮一盏从厨房里找到的油灯。白天时，电的供应时有时无；但傍晚时，电肯定会被停掉。提娅在熟练地敲击着钉子，油灯闪烁的火焰把她的身影跳动性地投射在墙面上，充满了活力。干完了，她从椅子上跳了下来，仔细查看油布的边缘。

"I think that will do for now."

“我想，先这么凑合着吧。”

He watched her hands neatly fold the bag of nails. "You seem to have learned some new skills since we were divorced."

看着她的手麻利地叠着装钉子的袋子，他说：“我们离婚后你好像学了一些新技能。”

"Yes, I have learned a great deal. My ex-husband taught me a number of things."

“是的，我学了很多。前夫教了我一些。”

"But he wasn't really a carpenter."

“但他并不是一个木匠吧。”

She didn't reply to this as she returned the hammer and nails to the cellar. Naat's ankle was aching more severely now, and he eased himself onto the couch. When Teea returned, he patted the spot beside him on the

她没有回答这个问题，把锤子和钉子放回到地下室。现在，纳特的脚踝痛得更厉害。他坐到沙发上，让自己舒服些。当提娅回来时，他拍了拍旁边的位置，

couch and nodded.

She sat down beside him. She wasn't close enough for their knees to touch, but her shoulders were turned toward him. He looked at her arms and saw that he had been deceived by his memories. When she had appeared on his doorstep, she had still looked small to him, as she had been when they were married, but now her muscles were defined, sinewy, like those of a cat.

"You're much stronger than I remember."

She shrugged. "I've had to be. I've gotten involved in rebuilding damaged houses."

"That must be hard work."

"It is. But at least it's a way to make a bit of a living."

"So," he hesitated for a moment, "so how come you're not rebuilding your own house?"

"Sometimes, things are too damaged to rebuild."

Naat nodded, struck by attractive she looked. "I can't get over how much you've changed."

"In what way?" There was no accusation in her tone, no edge. He was relieved by this.

向她点了点头。

她在他身边坐下来，但近得还不足以让他们的膝盖贴在一起。她把肩膀转向他。看着她的手臂，他发现记忆欺骗了他。当她在他的门口出现时，她看起来还是那么小巧，结婚以来她一直如此。但现在不一样了，她的肌肉像猫的一样有型、有力。

"你比我记忆中的要强很多。"

她耸耸肩。"我不得不。我已经加入了受损房屋的重建工作。"

"那一定不容易做。"

"是的。但至少可以让我挣点钱生存。"

"那么，"他迟疑了一会儿，"你怎么不重建自己的房子呢？"

"有时候，受损太厉害就没法修复了。"

纳特点点头，被她显露的魅力所打动。"我真是无法知道你到底变了多少。"

"在哪方面？"她的语气中没有指责，没有盛气凌人。他松了一口气。

"I'm not sure. You just seem so much more...alive, maybe."

"I was always alive."

"Yes, but when we were together, you always seemed to be so…bored…bored and tired. I suppose that was my fault."

"No, no." She put her hand on his. His arm jerked, as if shocked, and he had to force himself not to pull away. "We were both much younger then. We were different people. We have both changed. I mean, look at you."

He withdrew his hand from hers and laced his fingers across his stomach.

"Please, don't." Her eyes were barely visible in the wavering light. "I wasn't going to…"

"I know. You weren't going to hurt me. I've heard that before."

"I was just…just going to say how you seem to have matured. You seem so different now from that fiery journalist who was going to change the world, reveal the truth about everything. Now you seem to carry more… I don't know… wisdom maybe?

"我不确定。你好像比以前更……有活力。"

"我以前就有活力。"

"是的，但当我们在一起时，你总是显得很……无聊……无聊和累。我想这是我的错。"

"不，不。"她把手放在他的手上。他的手臂抽搐了一下，像是受到惊吓那样。他强迫自己不要把手臂抽开。"那时，我们都很年轻。我们是不同类型的人。我俩都改变了。我的意思是，看看你自己吧。"

他把手从她的手中抽出来，手指展开横放在自己的胸前。

"请不要。"在摇曳不定的灯光里，她的眼睛几乎看不见。"我没打算……"

"我知道。你没打算伤害我。这话我以前听过。"

"我只是……只是想说，你似乎已经成熟了。你现在看起来是如此不同于从前那个激进的记者，要改变世界、揭示一切事情的真相。你现在似乎多了……我说不好……也许是多了智慧？"

He released a breath and felt the corners of his mouth tighten, the hint of a smile creeping up his cheeks. "That's funny. I see you've actually developed a sense of humour since we've been apart."

"Don't be so hard on yourself."

"Why not? I don't have any wisdom. Look at me. Look at this place. I've got nothing. I've done nothing. Everything that ever mattered is…gone. I'm just hanging on right now."

"But I'm here now."

Naat chewed on his lip, as if he were trying to digest himself. "Yes, you are here now. But I still don't know what you really want."

Teea took a deep breath. "I want what I always wanted. I want you."

Naat was silent for a moment. "That's not what you said seven years ago."

"I know, I know. I can't tell you enough times that I'm sorry. But don't you understand what was really happening then?"

He crossed his arms. "Tell me."

他松开一口气，感觉嘴角在收紧，一丝微笑爬上他的脸颊。"这倒有趣。依我看，咱们分手后你是实实在在开发了一种幽默感。"

"别对自己这么苛刻。"

"为什么不呢?我没有智慧。看看我，看看这个地方。我什么也没有。我什么也没做。我在乎的都……离我而去。我现在只能勉强度日。"

"但我现在就在这里。"

纳特咬着嘴唇，好像要把自己消化掉。"是的，你目前是在这里，但我仍然摸不透你到底想要什么。"

提娅深吸一口气。"我想要我一直想要的。我想要你。"

纳特沉默了片刻。"这不是你七年前说的。"

"我知道，我知道。说再多的抱歉都不够。但你真的不明白那时发生的事情吗？"

他抱着双臂说："告诉我。"

"I was in pain then. You were always so strong, so self-assured. You always seemed to know what you wanted, where you were going, what you were going to do to the world. I felt like a passenger. I always ached for you, and I wanted to show you that I could be important too, that I could matter. I wanted to be your equal. And the more you…ignored me, the more I needed to show you that I could be important."

"我那时很痛苦。你总是那么强、那么自信。你好像总是知道你想要什么、你正要去哪里、要为这个世界做点什么。我感觉自己像一个过客。我总是为你而痛。我想告诉你，我也有价值，我也可能是重要的。我想和你平等。你越……不理我，我越需要向你证明我是重要的。"

"So that's why you went with…with all those men?"

"这就是为什么你出去会……会那些所有的男人？"

"Yes…yes." Teea's voice faded a bit. "Please Naat, we don't need to talk of them. That was long ago. I was weak. You pulled away from me then. I was…doing it all for you, to show you that I could be important, that I could be strong."

"是……是的。"提娅的声音渐渐低下去。"恳请你，纳特。我们不需要谈论那些男人。那是很久以前的事了。我那时脆弱。接着你离开了我。我做那些都是为了你，为了向你证明我也会是重要的，我也能强壮。"

"But you even married one of…"

"但你甚至和其中的一个结了婚……"

"Please…please. That was a mistake." Her voice was almost a whisper now, her eyes a lake under moonlight, steady, glowing. Naat's grip on his elbows began to slip.

"请你……请你……那是一个错误。"她的声音现在几乎是耳语，她的眼睛在月光下像两潭湖水，稳定，并泛着光。纳特握着自己胳

They had never talked like this before, never been able to speak through the poison that always coated their tongues. Seven years ago, his pride and her immaturity had fractured them, cleaving them the same way the Wall divided them from the Westers. Now she wanted a truce. The only words he could find were, "How can I trust you?"

"I can't make you trust me. But, I've lost everything and…you're all I've got now."

All the twisted words, all of the harsh echoes of their bitter fights came back to him. There was still a sting there, but time had numbed him. These past selves seemed like ghosts to him now, cold and barely visible. He didn't want to live with them anymore, didn't want his present anaesthetized by his past. He put his hand in hers, just as the siren started its slow, ascending howl. Outside, the Wall was blanketed in darkness, almost invisible.

"We better get back down in the cellar."

She put her arm around him to help him walk. He put his hand on her shoulder, his wife's shoulder,

膊肘子的手开始滑动。他们以前从未这样谈过。他们的舌头以前像是涂上了毒。七年前，他的骄傲和她的不成熟让他们之间产生裂痕。他们分开，就像那堵墙把他们和威斯特人分开那样。现在，她想要休战。他所能找到的唯一一句话就是，“我怎么能相信你呢?”

“我无法让你相信我。但是，我已经失去了一切。现在……你就是我的一切。”

所有扭曲的话、所有争吵时那些激烈的言辞又都回来了。它们仍然蜇人，但时间已经使他麻木。那些过去的自己现在对他而言都已经成为鬼魂——冰冷、若隐若现。他不再想拥有它们，不想让他的现在被他的过去麻醉。他把手放进她的手里。就在这时，警报响起，缓慢、由低而高。外面，那堵墙被笼罩在黑暗中，几乎看不见。

“我们最好回到下面的地下室里。”

她用一只胳膊搂着他，帮助他行走。他把手放在她——他妻子——的肩膀上，

and let her help him down the ladder, just as the first distant concussions shook the walls.

让她帮助他下梯子。这时，远处的第一声爆炸使墙壁开始震动。

Flight

飞行

Denis Simkin first noticed something wrong about an hour into Flight 873. He had been reading an article in the airline's magazine about wine tasting in the Sonoma Valley. The article had engrossed him, as all travel articles about places he would never go did, so he didn't immediately notice the urgent cluster of flight attendants at the front of the plane. Their insistent whispers eventually caught his attention. He leaned into the aisle to see what was happening, his elbow slipping on the hard, plastic chair arm.

All four flight attendants stood in the aisle by plane's main door. The only male attendant had the

873 次航班已经飞行一小时了，丹尼斯·西姆金开始感到有点不对劲。他一直在阅读航空杂志上的一篇文章，是关于在索诺玛山谷品酒的。这篇文章让他全神贯注。所有描写他永远都不会去的地方的文章都会让他着迷，所以他没有立即注意到所有乘务员已经集合到了飞机的前部，做出应紧准备。他们一直窃窃私语，最终引起了他的注意。他把身子探向过道，看到底发生了什么事，胳膊肘子在坚硬的塑料把手上滑动着。

总共四个乘务员都站在靠飞机主舱门的过道上。唯一的男乘务员忙着通话，手

phone to his ear. He punched the pale ivory buttons on the wall, his face creased, drawn. The three female attendants looked at each other, speaking in hushed tones. The youngest one, round cheeked with blonde hair pulled back in a pony tail, bit her bottom lip. Denis thought she had beautiful teeth. The other two attendants, both darker and a little older, leaned in close and whispered. One pointed to her watch, and the other just nodded. Nobody was smiling. To Denis, this activity did not seem like normal procedure.

指不停地敲打着壁上那排内部通话用的象牙色按钮。他的脸部表情时而拉扯、时而严肃。三个女乘务员互相张望，压低了嗓门说话。最年轻的那个有张圆脸，金发拢在脑后成马尾状，她咬着下唇。丹尼斯认为她的牙齿很美丽。剩下的两个乘务员皮肤稍黑，年龄也稍大点，她俩靠在一起小声嘀咕。其中一个指着手表，另一个只是点头。没人微笑。在丹尼斯看来，这一切似乎和正常程序不太一样。

He leaned back in his seat, placing his hand on his neck. He kneaded a stubborn cramp, trying to listen to the conversation at the front of the plane. The crew's tones were too muted to hear. As he slowly massaged the knot out of his neck, he turned toward the window, taking a glance at the girl he had been trying to ignore. She looked to be about ten years younger than him, maybe twenty-two, twenty-three. Her medium length hair, framed perfectly by the rounded contours of the window, was that brownish-

他抽身坐回到座位里，把手放在脖子上，捏着一个顽固的肿块，试图听见机舱前面的谈话。乘务员的声音太低，什么都听不到。他慢慢揉搓着脖子里的那个肿块，眼睛转向窗外，扫了一眼身边他一直试图忽略的女孩。她看起来大约比他年轻十岁，或许二十二三岁的样子。中等长度的头发，轮廓恰似机窗的轮廓，棕不棕、红不红的，是一种他永远都无法恰当描述的颜

reddish colour that he could never properly describe, the colour of an autumn leaf lying in a puddle. She was very pretty, much prettier than Charlotte, he thought. She had smiled earlier when she had asked him to move so she could use the washroom. Denis wanted to say something, to ask her if she knew what was happening, but the old, familiar fear cemented his lips. Charlotte was the only one who had ever unsealed his lips.

Only Charlotte.

****

Denis felt her staring at him across the kitchen table. Her spoon clinked rhythmically, annoyingly and he thought she must be trying to drown each Cornflake.

"So," he said, looking up from his newspaper, "looks like it might rain today."

Charlotte continued staring into the grey bubbles in her bowl.

"That's good," he continued. "It's been so dry recently".

She pushed more flakes under the milk.

"I think I might stop at HMV

色——就像是秋叶躺在一摊烂泥上。她非常漂亮，比夏洛特漂亮多了，他想。早先她去洗手间时，曾微笑着请他让一下道。丹尼斯想说点什么，问她是否知道发生了什么事，但过去的、熟悉的恐惧封住了他的嘴。夏洛特是唯一一个曾经让他开口说话的人。

只有夏洛特。

****

丹尼斯感到她的眼光越过餐桌盯着他看，勺子有节奏地捣着，挺烦人。他想，她一定是想淹死每一粒粟米片。

"哎，"他说，从报纸上抬起头来，"今天像是要下雨啊。"

夏洛特继续盯着碗里的灰色泡沫。

"这好啊，"他继续说，"最近这么干燥。"

她把更多的粟米片一粒一粒地用勺子压在牛奶里。

"我想我可能会在回家

on the way home today, see if they've got that new Radiohead CD." A pause. "And, I think I'll stop at the drugstore to get a new razor. Do you need anything?"

She slammed the spoon down. Milk drops skittered across the table.

"Do I need anything?"

Denis's mouth opened then closed.

She crossed her arms, but she couldn't look at him. "I can't do this anymore."

"Do—what?"

She grabbed the wet spoon and threw it at him, barely missing his head. It clattered on the battered linoleum. "Don't you understand anything?"

"I'm sorry," Denis began, his words sluggish. "I…I know you've been upset lately, but I don't really understand why." He felt his ribs start to uncurl from his spine, as if everything were unwinding.

Charlotte took a deep breath, released it in a huff. "This just isn't working. I need…I need to get away."

的路上去 HMV 看一下，看 Radiohead 新出的唱片是否到了，”停顿了一下，他接着说，“我想我会去药店买把新剃须刀。你需要什么吗?”

她砰地撂下勺子。牛奶溅了一桌子。

“我需要什么吗?”

丹尼斯的嘴张开又合上。

她抱着双臂，但无法看着他。“我再不能这样做了。”

“做——什么?”

她抓起湿勺子向他扔过去，几乎砸在他头上。勺子哐当一声落在被溅上糊状物的油毡上。“你什么都不懂吗?”

“对不起，”丹尼斯开始缓慢地说道，“我……我知道你近来一直很烦躁，但我真的不明白是为了什么。”他觉得胸腔膨胀，肋骨从脊柱那儿向外拉直，仿佛一切卷着的都在舒展开。

夏洛特深吸了一口气，然后怒冲冲地说：“这样不行。我需要……我需要离开。”

The walls of the room started to recede, tilting at crazy angles. The ceiling seemed to be expanding horizontally in all directions. Charlotte's face started losing colour. He tried forcing words out of his mouth, but his tongue was like a pillow, numb, fat. He bit down hard, tasting the sour iron. Okay, this is real, he thought. He swallowed the few drops of blood and cleared his throat. "What do you mean? Are you…leaving me?"

She took a deep breath. "No…yes…I'm not sure. I just need some time, some space."

Denis's body vibrated. "I…don't really understand."

Charlotte's eyes softened a little. She got up from her chair and walked to the window. The sun was already bright; lemony streams of energy soaked the earth. She stared into the glare for a moment. "You see how light it is out there?"

He was uncertain how to answer her, uncertain of her direction. "Uh, yeah, I guess so."

"I want to live there, in the sun, in the light."

房间的墙壁开始坍塌，以各种疯狂的角度倾斜。天花板似乎沿着各个方向无限延伸。夏洛特的脸开始失色。他试着强迫自己挤出几个字来，但舌头就像一个枕头，麻木、肥嘟嘟地。他使劲往下一咬，品尝着铁的酸味。好吧，这是真实的，他想。他吞下几滴血、清了清嗓子说，“你这是什么意思?你要……离开我?”

她深吸了一口气。“不……是的……我不确定。我只是需要一些时间、一些空间。”

丹尼斯的身体摇晃着。“我……真的不明白。”

夏洛特的眼睛柔和了些。她从椅子上站起来，走到窗前。太阳已经明亮，柠檬色的光线笼罩着大地。她盯着光看了一会儿。“你看，它就在那儿——多么明亮。”

他不确定如何回答，不知道她要说什么。“嗯，是的，我想是这样。”

“我想住在那里，阳光里，光里。”

Denis starting tapping his fingertips on the table, alternating his hands, left, right, left right. He wanted to say something, but the words were all jumbled, his guts tumbled.

丹尼斯开始用指尖交替敲打着桌子，左手、右手、左右手。他想说点什么，但所有的字都纠结在了一起，他的勇气丧失殆尽。

"Oh for God's sake, Denis, do I need to spell it out for you? I just can't live like this any longer." Her cheeks flushed; a small tear trickled like mercury down her cheek.

"哦，看在上帝的分儿上，丹尼斯。我需要替你拼写出来吗?我不能再这样生活了。"她脸颊通红，一小滴泪像水银般淌下她的脸颊。

His hands stopped drumming. He felt weighted down, a victim of a vicious gravity. "Why?"

他的手停止敲打。他觉得快要被重量压扁，成为邪恶地球引力的牺牲品。"为什么?"他问。

Her eyes glistened like steel spheres. "You're just not going anywhere."

她的眼睛闪出钢球般的光。"因为你哪里都不去。"

****

The blonde flight attendant tried to put a smile on her face as she moved down the aisle to the back of the plane, responding to a call. She looked relieved to have something else to think about for a few moments. The remaining three attendants looked like they had decided something, their heads nodding in unison. Denis swallowed,

有人按了服务指示灯，那位金发空姐脸上强挤出一副笑容，沿着过道从机前走到机后。她有一种如释重负的感觉，至少片刻之内她有别的事去关注。剩下的三个乘务员看起来已经有了决定，他们的头一致性地点着。丹尼斯咽

looked at his watch. One hour and fifteen minutes since take-off. The plane should have already started its descent into Vancouver. He looked out the window. All he could see was a uniform layer of white, billowy clouds. There were no breaks, no tiny spy-holes to give a hint of what lay below. He shook his head, thinking that they should have begun to feel the deceleration of the plane, the downward tip of the nose, the slight change in the pitch of the engine hum. But there was no change, everything was static. He peered over the seats. None of the other passengers seemed to have noticed anything unusual. They were all reading their books, conversing with their neighbours or sleeping. Denis wondered if he had miscalculated somehow.

His eyes were drawn back to the front of the plane. The male flight attendant stood by the cockpit door now. He raised a closed hand, striped sleeves rolled up, tight on his forearm. Knock, knock, knock. A pause. Knock, knock, knock again. This pattern was repeated several times, but the cockpit door never

了一口口水，看了看手表。飞机已经飞行 1 小时 15 分钟，早就应该开始降落温哥华机场。他望了望窗外，看到的是一层均匀的、汹涌翻滚的白云，没有缝隙、没有任何小孔可以让人看到白云下面是什么。他摇了摇头，心想他们早就应该开始感到飞机减速、鼻尖朝下、马达的轰鸣声有所变化；然而，没有变化，一切照旧。他扫视了一下其他座位。其他乘客中似乎没人注意到任何异常；他们或是在读书，或是在与邻座交谈，或是在睡觉。丹尼斯怀疑，是不是他弄错了。

他的眼睛被吸引回到机舱前部。那位男乘务员站在驾驶舱的门口。他伸出蜷着的手，把条纹衬衣的袖子撸起，露出小臂，袖口紧紧卡在那里。咚，咚，咚。停了一会儿了。咚，咚，咚，他又敲。这种模式重复了几遍，驾驶舱的门从未开过。

opened. The flight attendant turned back to the other two, his face taut. The three of them huddled together. The blonde flight attendant was still at the back of the plane, distributing pillows. She seemed to be avoiding the scene at the front.

他转过脸去看着其他两位空姐，脸紧绷着。三个人凑在了一起。那位金发空姐还在机舱尾部，分发着枕头。她好像在回避机舱前部正发生的事。

The three attendants nodded to each other. The taller female flight attendant picked up the phone and hesitantly pressed the intercom button. "Attention please. Your in-flight crew wishes to make an announcement. Our descent into Vancouver is going to be delayed slightly. We are currently dealing with some technical, communication issues. We should have these resolved in a few moments. We will let you know when we begin our descent. Thank you." She then repeated the announcement in French, her words becoming more rushed, as if she were straining to meet a deadline.

前面的三个乘务员彼此点了点头。个子较高的那位女乘务员拿起话筒，犹豫地按下了内部对讲机按钮。"旅客们请注意。机组人员希望发表一个声明。我们在温哥华机场的降落将延缓。我们目前正在处理一些技术、通信问题。我们在几分钟后会解决这些问题。一旦开始降落，我们会立即通知你们。谢谢！"接着，她用法语重复一遍刚才的声明，但吐字越来越快，就好像要赶在截止时间前把话说完似的。

As soon as the announcement was finished, the cabin came to life with murmurs and exclamations. "What do they mean 'communication issues'?" "That doesn't sound good." "I knew I

宣布刚结束，机舱内便嘈杂起来。有小声抱怨的、有叹息的："'通信问题'？什么意思？""听起来不妙啊！""我就知道不该做这趟飞机。"他试着

shouldn't have flown." He tried to tune the noise out as he attempted to organize his own thoughts. If the problem was with the radio, why didn't the pilot or co-pilot answer the knock on the door? Security protocols? But surely they would know their radio wasn't working, in which case they would be expecting the knock. Wasn't there a peephole in the door? They could see there was no threat from the knock. It didn't make sense.

不去理会那些嘈杂声，把自己的思绪理一理。如果是无线电出了毛病，为什么驾驶和副驾驶不对敲门做出应答？是安全协议吗?但可以肯定，如果他们的无线电坏了，他们会知道的。在这种情况下,他们会期待着敲门声。难道门上没有视孔吗？他们可以看到，那次敲门没有威胁。这一切都说不通啊。

The clouds grew thicker, puffy cotton balls that absorbed the streaking plane.

云变得越来越厚，棉花团似的，吞噬着快速行进的飞机。

****

Denis stood on the platform of the train station, his nine-year old body barely bigger than the suitcase that stood beside him. The train was gone, the platform was empty. He was waiting for his father to pick him up. For six hours he stood there, the sun sinking down over glowing rails. He tried to look into the swollen orange orb, to see if another train would come and take him back home, but no more trains came. As he stared, the rails seemed to bend

丹尼斯站在火车站的站台上，他九岁的身体比身旁的行李箱高不了多少。火车开走了，站台空荡荡的。他等着父亲来接他。他在那里站了六个小时了，看着太阳下沉到反射着耀眼的光的轨道上。他盯着那个肿胀的、橙色的球体看，试图看到是否有另一辆火车来，把他带回家。然而，没有火车来。盯着盯着，铁轨似乎顺着地表的曲线弯曲，他能看到一

around the curve of the earth. He could see a perfectly circular loop of steel, 40,000 kilometres long, slowly guiding a single train on its circumnavigation back to the lone station where he stood. The air chilled as the sun finally slid off the rails and Denis slowly paced the void of the platform to keep warm. Eventually, his father did show up, smelling of juniper berries and perfume, his cold hand guiding Denis toward the car, toward his required visitation.

个完美的圆形钢环，长40000公里，慢慢引导着火车沿着它的环行单轨回到这孤单的、他正站在其中的小站。太阳终于从铁轨上滑落，空气变冷。丹尼斯在空旷的站台上慢慢踱着步，这样能让他暖和些。最终，他父亲出现了，身上散发着杜松子和香水的味道。他冰冷的手引着丹尼斯走向他的车子，履行他要求的探视。

****

Denis looked over at the auburn girl. Her eyes were closed and her hands gripped the armrests. Her lips moved silently. He wondered if she was uttering a prayer, wondered if it helped. Denis sometimes considered whether he would feel the need to pray if he faced imminent death. He wasn't feeling any particular pull to prayer at the moment, but he also wasn't convinced that question of his mortality was about to be immediately answered either. There still must be a rational explanation.

****

丹尼斯看着那位皮肤赭色的女孩。她闭着眼睛，双手抓着扶手。她的嘴唇默默蠕动。他想知道，她是否正在祈祷；想知道那样做是否管用。丹尼斯有时会想，如果他面对突如其来的死亡，他是否会感到祈祷的必要。目前，他还没有感到任何特别的引力让他祈祷，也不相信他的死亡问题需要立即做出答复。一定还会有一个合理的解释的。

As he watched her narrow lips

看着她窄细的嘴唇蠕

move, her delicate fingers squeeze and release the armrest, he became aware of a hollow, anxious feeling in his stomach. Before he could even think about what he was doing, he grabbed her hand.

动，纤细的手指在扶手上抓紧、放松、抓紧、放松，他开始感到胃里有一种空荡荡的、焦虑的感觉。在还没有弄清楚自己在做什么之前，他抓住了她的手。

Her lips stopped moving. Her round, green eyes opened, looked inquisitive.

她的嘴唇停止蠕动。她睁开了绿色的圆眼睛，显得好奇。

"I…uh…" His mouth chewed glue.

"我……嗯……"他的嘴里像嚼着胶水。

"It's okay." She squeezed his hand. "I'm sure there's nothing to worry about." Her palm was warm. He thought he should let go, but she didn't seem to mind. "Are you a little scared?" Her eyes told him that she knew he was harmless.

"没关系。"她紧紧地握着他的手，"我相信没什么可担心的。"她的掌心是温暖的。他认为他应该放手，但她似乎并不介意。"你没被吓着吧？"她的眼睛告诉他，她知道他是没有恶意的。

"No… well yes, I suppose a little. I don't usually worry about things too much; I just let them happen."

"没有……是的，我想有一点吧。我通常并不太担心事情，我只是随他们发生。"

She nodded her head, a polite acknowledgement of the words, but with little understanding of the meaning. Denis sometimes questioned this attitude himself, wondered if he should worry about life more. Charlotte certainly seemed to think so. He always thought that

她点头，礼貌地认可这些话，但对其中的意思却并不理解。丹尼斯有时自己会质问这种态度，想知道他是否应该更多地担心生活。夏洛特似乎肯定会这样想。他总是认为，担心未来只是制造压力，而他不喜欢压力。

worrying about the future simply caused stress, and he didn't like stress. Charlotte wanted to make plans, wanted to build some certainty into her future. He always felt plans were too constricting. He remembered Mrs. Murray, his high school science teacher once telling him that "those who fail to plan, plan to fail". He actually had to muffle a laugh when she said this, but years later when Charlotte had used the same phrase it didn't seem so funny.

夏洛特想制定计划，想让她的未来有保障。他总是觉得计划太有局限性。他还记得默里夫人——他高中时的理科老师。她曾对他说"那些不做计划的人就已经在计划失败了"。当她说这话时，他不得不压低自己的笑声，但数年之后，当夏洛特说同样的话时，它却显得并不那么可笑。

"Well, I hope they get this problem fixed soon. My boyfriend is waiting at the airport for me, and he's probably wondering why we're late."

"唉，我希望他们很快就能解决这个问题。我男朋友正在机场等我呢，或许他正纳闷我们为什么晚点了。"

Denis quickly released her hand. His fingers flexed, started drumming on his knee. He looked at his watch. They should have just landed. He turned toward the cockpit. The male flight attendant was out of view, but Denis could hear him banging around in the service area. The other three flight attendants were in the aisle, calming and soothing passengers. Most of the voices were murmuring, but a few louder ones were making demands,

丹尼斯很快放开了她的手。他弯起手指，开始在膝盖上打着鼓点。他看了看手表。他们早该着陆了。他转向驾驶舱。男乘务员已经不见了，但丹尼斯能听到他在服务区间里忙乎着。其他三个乘务员都在过道上，安抚乘客，使他们平静。大部分的声音都是喃喃小声，偶尔也有一些高嗓门要求知道正在发生什么事，想和飞行

wanting to know what was going on, wanting to speak to the pilot.

员说一两句。

He looked back toward the girl. "You've just got to wait. Things always work out if you wait long enough." He tried to use the most reassuring tone he could, but the words seemed flat, dead even to his ears.

他回过头来看着那个女孩。"你只需要等待。只要你等得够长，事情总会解决的。"他试着用他最肯定的语气说这些话，但那些字在他听来却是瘪瘪的，毫无生气。

****

He drummed his fingers on the steering wheel, wondering what was holding up traffic. The row of cars in front of him seemed endless.

****

他用手指敲打着方向盘，猜想到底是什么让交通堵塞起来。他前面的车已经排了一长队，看不到头。

Charlotte had hurriedly packed a suitcase that morning. He didn't ask where she was going, knew there would be no point asking when she'd be back. He pleaded with her at first, then tried reasoning with her, tried to get her to rationalize her decision. This made her angrier.

夏洛特那天早上匆匆打包了一个行李箱。他没问她要去哪里。他知道，问她什么时候回来没有任何意义。他开始时恳求她，然后和她摆道理，试图让她更理性地做决定。这使她更愤怒。

After she had gone, he felt a sudden need to get out, to escape the smothering silence in the house. He still had five hours before he needed to be at the airport. He pointed the car aimlessly onto the freeway, looking for some relief in the hum of tires on smooth asphalt. But he had

她走后，他突然觉得需要走出去，逃离房间内那令人窒息的沉默。离他应该去机场的时间还有五个小时。他漫无目标地把车开向高速公路，希望在光滑的柏油路上、轮胎发出的嗡嗡声中找点安慰。他只开出了五分

only been driving for five minutes when he lurched to a stop, the road clogged with countless glowing brake lights. He assumed there must be some catastrophic event ahead that was obstructing progress. The air in the car was starting to get heavy. He opened the sunroof to get some breeze. As he peered over the glinting car roofs front of him, he could see an exit ramp clotted with cars. The ramp curved off to the right and over a hill. Pairs of brilliant red eyes shimmered in the bright sun, marking a trail of cars that seemed endless.

钟，便把车蹒跚着停了下来。路上布满了无数个发光的刹车灯。他猜想前面一定是发生了灾难性的事故，阻碍了车辆前行。车里的空气开始变得沉重。他打开天窗让一些微风吹进车里。当他的视线越过前面闪着亮灯的车顶时，他能看到一个出口匝道处车挤成了一疙瘩。匝道弯曲、向右爬上了一座小山。一对对锃亮的红眼睛在明亮的太阳下闪着光，标志着一眼望不到头的车队。

Charlotte had told him before she left that she was frustrated with his inertia. As his eyes scanned the stationary jumble ahead, he thought of Mrs. Murray, pounding on a desk, stating that a body persists in its state of rest. Charlotte had tried, with patience and love at first, to pull him up, to help him fly. She once told him that she thought he could soar like a bird if he could just crack the shell. He appreciated her kind words, her protectiveness, but he sometimes wondered if she thought it was her job to hatch him. Later, as

在离开之前，夏洛特告诉他，她对他的惯性很恼火。当他的眼睛扫过前方一动不动的混乱时，他想到了默里夫人。她敲着书桌说，物体具有保持静止状态的惯性。夏洛特在开始时，用耐心和爱努力把他往上拉，要帮他飞起来。她曾经告诉他，她认为他能像鸟一样飞翔——如果他可以击碎外壳的话。他欣赏她善意的话和她的自我保护。但有时他会怀疑，她是否认为孵化他是她的工作。之后，随着她话

her words became sharper, he wondered if he had really tried hard enough. Charlotte seemed to be in a hurry, but he couldn't understand where she was trying to take him.

语变得尖刻，他开始怀疑自己是否真的不够努力。夏洛特似乎很急，但他不明白，她要带他去何方。

The strong morning sun was laying a warm, heavy blanket across his arms. He felt energy pulsing into his skin. He looked up through the sunroof. The cloudless sky was a deep, vivid blue that could only be found on the prairies in the summer. Across the seamless azure canvas he noticed a jet trail slowly developing. The dual white lines moved diagonally across his field of vision, undisturbed by wind even at that altitude. As the trails lengthened, he thought about where that airplane was going, who was on it. Denis glanced back at the unmoving line of winking tail lights, but his gaze quickly returned to the tandem chalk lines that stretched across the sky to the west, toward the ocean. He pulled the airline ticket out of his pocket, scanned it, and wondered.

早晨强烈的阳光似在他的胳膊上盖了一层温暖、厚重的毯子。他感到能量像脉冲一样涌进他的皮肤。他抬头往天窗外看去。天空万里无云、一片湛蓝，这种生动的蓝色只有在大草原的夏天才能见到。在这一副毫无瑕疵的蓝色画布上，他发现了一架飞机的痕迹越来越明显。有两条白线呈斜对角从他的视野里划过，即使是在那样的高度仍然没被风吹乱。随着两条线加长，他猜想飞机会飞向何方、谁在飞机上。丹尼斯回过头来扫了一眼那排一动不动、眨着眼睛的尾灯。他的目光很快又回到了那串粉笔线，在天空中向西延伸，向着海洋延伸。他把机票从口袋里掏出来，扫了一眼，开始沉思起来。

****

"So why are you going to Vancouver?"

****

"你为什么去温哥华?"

Denis jerked in his seat, startled. She had been silent for a few minutes and he had been concentrating on the activities at the front of the plane. The male flight attendant had emerged from the service area, holding a slim piece of silver metal that he had tried to conceal in his palm. He began working on the cockpit door latch. He had pulled his sleeves up further, revealing coarse bristles that sprouted from his forearms. Although the flight attendant's movements were discreet, Denis could see that the object looked like some type of wrench. Several passengers had risen and were moving to the front of the plane.

丹尼斯吓了一跳，身子在座位上扯动了一下。她已经沉默了好几分钟了，而他也一直专注于机舱前部的活动。男乘务员已经从服务区走出，手里拿着一个小金属片，银色的，他极力想藏在手掌里，但还是没藏住。他开始撬驾驶舱的门锁。他把袖子卷得更高，露出前臂上又粗又硬的汗毛。尽管这位男乘务员的动作是谨慎的，丹尼斯可以看出来那东西看起来像是某种扳手。一些乘客已经站了起来，往机舱前面走去。

"I…I just had to get away for a bit."

"You mean like a vacation?"

Denis turned toward the girl. Her round eyes were inquisitive, but tense. He imagined she was trying to distract herself from their pressing reality. His own anxiety had been simmering, and he felt a sudden need to connect with this girl. "Not a vacation. I was actually supposed to go to Toronto. For a training session.

"我……我必须离开一段时间。"

"你的意思是度假吗?"

丹尼斯转向了那位女孩。她的圆眼睛里有好奇，但也有紧张。他猜想她一定是在极力分散自己的注意力以不受紧迫现实的影响。他自己的焦虑也一直在酝酿着。他突然感到一种需求，想和这个女孩发生点什么。"不是度假。我本应该去多

I work as a lab assistant, you see and there was this course…well anyway, I changed my mind. I had to go somewhere…else. I…think my wife just left me."

伦多，去接受一段时间的培训。我是一名实验室助理，你看，是这样的一门课……不管怎么说，我改变主意了。我不得不去个地方……其他的地方。我想……我老婆刚离开我了。"

"You think?"

"你想?"

"Well, I guess I know, really." Denis looked down at his hands. "She always thought I was too passive. She always wanted to do things. She felt like I was dragging her down."

"嗯，我想我知道，真的。"丹尼斯垂眼看着他自己的手。"她总是认为我太被动。她总是想做事情。她觉得我拖了她的后腿。"

The girl leaned in. "That's so sad."

女孩向他靠了过来。"这太令人伤心了。"

Denis looked up, looked into her melting eyes. "She was probably right, though. She deserved more…more than I have."

丹尼斯抬起头来，看着她动人的眼睛说，"她或许是对的。她配得上……比我能给她的更多。"

The girl put her hand on his arm. "Don't sell yourself short. Everyone's different; everyone's got to find their own place. Maybe she just didn't want to take the time to find out what you were really all about."

女孩把一只手放在他的胳膊上。"不要看轻自己。每个人都是不同的；每个人都必须找到自己的位置。也许她只是不想花时间去了解你到底是什么样的人。"

Denis doubted this, but he didn't refute it. He simply nodded, hoping she would keep her hand on his arm.

丹尼斯对此表示怀疑，但并没有反驳。他只是点了点头，希望她能把手继续放在他的胳膊上。

The flight attendant at the front of the plane was leaning against the door now, straining. The wrench suddenly slipped, clattering against the door as it fell to the carpet. A passenger, a muscular man in his late twenties, picked it up and offered to try. He braced his legs, jammed his elbows tight to his sides, and heaved on the wrench. A couple of grunts, then a frustrated shoulder slam on the door. The young man stepped back and stood with the flight attendant. Their heads nodded from side to side, their lips tight over their teeth. They surveyed the cockpit door, not seeming to find any answers. Then, as the young man began bracing himself for another assault, there was a quiet click. The flight attendant and the young man looked at each other, their faces frozen. The door had opened, just a crack. After a moment, the flight attendant slipped his fingers into the space between the door and the frame and eased it open.

"They're gone!"

The girl jerked her hand away. A silence blanketed the cabin, as if

在机舱前面的乘务员现在身体靠在了门上，绷得紧紧的。突然间，扳手滑落了，顺着门发出响声，落在地毯上。一名20来岁、肌肉发达的男乘客捡起扳手，主动提出让他试试。他弓起腿，胳膊肘紧紧夹在身体两侧，用力向上推着扳手。他吭哧了几声，然后用一只沮丧的肩膀撞击着门。年轻人退了回去，和那位男乘务员站在了一起。他们摇着头，嘴唇紧绷在牙齿上。他们检查了驾驶舱的门，似乎找不到任何答案。接着，当这个年轻人开始弓起身子做另一次进攻时，出现了轻轻的咔嗒声。那位男乘务员和年轻人互相看了看，脸上的表情凝固起来。门开了，但只是一条缝。过了一会儿，男乘务员把手指塞进门和门框之间的缝隙，把门打开来。

“他们不见了！”

女孩猛地把手抽走了。沉默像毯子一样笼罩着客

all lungs were empty. Then the dead air was overwhelmed by a cacophony of voices, questioning, crying, screaming, chattering voices.

舱，好像人们的肺都是空的。突然间，死寂的空气被刺耳的声音淹没，质问、哭泣、尖叫和喋喋不休。

Denis looked over at the girl. Her eyes pleaded, but he didn't have anything to offer her. Instead, he got up and tried to get a better view of the cockpit. The aisle was blocked now, the flight attendants trying to calm the passengers, get them back in their seats. The blonde attendant was sitting at the back of the cabin staring out a window, mouth slack, ignoring the chaos around her.

丹尼斯转过头去看那个女孩。她的眼睛在恳求，但他没有任何可以给予的。相反，他站了起来，试图能更好地看清楚驾驶舱。现在，通道已经被阻塞，乘务员们都在努力安抚乘客，让他们回到座位上。那位金发女乘务员坐在客舱的尾部，盯着窗外，嘴巴松弛，无视周围的混乱。

The clamourous air was fractured by a feedback screech from the intercom. Everyone stopped talking, and the taller flight attendant began speaking. "Everyone, please return to your seats. We are currently experiencing an emergency condition. Please fasten your seat belts and await further instructions."

喧闹的空气被对讲机发出的尖锐回音刺破。每个人都停止了交谈。那位个头较高的女乘务员开始说话。"各位乘客，请回到你们的座位上。我们正在经历紧急情况。请系好安全带，等待进一步的指示。"

"But what's going on?" The voice from the back of the cabin was insistent.

"但到底怎么回事啊？"有人从客舱尾部坚持询问。

The flight attendant took a deep breath. "It appears that our pilot and co-pilot have disappeared from the cockpit." Her tone was surprisingly

那位空姐深吸了一口气。"看来，我们的飞行员和副驾驶都从驾驶舱消失了。"她的语气出奇地中

neutral, as if she were making an announcement about a spot of approaching turbulence. Denis was at first surprised by her calmness, but then realized that this was part of the flight crew's training. "Our chief flight attendant, Jason, is in the cockpit assessing the situation. Please go back to your seats. We will update you as soon as we have more information."

立，就好像正在宣布飞机将要遇到一股气流一样。丹尼斯开始时对她的冷静很惊讶，但马上意识到这是机组人员受训的一部分。"我们的乘务长，杰森，正在驾驶舱里查看情况。请回到你们的座位上。我们一旦有新的消息会马上通知你们。"

Denis sat down and looked out the window. They were now well past Vancouver. The clouds had dissolved, the Pacific a greyish, green carpet expanding to meet the horizon. The girl beside him was quietly sobbing into her hands. He put his hand on her shoulder and stared at the formless sea, a feeling a calm beginning to blanket him.

丹尼斯坐下来，望着窗外。他们现在已经越过温哥华的上空。云已散，太平洋就像是一张灰绿色的地毯向着地平线扩展出去。他身边的女孩用双手捂着脸无声地啜泣着。他把手放在了她的肩上，盯着无形的海，一种平静的感觉开始将他笼罩。

Ten minutes later, the tall flight attendant came back on the intercom. "Attention, please. I have an update on our situation." She paused for a moment. "We've lost all communication. The auto-pilot controls are locked and cannot be disengaged. However," she looked around the cabin, scanning the anxious faces "our fuel tanks are

十分钟后，那位个头较高的空姐回到对讲机。"请注意。我有一个最新消息。"她停了一会儿，"我们失去了所有联系。自动舵控制被上锁，没办法解除。然而，"她环顾四周机舱，扫视着人们焦虑的面孔，"我们的油箱目前还满着。我们无法解释发生了什么，因为

now full. We can't explain what is happening, it doesn't make any sense. We are working to regain control, but there is no imminent danger. Whatever has happened here, it seems like the result is going to be a very long flight."

这解释不通。我们正在努力重获控制权，但也没有迫在眉睫的危险。无论这里发生了什么，但看起来这将会是一个漫长的飞行。"

Minutes passed or hours passed, Denis wasn't sure. The world began to shrink, as he watched the endless waves below. Time became seamless. The girl beside him had stopped crying, and a resigned, but tense peace spread through the cabin, an enveloping inertia. At one point, the girl turned to him, her eyes dancing with questions, with fear, with the angst that swallows those who have left something important behind, and asked "What do we do now?"

几分钟或几小时过去了，丹尼斯不确定。当他看着下面无尽的波浪时，整个世界开始收缩。时间不再是一个可分的概念。他身边的女孩已经停止了哭泣，缩在座位上。机舱内平静、紧张，一切随惯性走着。有一度，女孩曾转向他，眼里闪烁着问题、恐惧和焦虑，这些情感吞噬着那些身后还有重要牵挂的人，她问："我们现在怎么办?"

Denis leaned back in his seat, grabbed the magazine from the seat pocket and flipped to the article about the Sonoma Valley. "We wait," he said, his voice now confident, "and see what happens."

丹尼斯身体向后靠在椅背上。他伸手拿起前排座位后袋里的杂志，翻到那篇关于索诺玛山谷的文章。"我们等着，"他说，他的声音现在充满了自信，"看看会发生什么。"

Fred

弗雷德

Crystals of light were piercing my eyes the morning I saw my dead dog running down the path by the river. I know you probably won't believe this story but it did happen, last summer.

那天早晨，阳光像晶体一样刺疼我的眼睛。我看到了自己死去的狗，正顺着河边的小路在跑。我知道你或许不相信这个故事，但它的确发生了，就在去年夏天。

It was one of those sultry prairie mornings. The sun had risen at its usual uncivilized hour, and it was already twenty five degrees by nine o'clock. I was just in the middle of my ritual morning walk. See, I'm a school teacher so I like to savour my summers. No extra work for me, no toiling away on the rigs for a little extra cash. No, I like to take it easy in the summer.

大草原的早晨是闷热的，那天也一样。太阳一如既往地早早升起。9 点时，气温已达 25 摄氏度。我像往常一样正在散步。你知道，我是一名小学教师，我喜欢品味夏天。因此，我不做额外的工作，不会为一点额外的小钱劳累，去当钻井工。不，我喜欢在夏天放松身心。

Anyway, the walk had been good, nearly an hour and a half.

不管怎样，那天的散步一直不错，几乎进行了一个

When I had started, it had been a bit cooler, especially by the river. Wisps of steam rose off the mottled aspen trunks as the sun began to penetrate the dense fog that had settled in the valley overnight. I liked to stand on the smoothly arched pedestrian bridge, watching the lazy vapour meander up and out of the broad fissure carved by the sluggish river. I could spend half an hour or more looking down at the brackish surface, pondering all those things that needed pondering. I usually faced west while I did this, as the sun was too low and too bright to look at directly. On this day, maybe because it was the anniversary of my wife Kate's death, maybe because I needed to feel something, I had decided to look east instead and let the murderous rays bathe my face.

半小时。开始的时候，天还不是很热，尤其是在河边。在夜里，浓雾会积淀在河谷。当太阳开始穿透浓雾，一缕缕蒸汽顺着斑驳的白杨树干冉冉上升。我喜欢站在平缓的人行拱桥上，看着缓慢的河流在浓雾中切出一道宽缝，懒散的蒸汽在水面上游荡，慢慢散去。 我可以花半个小时或更多的时间看着微波不起的水面，考虑着那些需要考虑的事情。我通常面向西站着，因为这样可以避免直视既低又亮的太阳。也许因为那天是我妻子凯特的死亡周年纪念日，也许是因为我需要感受点什么。总之，我决定向东看，让凶残的光线直击我的脸。

I had been standing in that position for about ten minutes when I saw him. At first I assumed that it was just a stray dog. It clearly did not have an owner in sight as it bounded happily down the asphalt path. A dog off the leash wasn't common in our area, but it wasn't unknown either. I only gave the dog

我就这样在那儿站了大约十分钟左右，我看到了它。起初，我以为这只是一只流浪狗。当它顺着柏油路欢快地跑过来时，前后左右并不见其主人。它没有戴颈圈，这在这个街区是很少见的，但也并不是没有这种可能。它跑过时，我只是随意

a slight glance as it went by.

Except—

As I was turning my gaze back to the languid, lead-coloured water, I noticed something about that dog. It looked like a mixed breed; border collie, hound, God knows what else. A typical Humane Society special. Nothing remarkable about it.

Except the colour.

It was completely white, except for a black, heart-shaped patch on its left rear flank. I don't mean a Valentine heart either. This patch looked somewhat like a human heart; aorta, auricles, ventricles, the whole works. A very unusual marking for a dog.

Unusual, and exactly like Fred's markings.

Fred was a dog I had for five years when I was a kid. I was seven when we got him, a leftover from a litter of farm dogs. Fred was the most even-tempered dog I had ever met. Although he knew how to warn off strangers when necessary, he was never aggressive, never barked in anger. He was the perfect companion for an only child. We played for

看了一眼。

然而——

正当我把目光转回到慵懒的、浅灰色的水面时，这只狗的某个特征引起我的注意。它看起来像个杂种——边境牧羊犬、猎犬，或天知道什么别的品种。一个典型的动物保护协会对象。它没什么特别的地方。

除了颜色。

它通体白色，只有一块心状的黑色在其左侧、靠后的地方。我说的心状不是情人节常见的那类。它看起来更像人类的心脏：主动脉、心耳、心室，该有的都有。这对于一只狗而言，是个非同寻常的标记。

不寻常，简直就和弗雷德的一样。

当我还是个孩子的时候，弗雷德和我待了五年。得到它时，我七岁。它是一群农场狗里剩下的。弗雷德是我见过的、最随和的狗。尽管它知道在必要的时候如何警告陌生人，它却从不咄咄逼人，从未愤怒地咆哮过。对于一个独生子而言，它是一个绝好的伙伴。我们

hours down by the river, dodging through the trees, jumping over the reeds. Fred loved it. He seemed to have an infinite store of energy. He was always ready to play, and I never remember seeing him sleep. I suppose he must have slept while I slept, but as soon as I was awake, he was there, beside my bed, ready for another day.

会在河边玩上几个小时，穿过树林，跳过芦苇丛。弗雷德喜欢这样，它似乎有无限的能量。他总是乐于玩耍。我不记得曾见过它睡觉。我想，它一定是在我睡着的时候睡觉；但我醒来时，它就在那儿，在我的床边，准备新的一天。

That is, until he got run over by a car.

直到他被车碾了。

And now, running down the path, tongue hanging out, spittle spraying was that same dog, or at least one that looked the same. I couldn't believe what I was seeing. I had to get closer.

现在，吐着舌头、喷着唾沫、顺着小道跑着的正是那条狗，或至少是一条看起来一模一样的狗。我无法相信自己的眼睛，我得靠得再近些。

I started jogging slowly across the bridge, trying not to startle the dog. He seemed to be slowing, although he still didn't see me. As I stepped off the bridge, I slipped on some gravel, making a *shooshing* noise, like marbles in tin can. The dog looked up, finally noticing me.

我开始慢慢地、跑过那座桥，不想惊吓到那条狗。它似乎慢了下来，但并没有看到我。跑下桥，是一条铺满碎石子的路，踩上去既滑又弄出吱嘎的噪音，像是弹珠在锡罐里发出的声音。狗抬起了头，终于注意到我了。

One blue eye, one brown.

一只眼睛是蓝色的，另一只是棕色的。

Just like Fred.

和弗雷德的一模一样。

My breath was quickening.

我的呼吸加快。这不可

This couldn't be true. I had seen Fred's body writhing on the road thirty-five years ago, watched the light fade in those mismatched eyes as the thick liquid leaked out of his body. I watched him die.

Could it be?

The dog had stopped now and was watching me. His tail was wagging slowly, describing a lazy parabola in the air. He looked curious, not frightened, definitely not aggressive.

I stepped slowly toward the dog. I had to find out.

"Fred. Come here," I said, using my firmest dog-training voice.

The dog immediately started running toward me. He was bounding, his tail frenetic. When he came within about a metre of me, he veered off to the trees and began circling back. He was playing.

It was Fred, no question.

Before my brain could catch up to the undeniable reality in front of me, Fred took off, trailing an enthusiastic bark behind him.

I started running. Fred was

能是真的。35 年前，我看着弗雷德的身体在路上抽搐，随着血液不停地、从它的体内流出，那双颜色不一的眼睛渐渐失去了光泽。我看着它死去。

这怎么可能？

那狗现在不跑了，它停了下来，正看着我。它的尾巴慢慢晃动，在空中划出一个懒散的抛物线。它看起来更像是好奇，而不是害怕，但肯定不是咄咄逼人。

我开始一步步、慢慢向狗靠近。我必须搞明白。

"弗雷德，过来。"我说，声音坚定，是那种训狗时常用的。

那狗立刻向我跑来，蹦蹦跳跳，尾巴疯狂地摇晃着。当它跑到离我大约一米以内的时候，它转头向树林跑去，兜了个圈，又跑了回来。它在和我玩。

毫无疑问，这是弗雷德。

在我的大脑能明白眼前发生的、不可否认的事实之前，弗雷德又跑开了，身后留下一声欢快的叫声。

我开始跑，去追。弗雷

going down the path, toward the older part of town, the part of town where I had grown up. Even though it wasn't very far from where I now lived, I hadn't visited the old neighbourhood in years. I don't know why, I guess I just didn't see any need to go.

德顺着那条道、向着镇子里的老区跑去，那是我长大成人的地方。尽管它离我现在住的地方不是很远，我已经多年没去过了。没有什么具体原因，大概是没那必要吧。

But now, chasing this spectre, or reincarnation, or zombie, or whatever it was, I found myself in places that looked familiar, but not quite right. I had never been much of an athlete, and Fred had to wait for me several times, but our progress was steady. When I called to Fred he would wait, but as soon as I got near, he was off again, carving an invisible path, leading me somewhere.

然而现在，当我追逐这个幽灵、转世、僵尸或无论你叫它什么，我发现自己置身于熟悉的地方，但又完全不是那么回事。我从来就不是那种运动型的，弗雷德不得不停下来几次，等我；然而，我们就一直这么稳稳地进行着。只要我喊弗雷德，它就会停下来等；但我一靠近，它就会跑开，切出一条看不见的路径，把我引向某处。

He finally stopped under the old railway trestle. That bridge had been built nearly a hundred years ago, and was still used sporadically by trains coming from the lumber mills up north. When we were kids, my friends and I would climb the embankment and go up on the bridge, daring each other to wait as long we could when we heard the mournful whistle in the distance. Of

它终于在一个旧铁路栈桥下停了下来。那座木桥已经有近百年的历史了，偶尔还会被从木材加工厂北上的火车使用。当我还是孩子的时候，我和伙伴们会爬上路堤、上桥，听着远处火车的鸣笛，我们比胆大，看谁能在火车逼近前在桥上站的时间更长。当然，父母知

course, our parents always scolded us when they found out what we had done, telling us we would get ourselves killed. We kept doing it anyway.

道此事后，总会责骂我们，说这样会让我们送了小命的。但我们还是照做不误。

Fred was sitting directly in the middle of the path, under the blackened, crisscrossed timbers. As I got closer to bridge, I could see the faded white paint, the cross, barely visible on the greasy creosote. I knew immediately what it was; the hasty memorial painted by Maureen, the girl who had lived next door to me on the old street, a humble tribute to her brother who had launched himself off the top of the bridge when he was twenty-one, smashing his skull and his whiskey bottle all over the newly paved path. I remember she had taken it the hardest of the whole family, but I think everyone eventually came apart, and her family moved away less than a year later.

弗雷德正坐在路中央，头顶上是那座木桥。桥体是纵横交错的圆木板条，已经发黑了。当我离桥更近的时候，我看到了褪了色的白漆，是个十字架，在油渍渍的、经过木馏油处理过的圆木表面仍依稀可辨。我立刻意识到了这是什么—— 一个简单的纪念，是莫林画的。莫林是我住在老街时的邻家女孩。这是她对哥哥卑微的祭奠。21 岁时，他从桥上纵身跳下，头盖骨和威士忌酒瓶在新铺的路面上摔得粉碎、满地都是。我记得，全家人数她在这次事件中受到的打击最大；但我想，每个人最终都会支离破碎的。此后不足一年，她家就搬走了。

I wiped my drenched forehead with the back of my hand. Staring up at the oily logs, I was stunned by the vividness of the memory. I had long forgotten about that tragic event, but now found myself mesmerized by

我用手背擦着汗湿的额头。抬头看着那些油腻的圆木，我吃惊于自己生动的记忆。我早就忘记了那个悲惨的事件，但现在却发现自己沉迷于头顶上方那带角的、

the angular, pungent geometry above me, wondering what had happened to Maureen, and her family, and all those other people from the street that eventually moved away. I was one of them, of course, and I wondered if anyone ever thought about me the same way.

Fred seemed to sense that I needed some time here, so he sat patiently under the bridge, not close enough to touch, but close enough to see my eyes. Eventually he stood up and with one spirited bark was on his way again.

I had barely caught my breath, but I took off again. I was determined to keep him in sight. We wound our way further down the path, my eyes stinging with oscillating flashes of the sun carving its way through the trembling aspens, my soaked shirt sticking to my back. We had reached the end of the path when I realized that Fred was going to cross the road. Sour memories filled me as I screamed Fred's name. He ignored me, crossing the road at full speed. Miraculously, there were no cars and he made to the other side,

辛酸的几何图形，思讨着莫林后来不知怎样了，还有她的家人，以及所有最终从那条街上搬走的人们。当然，我是其中之一。我想知道他们中是否也有人会想到我，就像我想到他们一样。

弗雷德似乎意识到我在这个地方需要一些时间。它耐心地坐在桥下——在我够不着它、它又能看清我眼睛的地方。最后，他站了起来，欢快地叫了一声，又上路了。

我才刚刚喘过气来，但我又出发了。我下定决心不让它从我的视线里消失。我们顺着那条道继续往下跑。太阳光穿过白杨树，一闪一闪地刺痛我的眼睛。我的衬衫湿透了，贴在背上。当我意识到弗雷德要穿过马路时，我们已经跑到了路的尽头。辛酸的记忆涌上心头，我狂喊着弗雷德的名字。它不理我，全速穿过马路。真是奇迹，竟然没有车！它跑到了路的另一边，毫发无损。我冲刺般越过马路，在路的那一边，大口喘着气。

untouched. I sprinted across, gasping as I reached the other side. Fred waited about half a block ahead as I gulped the air, and when I stood up he took off again.

弗雷德在前面大约半个街区的地方等着。等我喘好了气、直起腰来的时候，它又跑开了。

As I jogged along, I looked at the old houses around me. They looked familiar, but a little more run-down than I remembered. I still couldn't work out what Fred was trying to do. Why was he leading me through my old neighbourhood?

我跟着它跑的同时，眼睛看着周围的老房子。它们看起来熟悉，但比我记忆里的更破旧。我仍弄不明白，弗雷德到底想干什么。它为什么要领着我穿过以前的老街区？

We were now crossing the dry, crisp soccer field. My feet stumbled on the clumps of grass and divots. Fred was starting to get ahead of me, but I could see where he was going; my old elementary school.

我们正穿过干巴巴、被晒焦了的足球场。我被脚底下凸凹不平的草疙瘩或小坑弄得磕磕绊绊。弗雷德开始和我拉开距离，但我仍然可以看到它正往哪儿跑：我从前的小学。

As I got closer, I was amazed at the consistency of the stark, utilitarian, Modernist architecture. The long, yellow Roman bricks, the flat roof, the alcoves; it all looked exactly as I remembered. The playground equipment was, of course, newer, safer. God forbid a child might actually get hurt.

当我靠得更近时，我惊讶于其建筑风格的一致性：简约、实用、现代——黄色的罗马长砖、平坦的屋顶、凹进去的壁龛。一切就如我记得的一样。当然，操场上的设备更新、更安全。上帝不允许任何一个孩子可能受到伤害。

Fred was waiting by the second alcove. I walked past the metal support pole that I had stuck my

弗雷德正在第二个壁龛处等着。我走过金属支柱。二年级时，我曾在冬天伸出

tongue to in the winter of grade two. I could still taste the bitter metal on my tongue as the principal poured hot water down the pole, soaking my jacket. How many other tongues had tasted that pole since then?

I slowed when I got to the alcove. Fred knew where this was. I had brought Kate here after the grade nine graduation party. We had stumbled down the hill from the junior high school, laughing, sucking in greedy mouthfuls of the fresh, June air. I had known Kate since the first grade, and we knew the alcoves would be secluded at this time of night. The memory of the fumbling fingers, the hot breath was once like fire in my head. Intensity like that didn't exist any more. Kate had been gone five years now, and it seemed that the night in the alcove pushed all the other memories aside. I couldn't picture her face anymore, except as two glistening lips in the dark.

I stepped back out of the alcove, into the morning light. Fred was still sitting there. He started walking and I followed. He didn't run this time, and I didn't try to

舌头舔它。当校长顺着柱子往下浇烫水时，我仍能伸出舌头去品尝那苦涩的金属味，任外套被淋透。从那时到现在，又有多少条别的舌头在这个柱子上舔过？

当我接近那个壁龛时，我放慢了脚步。弗雷德知道这是哪里。九年级的毕业晚会后，我带凯特来到这里。我们跌跌撞撞地从山坡上的初中校园跑下来，大笑着，张着大嘴贪婪地吸着 6 月的新鲜空气。我从一年级就认识凯特。我们知道，在夜晚的那个时候，壁龛是隐蔽的地方。记忆中那摸索的手指、滚烫的喘息曾像火一样留在我的脑海里。这样的强度已不复存在。凯特已经走了五年了，我们在壁龛里的那晚似乎把所有的其他记忆冲到了一边。我已经记不清她的脸是什么模样，除了黑暗中那两片闪耀着光泽的嘴唇。

我从壁龛里退出来，踏进晨光。弗雷德还坐在那里。它开始走，我紧随其后。这次，它没有跑，我也没想要抓住它。它仍然有目

catch him. He still moved with purpose, but he wasn't as frenetic as before. We crossed through the school yard and past the overturned garbage cans in the alley. A boy of about nine was kicking the chain link fence, trying to sculpt a shape into the barrier. Fred and I ignored the boy and move steadily through the alley. Finally at the end of the alley, we turned the corner and went about half a block down the street.

We were home.

This was the house I grew up in. I stared at the low, wide bungalow that lounged across the property. The cracked retaining wall had been replaced with terraced, landscaping bricks. The peeling, lime green trim was now a smooth grey. The sprawling willow that I used to climb was still there, but all the lower branches had been trimmed off. It was a beautiful, dense green canopy now; wonderful curb appeal, but totally unclimbable. The massive spruce trees had been trimmed, their bases surrounded by landscaping gravel instead of dead grass. It all looked so well manicured, so alien.

的地走着，但不像以前那样急切了。我们穿过校园，走过巷子里被掀翻的垃圾桶。一个大约九岁的男孩踢着铁丝网围栏，试图在这个障碍物上弄出一个形状。弗雷德和我没理那个男孩，不紧不慢地走过那个小巷。终于到了巷底，我们转了个弯，在那条街上，我们大约又走了半个街区。

我们到家了。

在这所房子里我长大成人。我盯着这处低矮、宽展的平房。那曾经裂了缝的挡墙已经被一排排垒放整齐的风景砖取代；曾经是柠檬绿的装饰边已经被换成了光滑的灰色。那棵曾枝叶茂盛、被我爬上爬下的柳树还在，但较低的枝条已经被修剪掉。现在，它可谓是一个漂亮的、浓密的绿色蓬冠；外观美妙无比，却无法让人再攀爬。那些巨大的云杉也被修剪过。其树根周围原来是死草，现在是景观砾石。这里的一切看起来都被修剪得很好，就像外星人的住所一样。

It wasn't my house any more.

I stood staring, lips parted, drowning in memories. Fred started to move slowly toward the massive maple tree on the boulevard. He lay down at the base of the swollen trunk.

He knew which tree this was.

This was where he died; where I had placed him when his writhing had subsided after my Dad had run over him with the car. His eyes looked older now, ancient bi-coloured pools. I came closer, reached out my hand. I could now smell the acrid, crisp stench of burning rubber, hear the desperate groan of the brakes. Fred's bright, white fur was starting to fade, looking more like the boulevard grass, the edges of the heart-shaped patch becoming more indistinct. I put my hand on his head. There was only cold air.

The edges of his body were haze now, but I could still see his face. I wanted to touch him, but there was nothing to touch. My fingers ached as they grasped the frigid air. His tail was still but that one blue eye and that one brown eye

这已不再是我的房子。

我站在那儿看着，微微张着嘴，完全沉浸在记忆里。弗雷德开始慢慢地向着大道上的一棵大枫树走去。它躺在其肿胀的树干边。

他知道这是哪棵树。

这就是它死亡的地方。我父亲的车从它身上碾过。当它的挣扎和扭动平息以后，我把它放在这里。它的眼睛现在看起来老多了，像两汪不同颜色的池水。我向它靠得更近，伸出我的手。此刻，我可以闻到胶皮燃烧的味道——辛辣、焦干，我可以听到刹车绝望的呻吟。弗雷德光泽奕奕的白毛开始变暗，看起来就像是大道旁的杂草，那心状的边缘也开始变得不甚分明。我把手放在了它的头上。只有寒冷的空气。

现在，它身体的边缘都是雾霾，但我仍能看清它的脸。我想去抚摸它，却什么也摸不到。抓着寒冷的空气，我的手指生疼。它的尾巴静静躺着，一只蓝色的眼睛和另一只棕色的眼睛一直

were smiling as he finally disappeared. I groped desperately at the grass, but there was nothing. I flexed my fingers as the air began to warm.

I got up and slowly walked away from there, from that neighbourhood, back to my home.

在微笑，直至它消失了。我绝望地在草地上抓着、摸索，但什么也没有。随着空气开始变暖，我展开了手指。

我起身，慢慢离开那个地方。从那个街区返回自己的家。